Arthur Sherburne Hardy, Arthur Sherburne Hardy

Passe Rose

Arthur Sherburne Hardy, Arthur Sherburne Hardy

Passe Rose

ISBN/EAN: 9783743303058

Manufactured in Europe, USA, Canada, Australia, Japa

Cover: Foto ©Andreas Hilbeck / pixelio.de

Manufactured and distributed by brebook publishing software (www.brebook.com)

Arthur Sherburne Hardy, Arthur Sherburne Hardy

Passe Rose

PASSE ROSE

BY

ARTHUR SHERBURNE HARDY

AUTHOR OF "BUT YET A WOMAN," AND "THE WIND OF DESTINY"

BOSTON AND NEW YORK
HOUGHTON, MIFFLIN AND COMPANY
The Riverside Press, Cambridge

PASSE ROSE.

I.

It was well known to all the inmates of the abbey of St. Servais that the abbot was ill, and it was whispered under the arcades of the great cloister and around the wooden tables of the refectory that his illness was unto death, — whisperings which were repeated by the guests in the hospitium and their servants in the monastery stables. It was known also that the monk Hugo, physician to the brotherhood, had exhausted to no purpose the herbs in the physic garden adjoining the dispensary, and that the abbot, who felt himself rapidly failing, had determined, as a last resort and without further delay, to have recourse to the blessed relics of St. Servais.

Many of those gathered about the refectory tables looked to see on this occasion the complete refutation of certain heresies which Hugo had brought from Salerno, touching the efficacy of herbs and potions apart from all intercession of God, invocation of the martyrs, or sprinkling of holy waters. On the other hand, without doubting the power of the martyrs to change the counsels of God, but remembering rather that to all men it is appointed once to die, the entire community were much disturbed by sundry signs and wonders foreshadowing the abbot's end ; and the recollection of these marvels filled their thoughts to the exclusion of the sober words which fell from the lips of the reader as they finished their noonday meal. Indeed, but an hour before, Lehun, the cellarer who drew the wine in the vaults below the larder, having fixed his light, as was his custom, in the iron ring of the pier between the casks, was suddenly enveloped in darkness, although no draught of air nor any other cause whatsoever could be assigned for the extinction of the torch. Thrice had he relighted it, and thrice was it extinguished in the same manner, as those with him also testified. Moreover, on the preceding day, one of the swallows having their nests within the west portal entered the church at the hour of morning vigil, and, after circling the nave at the height of the vaultings, passed suddenly within the veil of the sanctuary, extinguishing with its wings the light burning before the high altar. But most wonderful of all, before the abbot was seriously ill, being but slightly indisposed, and taking his repasts, for that reason, in his own house, while the two brothers who waited on him were serving his table, darkness filled the room where he ate, it being the sixth hour and the sun without shining brightly. Such were the marvels which agitated the minds of the monks, as the reader closed the volume on the pulpit at the sound of the chapel bell, and they rose from the refectory benches.

Meanwhile, the abbot slept on the stone seat in the convent orchard. Thither he had caused himself and his pillows to be carried, and there, to all appearance unconscious of the agitation of which he was the cause, wrapped in his long robe, he dozed, and woke, and dozed again.

No sound disturbed him. It was the hour between the noon repast and nones, when, stretched on their narrow beds, the monks were given over to meditation and prayer. At the extreme eastern end of the inner precinct, on the very brow of the steep hill overlooking Maestricht, the orchard was removed from the clamor of the great western court without the abbey close, while the noises of the town were at this distance blended in indistinguishable murmurs. In the valley below, the river crept lazily in the bed it had won from the hills. The sun filled this valley with a lucent flood of misty light. It trembled on the hilltops, whose summits emerged as islands from an amber sea; it overflowed the dim horizon, where the river shone like a mirror suspended in mid-air. This was the abbot's favorite seat, under the scattered trees whose fruits gleamed in spots of flame-like brightness, and whose boughs overhung the frail wooden crosses which served to mark for scarce a year the sleeping-places of the dead. It were no wonder if to his weakened sense the breath of the tasseled laburnum exhaled a celestial sweetness, or that the dark verdure of the almond-trees and the scant leafage of the peach-rows appeared radiant with the light that knows neither waxing nor waning. Perchance, dozing among the graves, he mistook the chant which came faintly from the church over the orchard wall for the choir of the world to which he seemed hastening so fast. But as the solemn sounds drew nearer, first in the pillared aisle, then louder under the porch of the parvis, the abbot opened his eyes, listening attentively; and when the orchard gate creaked on its iron hinges, he raised himself on his pillows, and turned his head to the entering procession.

The hour of last appeal had come. The monks had laid aside their frocks, for the labor of the afternoon was suspended, and clad in their church robes they filed through the narrow door, filling the inclosure from the wall to the crest of the hill. One might have thought the occupants of the scattered graves had shaken off their heavy sleep, and stood each beside the bed where he had so long slumbered in silence, to welcome to his place their dying abbot. Four of the brethren lifted the sick man upon a litter; then, resuming the chant, which floated away over the cliff to the city below, the procession slowly retraced its steps.

The great bell in the tower of St. Gabriel, which rang only when the holy relics were exhibited, had already given its warning, and the abbey gates had long been thronged with the sick and the poor. Mothers whose love no deformity of nature could weaken brought their misshapen offspring in their arms; cripples had toiled up the rocky road on their crutches; the blind man, led by the child, held fast to the little hand in the press of the crowd; and one, a mother, had brought her dead babe, hidden in the warmth of her bosom. All these wretched beings, animated by so many hopes, fearful of delay, eager to be nearest the shrine, crowding the leper whose contact they feared, forgetting in their passionate desire the very compassion they invoked, filled the passage from the inner gate to the church, and fought their way up the steps of the porch with a desperate expectation. Those who were fortunate enough to have reached the screen which, just within the door, separated the public from the body of the church, clutching fast the rail to hold their place or withstand the pressure of the throng behind, peered anxiously between the openings of the barrier, their haggard faces pressed against its latticed panels and their lips trembling with rapid prayers.

Within the railing, to and fro before these hungry eyes, paced Friedgis, the abbey porter. His head was tonsured, but in place of the monkish habit he wore a short tunic, girded at the waist by a cord from which hung a bunch of ponderous keys. From time to time he threatened some more daring one of the crowd, who, either pushed from behind or desirous of bettering his position, would have climbed the screen but for the porter's forbidding eye. An old man, whose thin legs trembled under his palsied body, gazed pitifully upon the broad chest, the strong, supple shoulders, the firm, elastic limbs, as they passed back and forth before him, envious of all that beauty which announced the power to execute the desires of the will. The mother with her dead babe sought to attract the porter's eye as it glanced over the surging crowd, in some vague hope of coming nearer to the screen; and a woman whose flushed face contrasted strangely with the pale, sunken cheeks of the mother peered eagerly over the latter's shoulder. Whole of body, her sore was of the heart ; for her lover had deserted her, and she had come to summon the aid of the saint to her fading comeliness, and to invoke that vengeance upon another which we so often secretly desire in claiming pity for ourselves.

On the stone floor, between the feet of those in the first row, crouched a girl of extraordinary beauty. The people called her Passe Rose. It was neither ill of body nor ache of heart, but only a burning curiosity, that had brought her to the shrine of the martyr. At break of day she had been first at the gate, waiting the hour when the public were to be admitted ; and profiting by the momentary absence of the porter, gone in search of the hospitaler, to announce the arrival of merchants having cloth to exchange for the *potus dulcissimus* of the abbey, she had stolen through the door in their train, hoping to find some place where she might hide till the opening of the gates, and thus enter the church with the first of the multitude. But finding no shelter, she was discovered by the porter on his return, and, seized like a child in his arms, amid the laughter of the merchants and the jeers of their servants, had been thrust without the gate. Notwithstanding this rebuff she had succeeded in reaching the screen, where, treasuring up the insult in her wounded heart, she muttered a curse under her breath whenever her assailant came within sight of her flashing eyes.

Heedless of all these emotions, Friedgis gave hardly a glance to the multitude. If he had cast Passe Rose rudely out the monastery gate, it was because the Prior Sergius, when instructing him in the duties of his office, had dwelt long upon this particular, affirming with much emphasis "that as neither David, nor Solomon, nor Adam himself, the perfect work of God, had escaped the caress or deceit of woman, so might one as easily hope to bear coals in his bosom without scorching his vestment as to do what had not been in their power," — instructions which Friedgis had not scrupled to carry out with the disdainful rigor of the Saxon slave who despised the strange conditions of life to which fate had subjected him.

Doubtless the Abbot Rainal, had he not fallen sick immediately on his return from the Saxon campaign on which he had accompanied the king, would have endeavored to bring Friedgis to a more loving service; for every serf of the domain, whether of those who belonged to the land when the king bestowed it upon the abbot, or of the Saxon captives whom the king had distributed among his vassals, knew that the welfare of his soul was the abbot's chief concern. But the Prior Sergius was more easily satisfied on this point, and, having administered baptism to all according to the canons, scrupled little to enlist the body in God's service, whether the mind were willing or not, — a service which Friedgis, notwithstanding his contempt for a monkish life, executed as porter none the less zealously, and with such impartiality that had it been forbidden the brethren to leave the abbey close he would have thrown the transgressor over the wall with as little compunction as he had ejected the maiden.

Now it happened that when the side door was opened, and the chant of the entering procession began to fill the arches, Friedgis stood in front of Passe Rose, hiding from her all that was taking place. For some time she bore patiently with this obstruction of her view, thinking the porter would change his place before the service was over. The minutes passed, and still he did not move. When at last the monks began to chant the Kyrie Eleison her patience was exhausted, and after having in vain essayed to reach him with her silver bodkin, furious lest she should miss the moment when the reliquary should be exposed, she spat venomously upon his bare legs. Turning with the rapidity of a panther, Friedgis recognized his assailant, and before she could divine his intention, leaping the rail, he had seized her in his arms, and was bearing her through the press as easily as a ship's prow divides the water. Locked in his grasp of iron, she could not utter a sound, though her nails were deep in his bosom, and, before she realized what was taking place, she found herself once more without the walls, and the gate barred behind her.

While yet panting for breath the gate was reopened, and to her surprise Friedgis appeared again. The frail bodkin was still in her tightly closed fingers, and she clutched it closer, resolved to break it in her enemy's heart; but as he drew nearer she recognized in his hand her necklace of gold, which had become loosened in her struggles.

"Whence hadst thou this?" he asked, holding it out to her. She extended her hand to take it, speechless with rage. "Answer," said Friedgis, with a gesture of impatience.

"Give it me; it is mine," she said, breathless.

"Answer," repeated Friedgis, advancing a step menacingly.

"Thief! brigand!" gasped Passe Rose, clasping her bodkin.

Seeing that he could effect nothing by violence, and fearful of remaining longer absent from his post, Friedgis resorted to persuasion.

"If thou answerest truly, thou shalt return," he insisted coaxingly.

"It is too late," she replied, tears of sullen rage filling her eyes.

"Nay, come," he said briefly.

She followed him, trembling with anger and joy, through the gate to the steps of the porch, crowded with those unable to penetrate within the church.

"Hold firmly," he said, lifting her to his shoulder.

"And the necklace, dear porter?" she whispered in his ear, encircling his neck with her arms.

"If thou wilt come to-night, and knock thrice at the small north gate, I will give it thee," said Friedgis.

"By St. Martin, I will come!" answered the girl quickly.

"Good. Hold fast," he replied; and, forcing his passage to the screen, he deposited her in the place whence he had so rudely torn her.

Careless of the wondering glances of her neighbors, she scanned eagerly the scene before her. The office was finished. The abbot's litter reposed at the foot of the choir stair; beyond, between the parted curtains, stood the reliquary, in front of the altar.

Whatever the record contained in the annals

of the monastery of St. Servais, or in what manner soever the relics of its patron saint are therein connected with the wonderful recovery of its abbot, this is what happened : —

Having been transported into the church, whether from the coolness of the air or because the fever approached its natural term, or whether from the virtue of the herbs of Brother Hugo or the sight of the Prior Sergius, who intrigued to be his successor, the worthy abbot felt at the same time both an abatement of his fever and a ravishing sense of slumber; so that even before the reliquary had been brought from the crypt below the choir, the chant of the brotherhood, echoing above his head, between the narrow walls of the clerestory, seemed like the soothing song of a mother, and the voice of the celebrant died utterly away to his hearing. When he awoke, the light reflected from the yellow sandstone walls was gone, and for a long time he searched his memory to explain the star shining so close beside him in the night; till at last, his eyes becoming accustomed to the darkness, he perceived the star to be the lamp of holy oil, and that two brothers watched and prayed near his litter. Remembering then all that had occurred, and recognizing by his refreshment the miracle that had been done, having offered thanks to God, he called to the monk nearest him. The

monk, thinking the abbot beyond even the succor
of St. Servais, shook with terror at seeing his
lips move, so that when the abbot bade him summon the porter to assist in carrying him to his
own room, the monk's knees sank under him and
refused their support; whereupon his companion,
who had also heard the abbot's request, hastened
in his stead to the passage which led to the porter's lodging. It was by this passage that Friedgis entered the church to ring the bell for the
daily offices. Muttering a prayer as he went,
Brother Dominic — for that was his name — hurried down the corridor, and, being in haste,
opened the porter's door precipitately, expecting
to find the room dark and Friedgis in the sound
sleep of midnight.

If from Passe Rose, who, faithful to her promise, sat on the edge of the low cot, the apparition
of the pale face in its black hood called forth a
suppressed shriek of terror, the sight of a woman
of such loveliness in the chamber of the porter
caused the monk a surprise greater than the
devil himself could have effected; and before
Passe Rose had finished her cry he was flying
down the passage, pursued by its echoes.

Now, however opportune for the abbot had
been his appeal to the compassion of St. Servais,
his return to consciousness was exceedingly ill-
timed both for Friedgis and Passe Rose; for the

latter had not recovered her jewel, nor the former learned how she had obtained it. Passe Rose, indeed, had but just come when the appearance of Brother Dominic in the corridor caused her to spring to the door by which she had entered. This door opened into the walk between the church and the hospitium, next to the small gate by which access was had to the abbey close without passing through the great courtyard. Unable to move its heavy bolt, the girl sank upon the floor, convulsed with terror, her eyes fixed upon the spot where the monk had stood.

Friedgis, more concerned for the information he desired than for the consequences of the monk's discovery, in vain endeavored to allay her fear. "Come," he entreated, kneeling beside her and drawing the necklace from his pouch. "What dost thou fear? See, here is thy collar. Tell me who gave it thee." But terror had taken away Passe Rose's power of speech. She had even forgotten her jewel, and continued to gaze at the passage as if she still saw the livid face of the monk looking at her from its dark recesses. "I tell thee they shall not harm thee," said Friedgis, closing the passage door and turning its heavy key. "Fear nothing. I will crack them one by one, like fagots, over my knee. See," he repeated, pressing the necklace into her hand, "here is thy collar."

"Let me go," implored the eyes of Passe Rose.

"On my faith thou shalt go. Look." The porter drew back the bolt. "Only tell me first."

As he spoke, footsteps were heard in the corridor. They did not escape the quick ear of the girl, to whom they imparted the energy of a fresh fear. "Save me! save me!" she cried, springing from the floor, and throwing herself upon the porter's neck.

"I will save thee; I will carry thee out myself," said Friedgis disdainfully, endeavoring to unlock the girl's arms. "See, we are going." And renouncing all hope of calming her, he lifted her in his arms. "Only tell me where I may find thee. Whisper it in my ear." But while he spoke the arms about his neck relaxed their hold, the head on his shoulder fell back, and the body slid from his grasp. Passe Rose had swooned.

Holding his burden as best he could with one arm, Friedgis sought to open the door by which the girl had come, and while his hand was on the latch the grating of a bolt was heard in the walk without. He threw his shoulder against the oaken frame.

The door was barred fast on the outer side.

II.

Passe Rose, when any one asked whence she came or who were her parents, lifted her eyebrows as if to say, What difference does that make? But when she chose to be communicative she had good listeners, whether her tale was grave or gay. Her family had fled from the vicinity of Toulon to escape the pest, which, however, overtook both her father and her mother before they reached the confines of Provence. She next appeared with a company of mountebanks and dancers at Chasseneuil, where the king was assembling his vassals to invade Spain. Fluttering like a rose-leaf in the storm, Passe Rose was swept along in the throng gathering from Burgundy, Bavaria, Lombardy, and Austrasia to follow the banners of Karle beyond the Pyrenees, and reached Chasseneuil in season to dance before Queen Hildegarde at the Easter fêtes, — a performance of which she boasted proudly, and which she assigned to her sixth year. For while Passe Rose knew very well, by counting her rosy fingers, that eighteen and six make twenty-four, this fact taught her no fear and hinted no caution. Life was to her no cup of doubtful flavor, gingerly drunk with an eye on the bottom, but an ocean, over whose sparkling expanse she smiled, her lips at the rim, drinking alike the sweet and the bitter, with that thirst out of whose fullness spring courage and joy.

It would appear that after Roncevaux she followed the army northward on its way to quell the Saxon insurrection, but abandoned both it and her mountebanks at the Rhine. It is even possible that she passed into Italy, but this is doubtful, for to follow the itinerary of Passe Rose by her descriptions would be to travel over the known world. Certain it is, however, that she came to the fair of St. Denis with a company of Frankish merchants, at an age when her mere presence was their fortune; for whether it were pearls or perfumes, Egyptian linen and paper, oil or wine, buyers were plenty within the sound of her laughter and the glance of her eye.

When the fair was over, and the merchants were about to set out for England for purchases of tin and wool, either because they treated her ill, or because she had no desire to travel so far, or perhaps for graver reasons, — for of this matter she would give no account, — Passe Rose fled secretly in the night; and going a long way in a thick wood without finding any shelter, she lay down beside a wooden cross near the road, where, after saying all the prayers she had ever heard, she fell asleep.

Now Werdric, a gold-beater of Maestricht,

returning from the fair with two donkeys and a servant, was hastening home to his wife Jeanne, whom he loved above everything else in the world, and with whom he lived in perfect happiness, except — for they had no children, a lack which both sorely lamented. It was all in vain that Jeanne fasted, and that Werdric made a golden image exciting the envy of all who saw it, and which he gave to the church of St. Sebastian; so that, being now old, he thought no more about it, but Jeanne still prayed and fasted. Passing through the wood in the early morning, Werdric was astonished to see so fair a girl sleeping alone in such a place, and descending from his donkey he awoke her, asking where was her home, and if she would go thither with him.

" Willingly," said Passe Rose.

" And where may it be ? " asked Werdric.

" It is where thou art going," said Passe Rose.

Thinking that she spoke of some village or hamlet to which they would soon come, he set her upon the servant's donkey and pursued his way, marveling at her dress, which had silver lacing-cords and a hood lined with vair.

" How far may thy home be ? " presently asked Passe Rose.

Then Werdric remembered the fasts and prayers of Jeanne, and deemed that God had answered them, — a fact of which Jeanne made no doubt when he told her how he had found the young girl alone and asleep by the roadside, under the cross.

Perhaps it was because she fared so much better with the gold-beater and his wife than with either the merchants or the dancers that Passe Rose remained with the former to this day. For Jeanne gave her a chamber above the shop, having a small turret in the corner overhanging the street, through whose window of horn one might see in both directions all who passed by or stopped below for affairs of trade. In the chamber was a bed with curtains, a prie-dieu chair with cushions on which were stamped a design of the sun, and a box for clothes, of which Passe Rose was very fond, although she had none to put into it except when she was in her bed, — a want, however, which Jeanne soon supplied. For there was nothing the goodwife would not have given her, even to a name. This name — Theodora — came to her thought in the middle of the night; but the girl would have none of it, and declared her name was Passe Rose. Perhaps this name recalled some vague memories of Provence. Certain it is that when she passed by, it was as a breath from the land of orange, and olive, and rosemary. The hues of the Southern Sea were in her eyes and under the rose-brown flush of her skin; the sound of its waves was in the ripple of her laughter; and the odor of samphire, myrtle, and lentisk, glistening wet in its spray, in her hair.

Nothing would persuade Mother Jeanne, as she might now in good truth call herself, that all this was not the gift of God; and when Passe Rose told strange stories or related wild adventures, Jeanne, with a faith undisturbed by such prattle and nonsense, smiled.

It is needless to say that many who passed the goldsmith's shop were fain to gather this rose, and that many a gallant would have given his life for one of its petals, — "So they say," laughed Passe Rose, knowing also that when the rose drops its petals, then it begins to fade. In a way she loved them all, at once and by turns, and so impartially that one would as soon think to be angry with the sun, which shines upon all, as with her. At all events, she was truthful and sincere. She hated when she hated vigorously and well, and laughed when she laughed from her red lips to her sandaled feet. If she spat on Friedgis's bare leg, it was because she desired ardently to see the shrine of the blessed St. Servais; and if she whispered softly in his ear, it was because she wished very much for her collar of gold. She wounded pride and she flattered self-love, just as the rain disappoints

and the sun cheers, as it were in the very course
of nature, with a naturalness and good faith so
complete as to disarm all complaint. If selfish-
ness had gotten hold of Passe Rose!—ah, that
would have been a different matter. Does any
one call the sun selfish, even when he hides his
face? When a lover tired her, Aïe! aïe! aïe!
said Passe Rose, and, like the sun, went to shine
elsewhere.

But the love of Jeanne Passe Rose requited.
Thus, for a whole year she hoarded every copper
denier in her chest, till one morning she set out
with three silver sous in her crimson purse, to
buy the marten's fur which she knew the dame
desired for the border of her dress. On her way
she met Adelhaïde, sister to Robert, Count of
Tours, master of the hunt and of the king's stables; and this lady was attired so richly and
had so great a retinue with her that at the sight
of such splendor the three silver sous of Passe
Rose seemed to her of no value. But after
Adelhaïde had passed by, Passe Rose laughed,
pressing the pieces together in her hand, and
having gotten, by fair words or a fair face, the
worth of four sous for three, ran home singing.
On her part, the goodwife did all in the power
of love to spoil Passe Rose; but the latter possessed too sturdy a nature to be far diverted
from her own course, — sturdy and willowy,

like a young ash in the wood, which sways to the wind, but grows straight upward without bend or flaw.

If one should contrast the safe and quiet life which Passe Rose now enjoyed with the troublous period of her early years, it might be thought that she had determined to close the chapter of her wandering existence, and to order the remainder of her days in sobriety. For with all the pleasures of roving, hunger and cold and harsh words had not been wanting ; and like one who, fleeing down a narrow street pursued by enemies, suddenly perceives an open door, and, entering quickly, closes it upon all disquietude, so Passe Rose had left all pursuing ills at the place where the goldsmith had found her. Such, however, is human nature, that no sooner are former evils passed away than those which are present call to mind the pleasures which disappeared with them, filling the heart with regrets and sighs. Passe Rose was not discontented, but in her new condition new hopes and ambitions assailed her. She had put aside her mountebank's dress even to the armlets of Greek coin whose jingle made once such pleasing music in her ears ; and with the garments which Jeanne gave her she had put on the disdain for her former companions which every good citizen felt, however eagerly they might flock to witness jugglers' magic or feats of dancers' skill.   Only, while Jeanne despised their mode of life and did not hesitate to call them children of Satan, Passe Rose despised their condition.   As to their mode of life, it pleased her well, for liberty was its motto ; and this liberty itself, as well as the love of it, she carried in with her to her retreat when she closed the door.   But whatever the plans she cherished or the hopes she nourished, her laugh was as merry and her hand as ready as ever.   There was no menial labor she scorned to do, nor any courtly service she hesitated to demand.   Jeanne herself scarce knew when to wonder most : whether when, in the kitchen, Passe Rose made savory pasties of cream and pounded almonds and pistachios, or when, having put on her favorite dress, fastened close about the waist and wrists, she went out to take the air.   For being the gift of God, how should she know the best flour was of the second grinding, or that jelly of apple was the better for rosewater, which on the other hand impaired the flavor of quince ?   Moreover, Passe Rose brought from God knows where new inventions : comfit of purslane, marchpane of honey and the white of eggs, and frumenty with poppy seeds.   " Who ever heard of fennel in cheese ! " Jeanne exclaimed ; or, " Balm of mint in the soup, indeed ! " she cried, opening wide her eyes.   But

Werdric smacked his lips, declaring such cheese and such broth were never tasted in Maestricht before.

As for the manner in which Passe Rose wore her apparel, it was not strange that Jeanne wondered; for however simple it was, whether because of her girlish beauty or her unconsciousness, the Lady Adelhaïde herself was not so agreeable to the sight. So that while the knowledge Passe Rose had of houschold affairs caused Jeanne surprise, her knowledge of the art of dressing caused Jeanne fear. For it was neither right nor safe that the daughter of a goldsmith, selling at retail for the worth of two sous, should have a finer mien than the sister of the master of the king's horse. Be that as it may, it is sure that Passe Rose, unworthy as she thought the condition from which she had escaped, saw none above her to which she might not attain. If the sunlight is not altogether free, yet if the king's window be open it will enter without leave. Had not the slave Ingonda become Clother's wife? Had not Haribert of Paris raised Merofleda, the daughter of a woolcomber and Theodehilda, the shepherdess, to his throne? And did not Hilperic, king of Neustria, choose Fredegonda from among the women of the royal service, and marry her with the ring and denarius, according to the laws of

the Franks, thus making her his queen? So
Passe Rose, when she walked abroad, without
fixing her eyes upon any individual star, saw
them all, none the less, and the songs which related these events lingered in her ear longer
than the chantings of the monks of St. Servais,
which sometimes floated down from the abbey
hill among the busy people of Maestricht. Yet
for all her shortcomings Jeanne's love for her
grew with the years, and although accurate com-
parisons are impossible in view of the uncertainty surrounding her previous career, it is
quite likely that Passe Rose herself improved
vastly. It is so much easier to begin a new life
with new friends and fresh faces.

III.

So curiously in this world are trifles linked
to things of moment that if Passe Rose had not
known somewhat of cookery she would never
have been imprisoned with Friedgis in the abbey
of St. Servais. For it happened one morning,
as she watched the spit turning before the fire,
that she said to Jeanne: —

"In my country there grows an herb, in the
wet places of the wood, very fit to serve with
roasts and all kinds of sauces."

"What is its name?" asked Jeanne, at that very moment preparing the basting.

"I know not its name," replied Passe Rose, "but I know it well when I see it; and if thou likest, to-morrow we will search for it in the wood beyond the river."

And although Jeanne had great fear of the wood fays, she promised to go the following day, after exacting from Passe Rose the pledge that she would not trouble the pools, should they chance to come upon a wood spring. So in the early morning they set out, with an osier basket for the herb and a vial of blessed water for the fays.

Nothing was sweeter to Passe Rose than freedom. When the gate was passed and the walls of the town were behind her, she was as one who has recovered her patrimony. The sunlight entered at every pore; the rills running under the cresses by the roadside and the flowers distilling perfumes in the shade whispered to her, "We are yours;" and she, seeing everything, hearing everything, answered with a familiar nod or smile all these signs and tokens, like a proprietor going over his estates. Jeanne must needs stop to inquire of every fowler they met the price of his starlings, and whether the quail were yet full fledged; of the fisherman at the river-bank whether any pike had been taken in his net,

and what barbels would fetch a pound ; and of
the miller, whose water-wheel was midway on
the bridge, what was the grinding-tax this year.
" At last!" cried Passe Rose, when all these
obstacles were passed. " Mother of God, defend
us !" signed Jeanne, thinking of the fays. Indeed, at the border of the forest Jeanne declared
she could go no farther, that breath failed her,
that the clouds boded rain, — in short, that she
was no longer young and able to walk such a
distance, but would wait in the open field till
Passe Rose should return. So the latter, who
neither lacked breath nor feared the rain, and
would not be dissuaded, went into the wood
alone. When she returned her basket was
empty, her cheeks flushed with flame, and about
her neck was a collar of gold.

It is certainly strange that Passe Rose, who
when she danced before Queen Hildegarde
neither felt abashed nor was confused, should
stammer and cast down her eyes before Jeanne,
who was nothing but a little wrinkled old
woman, with a vial of blessed water in her
pouch. But so it was, and at the questions
which assailed her she faltered and turned
away, till at last she declared boldly that the
collar was given her by a fay. Having made
this assertion, her tongue was loosed and hesi-
tancy disappeared : for the first step it is that

costs; only let this be taken, necessity and invention will manage the rest.

She told Jeanne that after searching far and wide she came to a spring which trickled over a mossy stone into a pool, and that while she sought the herb about the water's edge she saw a golden comb (Oh, Passe Rose!) lying among the wet leaves of an ivy branch. No sooner had she taken it in her hand than she heard wailing and sobbing, and, looking up, saw the fay, with no other garment than a veil, clasped about the waist by a girdle of gold, wringing its hands, and beseeching her to yield up the comb. "Then said I," continued Passe Rose, "'If I give thee the comb, thou wilt bewitch me with thy breath.' 'Nay,' replied she, unloosing her belt; 'only give me my comb, and thou shalt have my girdle, which is a charm against all fairy power so long as thou hast it clasped on thy neck.'" (Oh, Passe Rose!) "'Give me first the belt, then,' said I. So she gave it, and when I had fastened it I put back the comb between the leaves and ran. For this reason am I hot, and my power of speech is gone."

This and much more of the same sort she told and repeated to Jeanne, till, like one who sees a patch of shadow afar on the plain, and at one moment thinks it a tower, and at the next is ready to swear it to be a tree, she began

to waver in her own mind between the false and
the real, almost ready to put faith in her own
words. But this was not at all the tale she told
to Friedgis; for just as the sun sometimes
shines fiercely on the tower till every line and
angle of its stones stands out among the trees,
and sometimes with mists and shadows confuses
tower and trees together, so Passe Rose dis-
closed to Friedgis what she had concealed from
Jeanne; and as sometimes, shining neither
fiercely nor faintly, but obliquely, the sun shoots
a slanting ray which illumines but a part of the
tower, and leaves the rest in the trees' shadow,
so it were best to follow Passe Rose herself into
the wood, lest, trusting only to what she revealed
to Friedgis, some doubt should still linger as to
what there transpired.

Albeit the great forest lying between Maestricht and Aix was well known to be the abode
of fays (which were none other than Frankish
princesses who had refused the religion of
Christ), besides dwarfs even more venomous,
and although the spirit of Fastrada, the wicked
queen who had bewitched the heart of Karle,
wandered here nightly in search of her magic
ring, and although it was neither Saturday nor
Sunday, evil days for all evil spirits, yet Passe
Rose entered the gloomy shadow of the trees
fearlessly. For a long time she sought faith-

fully for the herb among slender stems and powdery leaves, in the dark places where the woodlilies delight to grow, under the junipers and pines whose resinous breath the violets love, in wet patches of woolly moss wherein her feet sank to the cross-bandage of her sandals; lifting every leaf which might hide her quest, turning aside for no vine which barred her way, till, discouraged in her search, she gave it over altogether, and began to fill her basket with beechnuts, and seek for the late strawberries nodding among feathery shoots of grass and mould of last year's leaves.

While thus engaged she heard the faint blast of a horn, and, setting down her basket, listened. Presently she heard it again, nearer this time, and now its mellow echoes were lost in the quick, short bark of hounds. Passe Rose began to listen in good earnest, half rising to her knees and sitting back on her heels, her lips parted as if they could assist her ears to locate the place whence the sounds came. The intermittent cry of the dogs became more distinct, the blast of the horn was mingled with the shouts of men, and in the pauses came the sharp snap of a dead branch or the crash of young summer trees, till the beat of her heart grew loud and fast in her ears, like the muffled sound of the grouse's wing when he calls to his mate from the thick copse.

Tales of the fierce urus and savage boar rose to her mind, and, overturning her basket of nuts, she sprang to her feet, seeing already in every dark thicket the cruel tusk or foaming mouth of some desperate beast, and bewildered by the gathering storm of sounds. So near were they now, and on every side, that if she had stopped to weigh the evidence she would not have been able to take a single step; but fear got the better of reason, and not knowing whither she went, holding fast, in her terror, to her empty basket, she fled between bush and tree wherever an open space beckoned her.

Whether because St. Martin, upon whom she called only on grave matters, was otherwise occupied, and St. Servais liked not to be thought second even to St. Martin himself, Passe Rose, invoking the aid of each alternately, thought herself abandoned by both; for at the very instant that a crash in the thicket before her drained the last drop of blood from her heart and all remaining strength from her limbs, her feet caught in a trailing vine, and she fell headlong. But as often, when the saints abandon us, we discover some hidden power of our own, so Passe Rose, caught like a sheep by the fleece in a thorn-bush, and expecting nothing but certain death, bethought herself suddenly of the knife she carried to loosen the roots of the herbs, and, grasping it tightly in her hand, closed her fingers about the haft with the nervous determination of one brought to bay. Great, then, was her surprise, on lifting her head from the ferns and stems where she had fallen, to see a youth, mounted on a black horse, and gazing at her with a surprise equal to her own.

This youth was no other than Gui of Tours, son of Robert, Count of Tours, and master of the king's hunt. This, indeed, Passe Rose did not know, but certain other things she discovered in less time than they can be told, namely: that he was of middle height, neither too heavy nor too slender, sitting well on his horse, and light of foot; that the hand which held the rein could hurl a spear adroitly and lance a javelin far; and that neither peril, nor thirst, nor hunger could turn his step aside from what his heart desired. All this she saw while the youth was dismounting from his horse and approaching her.

"Art thou hurt?" he inquired eagerly.

"Nay," she replied, regaining her feet, and shaking the leaves and mould from her dress as a bird shakes the dew from its wings.

"Surely thou art hurt," he repeated, stooping to look into her downcast eyes, for her cheeks were flushed with running and her bosom heaved.

"Nay; give me my basket, and let me go."

Such liquid eyes he had not seen nor heard such soft Roman speech since he marched against Arigisus, through the orchards of Campania.

"Go thou shalt, and where thou wilt, but I with thee; for if the stag turns there will be need of my spear."

"Thou wilt lose the hunt," objected Passe Rose, recovering her composure, and fixing upon him her brown eyes. His were an honest blue, and his skin fresh as an apple, without speck or flaw.

"I will not leave thee so for all the stags in France!" exclaimed the youth hotly.

"Set me, then, on thy horse," laughed Passe Rose, "for I think my ankle is sprained."

Alarm had died out of her eyes and confusion from her voice, but the flush that disappeared from her cheek seemed to rise on his. He called the horse to his side, and, holding the stirrup till her foot was secure, would have lifted her to the saddle; but she, grasping with one hand his lancewood spear, sprang lightly to her seat, while the horse, docile enough before, feeling now a rider on his back, and hearing the noise of the hunt drifting away, began to chafe and tremble.

"Never fear," said Passe Rose assuringly. "Only do thou hold the bridle, for the branches are low."

Urged forward by the impatience of the horse, the youth had all he could do to check its speed and guide its way through the thick wood, while Passe Rose, bending now this way, now that, to avoid the branches, smiled whenever he turned to look at her winsome face and lissome form.

Mastering at length the confusion which tied his tongue, " What is thy name ? " he asked.

" Passe Rose. And thine ? "

Either her question was so sudden or her name so strange that he stammered over his own in reply ; and then there was silence till the wood began to open, the sunlight to enter more freely, and between the trees appeared the fields of grain.

It was then that Passe Rose bethought herself of Jeanne, and sliding from the saddle to the ground said, " My mother is here waiting, and the way is clear. Give me my basket, and I will give thee thy spear ; " and holding it out in her hand, " I thank thee much," she added.

" Where shall I find thee again ? " asked Gui, recovering his speech at the thought of seeing her no more.

" It is very hard, — the world is so wide," laughed Passe Rose.

" Every bee that roves in the wood has somewhere a nest " —

" Which he hides lest the wild bear steal the comb," interrupted Passe Rose.

" I am no wild bear for thee," the youth retorted impetuously, unclasping at the same time the bracelet he wore on his arm. " But if ever thou hast need of the bear's claws, send me this token, and by the faith of Gui of Tours " —

" It is too large," interrupted Passe Rose again, looking from her arm to the band of gold.

" For thine arm, indeed, but see ! " and passing the collar about her neck, he essayed to fasten the clasp at her throat.

Now it was impossible to fasten this clasp while looking into Passe Rose's eyes, and for this reason, doubtless, Passe Rose, losing patience at his clumsy fingers, pushed them aside, and clasped it deftly with her own; so that while the king's captain, the point of whose spear could find the heart of the stag in flight, was marveling that the clasp would not hold, the eyes into which he looked disappeared, and Passe Rose herself vanished with the rapidity of a startled deer.

IV.

Unknown to herself, the account which Passe Rose gave to Jeanne of the acquisition of her collar had made such an impression upon her mind that on recovering from her swoon in the porter's cell, being still afraid but not yet remembering why, conscious that something had transpired but not yet recollecting what, she murmured, "This had not happened had my collar not been lost." Then seeing it was Friedgis, and not Jeanne, who bent above her, a faint blush rose to her cheek and a smile passed through her eyes. Whether she smiled at mistaking Friedgis for Jeanne and blushed at repeating a lie to no purpose, or blushed to find herself alone with Friedgis and smiled at being entrapped in her own invention, there is no way to know; for immediately on raising her head from the couch on which she lay, the room began to swim once more, and, falling back again, both the smile and the blush vanished.

"It is better to lie still," said Friedgis, watching her. "There is nothing to fear."

Passe Rose, finding that by obeying this injunction she could open her eyes without dizziness, lay still, examining Friedgis attentively.

"I was not afraid," she said presently.

Friedgis smiled.

"I was only startled," she added, continuing her examination.

With the return of her strength came the pangs of curiosity. A hundred thoughts and questions succeeded each other. Who is he? Whence does he come? What grave eyes he has! How blue the veins on his arms, — and what arms! What can he wish with my collar? What does he think of me? Are there no women in Saxony? And although these arms had handled her roughly, the eyes imparted a sense of security. A feeling of confidence, mingled with a desire to strike a spark from the steel, possessed her. She had seen many of the Saxon prisoners dispersed in bands throughout the kingdom, and in spite of his shaven head had guessed his nationality aright.

Thus they gazed at one another in silence. For the first time the Saxon looked into the eyes of the South, — limpid, eloquent, idolatrous. Frisia had none such among its fens and snows, under its sad northern sky. Had the blood returning to her cheeks burst its channels, that it should suffuse itself, like the violet lustre of the sea, under the transparent skin?

Rising from his seat, Friedgis took a cup from a sort of embrasure in the thick walls, and filled it from a black jar. "Drink," he said, offering it to her.

"Great northern wolf!" said Passe Rose to herself, sitting up on the edge of the couch, and looking over the rim of the cup as she drank, "what kind eyes thou hast!"

"Hast thou my collar?" she asked, returning the cup. "I must go."

He took it from his tunic and handed it to her,

draining at a draught the hydromel left in the cup, while she fastened the collar about her neck.

Having adjusted the collar and shaken out her dress, Passe Rose went to the door.

"Thou canst not pass that way," said he; "it is barred on the other side." He looked to see the color die out of her cheek again; but Passe Rose only opened wide her eyes as the remembrance of what had taken place returned, and, resuming her seat on the couch, looked gravely into his face.

"What is to be done?" she asked energetically.

For an answer Friedgis moved aside a wooden bench in the corner of the room, and, lying on his back upon the floor, pushed with his feet one of the large stones forming the outer wall. The stone, from which the adjoining cement had been loosened, receded slowly, and suddenly fell with a dull sound on the ground without, leaving a black hole through which the night air entered.

"Is it far?" asked Passe Rose, who needed no explanation of this proceeding.

"The height of a man."

"Do thou go first," she said, peering on her knees through the opening, and hearing indeed the rustle of the leaves without.

Sitting on the floor in front of her, Friedgis made no reply to this proposition. His eyes were fixed upon the necklace, and Passe Rose saw plainly that she had first to answer some questions. To this, however, she offered no remonstrance, merely sliding from her knees into a sitting posture, and leaning her head against the wall. She had no intention of repeating the story of the golden comb, much as she prided herself upon the sharpness of the bargain she drove with the fay; but she did meditate between the truth and some new invention, better suited to the occasion.

"What is that to thee?" she said, answering his look.

Friedgis seemed to hesitate between prudence and desire.

"Is it thine, perchance?" asked Passe Rose ironically, urging him gently on.

He looked at her distrustfully for a moment; then rose to his feet, walking slowly to and fro in the narrow room without paying any heed to her, as if turning over some serious question in his mind. The feeble flame floating on the oil scarce reached Passe Rose. One would not have seen her at all but for a gleam which flashed now and then in the corner, from the polished surface of the jewel, when she moved. She knew that she had only to wait; but it taxed her patience sorely that a man should dally and turn like a sluggish stream in the meadow, which is sure

after all to come to the sea. For Passe Rose
made up her mind without delay, — like a mountain brook that leaps straight out from the crest
of wood, and shoots the cliff at a single bound.

Suddenly, when near her, the Saxon stopped.

" Hast thou seen the sea? " he asked abruptly.

She nodded assent.

" But thou knowest not its boundaries. Beyond Strandt there is the sea. Beyond Fosset-
island — the sea. Beyond Anglia — still the sea.
Will the keel which follows the north wind along
the sands of Frisia return again to its haven in
the Elbe, like a swallow following the lake's
margin? Surely its waves have space enough
wherein to sport. Wherefore, then, are they so
greedy, that they should call to the winds, saying, ' Come! here is a green land glad with
flocks: let us devour it'? Then the winds
gather the mist maidens, the waves hurl themselves upon the coast, the rivers, beaten back,
overflow, the fields become a marsh, the flowers
swim, the trees rock, and the sea, rejoicing in
their fall, covers all things."

Passe Rose from her corner regarded him
with increasing interest. What had this to do
with her collar? Moreover, the sea which she
knew did not behave in this manner.

" It is thus thy people have wasted Saxony.
Is the bridge of heaven so small that they can-

not breathe, — that they must creep from the
Rohr to the Weser, and overflow the Weser to
the Elbe ? The grass which the flocks cropped
is soaked with blood, the plains smoke, the
altars of the gods are thrown down. Of what
avail the gods, if they do not hear! Henceforth
they are nothing to me. Does Freya listen?
Does Odin see?"

"Peste," thought Passe Rose, carried away
by this eloquence, "it is true."

"If I return thither, who will say to me
'Brother,' or 'Friend'? The people are scattered
as leaves, the sword is broken, and Frankish women wear the jewels of the Saxon maidens."

"I am no Frank!" exclaimed Passe Rose indignantly, and coloring under his gaze. "My
collar is no spoil, but a free gift. If it is
thine" — She unclasped it quickly, and held
it out to him.

"Tell me whence thou hast it," replied Friedgis disdainfully, "that I may find her to whom
it belonged."

Passe Rose had to all appearances anticipated
this refusal, for she was already refastening the
collar about her neck. Her fingers proved as
clumsy as those of Gui in the wood, and thus
occupied she had time to reflect upon her answer. Living with the goldsmith, who had examined the fay's girdle and pronounced it of

Greek workmanship, she had devised a very
natural explanation of the manner in which it
came into her possession; but being of a gen-
erous nature, which opened readily at the sight
of misfortune, and having a devouring curiosity
to reach the bottom of all mysteries, she put
this temptation aside, and answered honestly
that she had found it in the wood of Hesbaye.
Thereupon she related how she had gone thither
to gather herbs on a day when the king hunted;
and how one of those who followed the hunt,
being thrown from his horse, which fell in a
thorn thicket, had left the collar on the ground,
it having doubtless been loosed by the fall; and
that she, hastening homeward from the place
where she lay concealed, had seen it glistening among the leaves. On finishing her tale,
Passe Rose leaned back against the wall in the
shadow.

Friedgis looked at her no longer; disappointment had succeeded the interest with which he
had first listened, and he turned away.

"Is the maid of thy kin?" asked Passe Rose,
watching him.

He turned again, and their eyes met.

"Aïe!" she cried, leaning forward and clapping her hands; "maid or wife, thou lovest her
well." The Saxon frowned, but Passe Rose saw
only the color which rose to his cheek. "Was

she also made prisoner with thee?" she asked
eagerly. "Where sawest thou her last?"

"At Ehresberg, where the spoil was divided."
He had sat down on the edge of the bed, and
covered his face with his hands.

"At Ehresberg?" repeated Passe Rose.
"Aye,"— prolonging the word with a sympa-
thetic sigh, and nodding in token that she understood everything. "And then — ye were scattered as leaves." Suddenly her face kindled.
"Wouldst thou know where the maid is?" She
had risen to her feet, and touched him on the
shoulder. He lifted his head, looking at her incredulously. "Listen. There is a blind woman
who sits in the porch of the church of St. Sebastian, of whom the people say that she hath power
to see what those who have eyes cannot discover,
and that for a copper piece she will tell in good
Latin speech whatever one desires to know.
Tell me only the maid's name, for I have two
silver sous in my chest " —

He hesitated, and the eager expression on her
face changed to one of disappointment, the red
lips pouted disdainfully, and, shrugging her
shoulders, she was about to turn away, when
Friedgis seized her by the arm.

"Stay! Her name is Rothilde."

"Rothilde?" repeated Passe Rose softly under her breath; then turning full upon him her

large eyes, " I like thee well," she said, with a candor so sincere that the Saxon's heart warmed towards her. " Thy hand is heavy, and thou shoulderedst me yesterday as I were a miller's sack, but I believe thee as I would not the prior himself, and as sure as my name is Passe Rose I will not fail thee. Look! " she exclaimed, drawing a small dagger from her bosom. " When I came for the collar I said, 'I will have mine own, though it be in the wolf's den.' Take it; with thee I have no use for it; keep it till I come again."

Friedgis looked at her in amazement. There was not a trace of coquetry in her manner.

" Thou art not afraid."

" True," she replied, replacing the dagger in her dress, as she recollected the lonely road from the abbey to the town. " Give me now thy cord."

" There is no need. Hold my hand, and thy feet will touch the ground."

" But the stone," said Passe Rose.

He loosed the cord from his waist, and without further delay the girl slid, feet foremost, through the opening, holding fast to his hand.

" For whom didst thou make this hole ? " she asked, as she was about to disappear.

"The wolf has two holes to his den," replied Friedgis.

Passe Rose laughed. " Let go thy claws, —
my feet touch," — and he loosed her hands.

She secured the rope about the stone that he
might draw it up in its place, and while thus
occupied imitated softly the note of the cuckoo.

" Didst thou hear the cuckoo calling in the
wood?" she whispered, standing tiptoe on the
stone. " Listen for it again in three days' time.
But stay thou here. They have shaved thy
head; the next time they will slit thine ears.
Farewell."

Then he heard the sound of her feet running
on the road.

V.

To keep her dagger company, Passe Rose
carried a key, which gave her infinite trouble;
for the former was slender and admirably concealed under the fold of her garment, whereas
the latter — although it opened only the small
door into the garden, under which Jeanne herself, who was both short and fat, stooped in passing — was of extraordinary size, and hidden
with difficulty. Having locked this door behind her, on her return from the abbey, and
entered the kitchen softly, she hung the key on
the peg, that the boy who drove the geese to the
fields might find it in the morning. She even

looked into the adjoining apartment, a sort of shed filled with straw and hay, where the lad slept with the donkeys, to see that he slept well, and, being satisfied of this by his breathing, closed the door carefully and went to her own chamber.

Jeanne's garden lay to the south, and was separated from the street by a wall nearly hidden within by the plum-trees, which, trained against its surface, seemed all to be vying with each other as to which should first peep over the top to discover what was without. At the farther extremity the wall was pierced by a large gate, with double doors, leading to the market-place in front of the church of St. Sebastian, whose tower threw its shadow into the garden, and thus furnished Jeanne an excellent clock for nearly half the day. " It is time to put the soup on the fire, — the cabbages have got the sun," she would say; by which she meant it was nearly ten, and that the hour when all good citizens had their dinner was near at hand. The remaining side of the garden was bordered by houses whose windows overlooked the entire inclosure, much to Jeanne's discomfort; for though she not infrequently gossiped with her neighbors, she liked not to be under their observance; so that to escape this she had caused to be planted on this side a row of wild carnelian cherry-trees, which, in time, not only yielded excellent fruit, but also interrupted her neighbors' view, while in no way intercepting their gossip.

It must be admitted that both Werdric and Jeanne made good all observance of Lent and holy-days by plenary indulgence the rest of the year. "Of what use are fine garments," said Jeanne, "except it be for the priest who serves God at the altar? They neither warm the body better than coarse ones, nor preserve the health; neither can they be taken into the other world. But God hath provided all manner of food to nourish his creatures." Passe Rose, who, in the course of the many vicissitudes of her fortune, had often eaten bread of millet and even of beechnuts with relish, did not fail to appreciate the unending supply of soft loaves, kneaded with milk and butter, which came from Jeanne's oven; for the latter not only made those pasties with yeast which could not be had of the public baker, but also baked her loaves over the embers of her own hearth, having an oven expressly for this purpose, in addition to the iron tripod over the fire on the earthen floor of her kitchen. Indeed, it was the pleasantest thing in the world to sit in the morning sun, as Passe Rose was doing the day after her adventure in the abbey, and watch the good dame as

she went about her matin duties. The kitchen
projected into the yard, and, the wooden parti-
tion between the posts supporting the roof being
removed during the summer, there was no lack
of fragrant air from the garden. The cherries
shone among the dark leaves, and the plums
made a purple mist against the wall. Little
birds hopped boldly up the path leading from the
gate, on one side of which stretched lines of cab-
bage and shallot, beet-root and parsley, while on
the other was a pleasance of grass growing lux-
uriously in the shade of the cherry-trees. Under
the eaves hung branches of sweet herbs; within,
on the shelves, were apples and plums dried in
the oven for winter use; on the walls shone
vessels of iron and copper; and from the pot on
the tripod, or the spit attached to its legs, came
always some smell so savory that the pigs in the
street without paused to sniff the air.

Jeanne, intent upon the contents of her stew-
pan, would certainly have been astonished could
she have known the projects which filled the
small head of Passe Rose. Nothing is so easily
forgotten as that gay pageant of dreams which
troop like an army with music and banners
through the mind of the young. When the
music is hushed and the banners no longer flutter, it is almost in vain that any one tries to recall the display; its figures are scarce more

than dumb, colorless ghosts, so that one doubts
if ever they were anything else. If once they
had witched the mind of Jeanne, in the growth
of her girdle she had clean forgotten them.
Passe Rose, on the contrary, at the very instant
Jeanne seasoned the stew, was listening intently
to the dream music and watching the dream
banners. Neither assisting Jeanne nor busying
herself with spinning, as was her wont, she sat
idly clasping her knees with her hands and gazing at the church tower. So still was she that
the little birds hopped nearer and nearer, and,
after inspecting her from all sides, and conclud-
ing that she was no more to be feared than the
statue over the church portal, would certainly
have flown to her knee or shoulder, had not a
wooden shutter in an adjoining house opened
suddenly, and a voice, which caused Passe Rose
to turn her head, cried, —

"Neighbor Jeanne, hast thou heard the news
from the abbey?"

Jeanne, seeing that it was Maréthruda, the
wife of the notary, ran to the wall beneath the
window, her spoon in her hand, while Passe
Rose listened.

"Nay, what has happened?" said Jeanne.

"The abbot has recovered"—replied Maréthruda.

"Praise be to God and the blessed martyr!"

interrupted Jeanne. "When did the fever leave him?"

"It was no fever at all," rejoined the other. "Have patience," for Jeanne was on the point of interrupting her again. "As thou knowest, the blessed saint came not at once to his aid; so that after the relics were brought from below and mass was said, all withdrew except two who watched beside him, praying. Towards midnight one of these perceived that the abbot moved his lips whenever, in his prayer, he repeated the name of Christ our Lord, and, thinking he would speak, laid his ear to the abbot's mouth. No sooner had he done this than he heard a most horrible hissing, as of fat on the coals" —

"Mercy of God!" ejaculated Jeanne.

"Amazed at this, he asked the abbot what he desired, and the brother with him came also, asking the same question. Then a voice, very harsh and not at all like to the abbot's replied, 'Abbot I am none, but a satellite of Satan, who has given me orders to torment the souls of all who love justice and pity the poor. To this end have I power to enter their bodies, or take upon me any form of man or of woman.' Then they ordered the demon, in the name of the saint, to come out, and he replied, 'I will, not because of your authority, but because of the power of the martyr.' This the demon said, shuddering and breathing rage, through the mouth of the abbot. Immediately afterwards he came out, and the abbot, speaking in his natural voice, bade them seek the serf who keeps the gate, that he should carry him to his own house, — for thou knowest the abbot is heavy. So he who came last went to the room which is by the gate," — here Maréthruda paused to recover her breath, and Passe Rose, unclasping her hands from her knees, leaned forward her head to listen, — "and, opening the door, what thinkest thou he saw?"

Jeanne, long since lost in wonder, was ready to believe it was Satan himself, but fear had reduced her to such a state she could offer no conjecture.

" A girl of surpassing beauty, who was none other than the demon himself."

Passe Rose laughed softly. " How knowest thou certainly it was he?" she asked gravely, approaching the window.

" Because," rejoined Maréthruda sharply, not liking that any one should doubt the power of the blessed martyrs, "for many reasons. First, there was about the neck a circle of fire; and secondly, no sooner did the fiend perceive the monk making the sign of the cross, than it uttered a piercing shriek and fell upon the floor. And, indeed, that it was no young girl is plain, for immediately the doors of the room were closed and barred, and when morning came the prior went in person to see whether it were so, finding no trace of any one but the serf. Can a young girl of flesh and blood like thyself pass through walls of stone?" asked Maréthruda triumphantly.

"True," replied Passe Rose.

"Moreover," added Jeanne, "devils often take the form of beautiful girls to tempt the saints; that is well known."

"God forbid!" said Passe Rose thoughtfully.

"Do thou go and buy a wax candle of four deniers," said Jeanne fervently, as she returned to her soup, "and light it at the altar of St. Servais in the church of St. Sebastian, and after dinner is over we will go to implore his succor, lest this devil enter one of us."

Whereupon, with a trembling hand, her thoughts flying hither and thither in her brain, like a swarm of bees which have lost their hive, Jeanne stirred the soup, and Passe Rose went down the path to the gate, driving the birds before her, and smiling at their noisy chatter.

It was indeed strange that Passe Rose, who was on her way to consult the pythoness in all sincerity, should at the same time find such cause for laughter in the fact of the abbot's possession by a demon. Yet so it was. So com-plex is the mind of man, and so various are the aspects of all which surround him, that in every age he is seen to deride the powers in whose fear he lives, to seek what he despises and contemn what he desires, to slight what he loves and caress what he loathes; and thus Passe Rose, on the way to the sorceress, made all manner of merriment of monkish superstitions, just as Jeanne, while powdering her cakes with coriander and adding the saffron to her soup, said to herself that only by resisting all carnal appetites could one be sure to escape the power of devils.

Having purchased the candle, Passe Rose approached the church portal slowly, looking for an opportunity when she might address the woman without being observed; for although the latter lived altogether upon the alms she received from those who sought her counsel, there was not one in all Maestricht who did not agree with the abbot that every such practice was contrary to the word of God and altogether unlawful. So Passe Rose lingered on the way, and, coming into the porch, began to admire the carvings over the door, although she had seen them often enough, and indeed much finer elsewhere; and when no one was by she pressed her sou into the old woman' hand, and, stooping to her ear, whispered : —

"I seek a Saxon maiden whose name is

Rothilde. Tell me quickly where she is to be found."

One might well think that God had forgotten the work of his hand at the sight of this creature, whose body was so curved by the rickets that her knees were close to her chin.

"Hasten," said Passe Rose, her rosy cheek next the yellow skin.

"Come again at the vesper service," replied the sorceress, "and I will tell thee all thou desirest to know."

Passe Rose was disappointed at this delay, but, restraining her impatience as best she might, went in and lighted the candle at the altar of St. Servais, where already others were burning, and before which were many people praying; for the rumor of what had transpired was spread abroad through the whole city. Thither also she returned with Jeanne in the afternoon, and again after the vesper office, when the sorceress told her that if she would compass her quest she must pass that night in fast and prayer in the oratory, and at vigils open the gospels which were on the altar, and it would be told her what she was to do.

Now it was no hardship for Passe Rose to fast only one evening and night, for she had often fasted perforce longer than that; neither did she fear to watch by night in the oratory. But it troubled her sorely to open the gospels, for she could not read. However, she made known to Jeanne her intention of passing the night in fast and prayer, — a resolve which Jeanne applauded heartily, it being easier for her to commend the abstinence of another than to practice it herself. So when night was come Passe Rose entered the church again, and prostrated herself before the altar in the oratory set apart for St. Servais.

There were others also with her : a woman who was a serf, belonging to the royal domain called Estinnes, suffering from a grievous paralysis, so that she could lift her hand neither to clothe nor feed herself ; a young man having a malady called by the Greeks spasm, whereby his hand shook continually ; and others tormented by various judgments of God, or having sins to expiate by prayer and fasting. Presently the sacristan closed the doors, and the sound of his footsteps on the stone flags having ceased, Passe Rose knew that he had retired. Then she raised her head and looked about her.

The feeble lights around the altar were unable to penetrate the darkness, and the shadows behind her seemed momentarily to advance and retreat, as if contending with them. Occasionally a groan or an invocation from some one of those near her rose like a spirit into the dome, beating back and forth from side to side, as a bird seeking to escape its place of confinement. Truly it did not occur to Passe Rose, as it might have to the learned abbot, that the altar, with its precious vessels and struggling tapers, before which these unfortunates were kneeling, surrounded by the darkness and overarched by the dome which flung back their supplications, represented in some manner the Church of God, so feeble amid the suffering, crime, and ignorance of the world, yet calm with patience and an invincible faith in its own destiny. Surely, of all this Passe Rose understood as little as she understood the characters on the pages of the gospels. Yet she knew well that there was here something too vast for understanding, in whose mysterious presence kings bowed and her own spirit trembled; and for a while she remained on the cold floor, repeating her prayers in good earnest without lifting her eyes. But being in vigorous health and of active mind, soon her thoughts began to wander, so that even with pinching herself she could scarce keep from dozing. At last her head fell to one side, and, anxious lest through sleep she should miss the hour, she rose softly, walking to and fro in the darkness, behind the others.

There was yet some time before the monastery bell would announce the hour of vigils;

there was nothing for her hand to do nor anything to divert her attention; so she gave herself over to her thoughts, following wherever fancy led her, as when one who is half asleep abandons himself to conscious dreaming. At first she debated with herself whether it were necessary to open the gospels at the hour which the woman had indicated; for although this manner of divination had been practiced by kings and was yet much esteemed by the people, it was under the ban of the Church, and expressly forbidden in the articles which Karle had caused to be written in his councils. This thought disturbed her, for there were many others present, and she wondered whether it would not answer her purpose to open the book on the reading-desk near the high altar. But aside from the fact that she had been particularly enjoined to consult the gospels in the oratory of St. Servais, there was only a single lamp burning before the high altar, and its light was so feeble that she could distinguish nothing.

Perhaps her strange adventures in the wood and the abbey recalled to mind somewhat of her former manner of life; or perhaps, being alone in the darkness and solitude, apart from the others, a sense of freedom possessed her which it was not possible to feel in the garden of Jeanne; or it may have been the influence of the night hours, which often set free thoughts and imaginings that, like many winged and creeping creatures, lie hidden during the day, — at all events, whether for these reasons or not, Passe Rose began to dream and indulge her fancy in visions wherein neither Jeanne, nor Werdric, nor the boy who tended the geese, nor any familiar objects had part; not even Passe Rose herself in her simple dress and sandals, but Passe Rose in silken shoon and a pearl girdle, Passe Rose on a white mare, with a page at the bridle rein. Now she traveled with Friedgis in a great wood, seeking the Saxon maiden, and now she sat with Gui of Tours at banquet; now Friedgis defended her from some wild beast whose covert they disturbed in passing, and now she rode in the train of the king's daughters — when suddenly the monastery bell sounded faintly from the hill, all these things vanished, and she saw only the altar surrounded by the candles and the gospels lying upon it. Yet on the background of her sight the dream lingered, so that she was conscious both of it and what she was doing as, going boldly forward, she opened the gospels, noting well the miniature which adorned the page, and making a mark with her nail against the passage she selected.

In the early morning came one of the clerks who had charge of the church, to prepare for the morning office.

"Sir," said Passe Rose, pointing to the gospels, "is that the Scriptures which the king gave at the feast of Noël to the church of St. Sebastian?"

"No," he replied; "the book of which thou speakest is used only on holy-days."

"I have heard it said that it is ornamented with most wonderful pictures."

"That is true," answered the clerk, "painted in gold and vermilion upon purple vellum."

"In gold and vermilion," repeated Passe Rose; "that were indeed wonderful."

"Moreover," said the clerk, "it is written in new characters, very easy to read" —

"Like those of the notary, which Maréthruda has shown me," suggested Passe Rose.

"Nay," replied the clerk, "that is an ordinary manner of writing very different" —

"Show me, I pray thee, in thy missal," said Passe Rose.

"I have it not with me," he replied, "but come hither. Seest thou these characters?" — opening the gospels, — "how long and thin is the stroke of the pen? Those in the king's parchment are round, and" —

"What astonishes me," interrupted Passe Rose, turning over the leaves, "is that any one should find meaning in such marks."

"It is very easy," said the clerk complacently.

"Tell me, now," asked Passe Rose, putting her finger on the page, "canst thou read this?"

"Certainly. That is the Gospel of Saint Matthew, who is here relating what the blessed Christ said to the multitude, and there where thou hast thy finger it is written: '*Behold, they that wear soft clothing are in kings' houses.*'"

"Aïe, Aïe," ejaculated Passe Rose, lost in wonder, and repeating the words under her breath.

Recalled at this moment to his duties by those who came to the morning service, the clerk closed the book, while Passe Rose, whose interest in the art of the copyist seemed to have been satisfied, went slowly away, saying to herself, "In kings' houses — in kings' houses."

VI.

A rise of three degrees in the temperature of the blood is fatal to ceremony, and so trifling a change often discovers a secret one might otherwise seek in vain to know — whether the bond which attaches others to us be one of interest or affection. Thus it was that the abbot, though his chaplain and servants neither asked permission to be seated in his presence nor received his wishes kneeling, as they did when he was in health, perceived from his sick-bed the evidence of a solicitude on his behalf which imparted to the thought of returning life a satisfying pleasure.

This was no more than he might rightfully have expected. His rule had been firm but mild, and setting forth doctrines strange to his times, namely, that power was for the protection of the weak, and not for their oppression, and that no man or woman, however unfit for labor or war, might not become useful to God, if only by exhibiting virtues of meekness and patience. Yet the abbot was always surprised as well as pleased that men should either love or praise him; for it was a noteworthy fact that of all who knew him none held him in less esteem than did he himself. Whereas in later times Pascal said, "I cannot forgive Montaigne," Rainal, abbot of St. Servais, used continually to say, "I cannot forgive Rainal."

Wearing ordinarily the common dress of a monk, except that all rose and bowed when he came into the refectory or chapter-house, none who saw him would have suspected that one of so modest a manner had been first chaplain to the great Karle, and loved by him above other counselors. Not only had he frequently served the king among the *missi dominici*, de-

termining pleas and judging causes of every
kind, but he had also been sent upon distant
missions both of church and state, — to the
pope at Rome, and to the dukes of Bavaria
and Spoleto.　How he had discharged these
duties was recorded over the king's own signa-
ture in the grant of his benefice, wherein it
was written that " by faithful service and a de-
voted obedience he worthily deserves the favor
of our generosity."　And it cost the king more
to part with his person than with the gifts
whereby he honored him ; for not only in his
palaces of Aix and Ingelheim, when, resting
from war, he refreshed his mind with learning
and the arts of peace, but also in the wastes of
Saxony, when he launched his *leudes* against
the rebels, at the siege of Pavia, and in the
grievous retreat from Spain, Rainal, no less
sturdy and tireless in the saddle than his royal
master, had shared his triumphs and reverses.

From these scenes he withdrew at his own request.　" For the child the hour of death may
be near at hand," he said to the king ; " for the
old man it must be.　Suffer me, then, to retire
from the affairs of this world, that when that
hour comes it may not surprise me occupied
with passing things, but applied to prayer and
meditation on the divine word."　Upon this
entreaty, oft repeated, the king released him

from daily attendance upon his person, as also from visiting the court yearly as others were required to do; and having thus given him control over himself, following the custom of his predecessors, was pleased further to make him abbot of St. Servais, with jurisdiction over the neighboring convent of Eicka and all its dependencies and granges, besides granting him certain villas with their adjacent forests and fields, pastures and meadows, formerly belonging to the royal domain, together with all servants and serfs attached thereto, to have and to hold in quietness, and to leave by will to whomsoever he wished.

It is not to be wondered at that the king, loving the abbot so well, should desire to be informed of his health; and to this end he sent frequently from the castle of Immaburg, near to Aix, where he was then passing the autumn hunting-time, inquiring how the abbot fared; and on the evening of the second day following the invocation of the relics came Gui of Tours on the king's errand.

Jeanne and Passe Rose were returning from afternoon service, and were leaving the open space before the church of St. Sebastian, near the corner of the garden wall, when the troop entered at the opposite angle, and at the sound of the horses' feet they turned to see what was approaching. Perceiving that the horsemen were riding furiously and directing their course to the street where she was, Jeanne seized the hand of Passe Rose, who would fain have loitered, and hurried her towards the garden gate, for the street was narrow, and she feared to be caught between the walls. So fast did the troop approach that the clatter of hoofs resounded in the street before the gate was reached, so that Jeanne was forced to run, and had well-nigh exhausted her strength when she reached the door. Here, although perfectly safe, she fumbled the key in her haste, and thrust it awry in the lock, while Passe Rose, there being room for but one under the arch, stood without, her hands and back pressed against the wall. The passing of the troop was the affair of a moment ; but when Jeanne had succeeded in opening the door, and, though all danger was over, had excitedly pulled Passe Rose into the garden after her, the girl carried in with her a picture as distinct as if she had seen it quietly in her own chamber, and not for a moment only, through a cloud of dust and amid a tumult of arms and horses' feet. This picture was none other than that of Gui of Tours at the head of the horsemen, a picture complete from the short-sleeved tunic which left bare the knees, the fur-lined jacket, and the baldric from which hung the sword, even to the shoes fas-

tened about the legs by leather thongs. On his
part, although swept on by the impetus of those
who came after him, Gui of Tours saw plainly
his collar of gold about a neck of equal lustre,
and two brown eyes, which, without any effort,
or perhaps knowledge, on the part of their pos-
sessor, shot a glance of recognition sharper than
an arrow's point through the dusty cloud.

"The world is not over-wide after all," said
Gui to himself, smiling as he galloped on.

Beyond the city the cavalcade left the Roman
road leading southward for that up the monastery hill. The way was steep, but the jaded
horses climbed it eagerly, their ears pricked
forward as if anticipating already the abbot's
oats. The slope on either side was covered with
vineyards, whose fruit was beginning to ripen,
and the full clusters, shaded with golden-yellow
or purple, might plainly be seen between the
bright green leaves tinged with autumn bronze.
Vine-dressers were tying the bending branches
to the stakes with willow withes, or spreading
ashes about the roots to hasten the work of the
sun ; and on reaching the brow of the hill, fields
sweet with odors of drying grass, interspersed
with patches of wheat and rye, flax and hemp,
appeared on the plain. The sun was low in his
arc as the abbey towers came in view, overtop-
ping the trees which shaded the fish-ponds, and

the sound of the wooden hammer on the bell was heard calling the laborers home. From the vines and the fields, the vegetable gardens about the ponds, and the blue line of forest to the west, they came in groups, laughing and chatting together, their tools in their hands; others were laden with baskets of provisions, while across the pastures, between the lowing of loitering cattle, might be heard the song of the goatherds and shepherds, and the wood-cutters chanting hymns and prayers as they emerged from the forest with their bundles of fagots and poles.

The vast court within the outer wall, extending on this side the length of the abbey close, with its small wooden houses, its workshops, granaries, and sheds, swarmed at this hour with a motley population. Wagons loaded with grain were drawn up within the gate, their unyoked oxen gazing stupidly around; donkeys, almost hidden by their burdens, waited patiently before the stalls; herdsmen carried milk-pails, whose white froth gave forth a pleasant odor, to the bakehouse, or filled the cribs in the cattle-sheds; workmen were preparing the wine-presses for the vintage, and rows of casks banded with iron stood ready for the coating of pitch and soap heating in caldrons over the fire. In the middle of the court was a small wooden basilica, in front of whose portico, under the shade of a few trees festooned by vines, a table was spread with loaves and dressed meats for the poor seeking food and shelter at the abbot's hands.

Through this throng Gui and his company made their way slowly, saluting the almoner at the table under the trees, and the monks in the doors of the workshops along the way; and coming to the high wall dividing the court from the monastery close, Gui struck with his sword-hilt upon the oaken gate.

Having given his horse to his servant, he, with two of his companions, entered, and were conducted to the hall reserved for the abbot's guests.

An atmosphere of peace and quietude, in striking contrast to the activity without, pervaded the inner inclosure. The very language was different, for the vulgar tongue was prohibited within the abbey proper.

Learning that the abbot was mending fast, Gui retired to the chamber assigned him, and after a bath, which he found already prepared in the large tank of warm water, returned to the hall into which his chamber opened. There Sergius the prior, dispensing the hospitality of the house in the abbot's absence, awaited him, as also a goodly smell of cooking which came from the adjoining room, through whose doorway might be seen figures hurrying to and fro in the flaring firelight and smoke.

The Prior Sergius was very agreeable in conversation, though he said little. Those whom he addressed were at first charmed by a certain Roman elegance of manner consorting strangely with his robe. Afterwards, whether because of his small white hands, or a fire which slumbered in his eyes, one began to entertain all manner of absurd conjectures; as that, if he had not been a monk, the love of luxury and pomp, or the greed of power and gain — but no, that were impossible, and while putting away the suspicions, the soft reserve of his speech gave to them so fresh a force that one looked askance at his pale, thin face, saying, "God keep him the monk, else the Devil will possess the man."

If young Gui of Tours did not observe this, it was either because he was hungry and the table well served, or because his thoughts were on other things. He listened to the account of the interposition of the saint in the abbot's behalf, and he in turn told the prior the news of the outside world, — of the ambassadors from the newly elected pope, who brought the keys and standard of the city of Rome; of the end of the war against the Avars, the destruction of their fortified camp, and the fabulous treasures found in the royal residence of the Kan;

of the expected coming of Pepin, the king's son,
to Aix; and then, suddenly turning to Sergius, —

"Prior," he asked, "tell me who it is that
dwells in the house by the square of St. Sebastian, at the corner of the street leading thence
upon the road to Liege."

"It must be Werdric the goldsmith," replied
the prior, after a moment's reflection.

Now the prior had one habit which, when it
overcame him, greatly marred his Roman manner. This was to fix his eyes upon those who
conversed with him. A straightforward gaze
which follows the motion of the heart troubles
no one, but to be watched and, as it were, studied like a book is far from agreeable. For this
reason, while the prior was telling who Werdric
was, — that he was born a royal serf attached
to one of the granges which the king had given
the abbot; that the latter had released him
from the yoke of servitude for his skill in gold-
working, and given him the house where he lived
with ample freedom to use it and all he might
thereafter make in his trade, according to the
canons and his own will, like other Roman citizens; how he lived in peace with his wife and
four others, one being a serf of the abbey, also
very skillful in the setting of gold, one a boy
who tended the geese in the meadow on which

the abbot had granted Werdric the right of pasturage, and two women, also serfs, spinning and weaving exceeding well ; and that there was, moreover, he believed, a young maiden in the household who passed for Werdric's daughter, an idle girl received out of charity, whether freeborn or not he could not tell, — while, as was said, Gui listened to this information, he felt the espial of the prior's eye like the pry of a lever under a stone ; so that although learning exactly what he wished to know, he nevertheless muttered to himself, " May God wither such eyes ! " and again, " This monk is both shrewd and audacious ; " and at last, when the prior came to the young girl, as if weary of the whole matter, he flung down his cup on the board, saying that if it pleased the abbot to receive him that night he was ready, and if not he would go to bed. Upon this the prior, who studied to live in perfect understanding with all, and knew how to preside at a table though partaking of nothing himself, filled the young man's cup and said he would ascertain what was the abbot's pleasure.

Gui's two companions, their faces hid in their arms and their arms on the table, were already asleep; for the ride had been long and the abbey wine was heavy. Indeed, young Gui himself, when he looked into his cup, could see nothing but a golden collar and two brown eyes which laughed and vanished when the wine was stirred, and reappeared when it was still again. He rose from the bench, walking to and fro, deploring the necessity which forbade his remaining in Maestricht, and endeavoring to devise some plan by which he might accomplish his mission without returning at once to Immaburg. Often he abandoned the thought as impossible to realize, being the king's messenger; and then, when he lifted the cup to his lips, the eyes in the wine shone and laughed again, and such perfumes rose from it as filled his brain with new devices, — in the midst of which he walked through the archway into the kitchen, nor knew where he was till the smoke lingering in the rafters and the shining of vessels in the firelight recalled him to his senses. While thus debating what he should do, a servant came, saying that the abbot had just awakened from refreshing slumber and would receive the king's message.

The effect produced upon the abbot by the relation of the events which occurred the night Passe Rose visited the monastery had been little short of stupefaction. He was not free from the naive credulousness which tinctured the piety of his day, a piety which if thus sometimes degraded to superstition was also often elevated to the heroism of faith. He had not the slightest doubt that the traces made by the chariot-wheels of Pharaoh on the Red Sea bottom were still visible, as affirmed by travelers who visited the spot, and that if effaced by the violence of the waves they reappeared by the will of God when the sea became calm again. But it perplexed him to believe that God had given over his body to be the abode of devils. That such should assume the form of a beautiful woman was credible enough, but that they should find shelter in the temporary dwelling of the soul of an abbot was unheard of and contrary to reason. Reflecting upon this matter as he lay on his bed, he endeavored to put away the temptings of spiritual pride. How should he justify the ways of God? When he looked about him did he not see bishops seeking honors rather than to honor God, magistrates loving presents more than justice, nobles glutted with spoils, — everywhere war, the war of the vulture upon the defenseless, the war of the kite upon the dove? How should he reconcile these things to the providence of God? Abbot though he was, he understood them as little as did Passe Rose what she saw when repeating her prayers before the shrine of St. Servais. Yet he knew, as she did, the presence of something mightier than he, — the spirit brooding above the waters. When perplexed by such thoughts the abbot instantly

addressed himself to prayer. He knew very
well that the tendency to think was one of his
besetting sins. His mind, vigorous as had been
his body, loved to try its wings. He longed for
the upper space in the presence of whose sun
no cloud can form. A demon was thus ever
opening the window of his soul and tempting his
thoughts to flight; but like the dove loosed by
Noah on the waste of waters, the thought of
the abbot always returned to the ark of God.

Following his conductor, Gui traversed the
shady walk between the church and the school
to the abbot's lodging, and when the door was
opened perceived the prior with two others
standing at the foot of the bed. Gui had seen
the abbot about the king's person and knew
his face well; for even after Rainal's retirement
from the court he had accompanied his master
upon the expedition to Saxony, and this the
more willingly in the hope of moderating the
treatment of the captives. Yet Gui was astonished to see the ravages of the fever. Approaching the bed, he knelt by its side; whereupon
the abbot laid his hand on his head and blessed
him.

Then said Gui, "Our sovereign master, the
very glorious Karle, to Rainal, his faithful serv-
itor and friend, sends greeting. He desires me,
his messenger, to say to you that your health is

his joy, and your joy his happiness, and may you continue in the grace of Jesus Christ and of all his saints."

It was more from emotion than from weakness that the abbot's voice trembled in reply.

"Say to the king in my name that the assurance of his friendship is consolation to the mind and medicine to the body, being after the grace of Heaven the support of failing years; and that if God deigns to give me life and health I shall speak in person those things which weakness of body now forbids the tongue to utter."

As Gui, rising from his knees, waited a sign that he might retire, the abbot, regarding him intently, as if searching his memory, asked his name.

"Gui, son of Robert, Count of Tours," replied the youth.

A shadow passed over the abbot's face as he heard the count's name. "Christ preserve you," he said, lifting his hand in sign of dismissal.

Now the abbot had caused to be written an account of the interposition of the saint in his behalf, duly signed by witnesses, and this document, together with a portion of the silken cloth which covered the reliquary, he desired to transmit to the king; so that when the morning was come, and Gui, preparing to leave the abbey, was about to mount his horse, he received a message from the abbot to the effect that he sent by a faithful brother, by name Dominic, certain papers to the king; and in order that the said brother should suffer no inconvenience on the way, he committed him to the safe conduct of the captain. Immediately after, riding a gray mule, appeared Brother Dominic himself, a fitting witness to all in the abbot's letter, having watched at night beside his litter and seen the shape taken by the demon in Friedgis's cell.

Young Gui of Tours was hot of temper and could scarce restrain his wrath; for his mind had but one thought, — to discharge the king's mission as speedily as possible, and return to Maestricht. But with a monk riding a mule, there was little chance to use the spur, and the day would scarce answer to compass the distance. Help for it there was none, however, and saluting the monk with scant grace, he rode slowly through the courtyard and out of the gate upon the road between the vineyards.

Never before was a man in so fit a temper to bear with discourtesy as was Brother Dominic, ambling along on his gray mule. Not since the day he came with letters from the convent of St. Bavon to the abbot of St. Servais, commending him as very dextrous in every art of the scribe, had his heart overflowed with such contentment.   For he had in his pouch, besides the manuscript for the king, the epistles for every day in the year, done by his own hand and destined for the queen.   The long months spent at his desk and the cramp in his right thumb were forgotten in the thought of the allegorical figures, the gigantic capitals, whose admirable drawing and soft coloring had cost so many hours, and which were now to be examined by a queen.   Though the missal was safely inclosed in the silken altar-cloth and thrice enveloped in thick parchment, this did not prevent him from turning over in his mind every page and examining with pride every well-known stroke of the pen.   Then again, like the apostles of old who had witnessed miracles and cast out devils, he also had seen the power of God, and it pleased him mightily to think that a poor monk should have been concerned in such weighty matters; so that between the praise he put into the queen's mouth and the wonder he foresaw on the king's face, the recollection of his gold-dotted miniatures and the rehearsal of the story of the demon, he had little time to complain that Gui of Tours rode moodily before him in silence.   Without his window, almost within reach of his hand as he sat at his copying-desk, a bird had her nest in a vine, and the view opening before him from the brow of the hill was to be seen also from the orchard within the abbey walls. Yet, riding to Immaburg on the high-road was a very different thing from sitting at his copying-desk ; and the boundless plain, the river smoking in the morning sun, the scent of dew-covered hay, the thrill of the air when a bird sang, all seemed new to him. The very motion of the mule was agreeable, although Brother Dominic was neither well-knit like the abbot, nor graceful like the prior, and the mule staggered at times on a rolling stone.

A temper quick to rise is soon appeased, and Gui of Tours had not reached the foot of the hill before his mood began to change. "By Heaven," he said half aloud, "the monk is not to blame, and I do him wrong." At the same instant came the thought to give the mule to one of the servants, and seat the monk on the servant's horse. "God willing, he may hold fast at a gentle pace, and compass a gallop before the day is over," thought he. Full of this thought, he reined in his steed, for the horses were fresh, and, stretching their necks to loosen the rein, had gained at every step on the mule.

At this place the road dipped to cross a running brook, and rising in both directions, was visible but a short distance. Thinking that the brawling of the stream drowned the sound of the mule's feet, and expecting every moment to see its ears over the top of the rise, Gui waited awhile, ashamed of his discourtesy, then rode backward to greet the monk with a pleasant word. But before reaching the brow of the hill he saw, to his astonishment, that the mule and the monk had parted company, whether in wrath or peace were hard to tell; for the mule was returning leisurely to the abbey, while Brother Dominic, the signs of terror on his face, ran in the opposite direction with such speed as his habit of body and dress would permit.

VII.

Was there ever any one who once in his life did not feel happiness, not flowing in from without, but welling up, as it were, from an unsealed spring within? The world and all about are the same; the springs are not there, but in ourselves. The eye sees and the ear hears what never were seen nor heard before; for once soul and sense minister to each other and agree.

It was not because of the sun struggling through her window of horn that Passe Rose, the morning on which Gui of Tours set out from Maestricht for Immaburg, rose so blithe from her dreams, — for this it did every fair day in the year, — nor could she honestly have told what had unsealed her heart's spring. Yet never had grating of shutter as Werdric opened his shop below, nor knocking at panel slide as some passer-by stopped at the window in the wall of the tavern across the way for his morning beer, nor braying of loaded mule passing down the street sounded as they did that morn. There was nothing so common or so trivial that her happiness could not give it value, just as every vulgar pebble twinkles, or blade of common grass revives, when the spring water overflows them. It was nothing to her that Jeanne's cakes were underdone; that the bees in the garden were making less honey than last year; that the boy who tended the geese was sick from overeating of green plums. She ate the cakes with a laugh, vowing that if the honey was less in quantity, the quality was better than ever before, and seeing Jeanne anxious for the geese, offered to drive them herself to pasture in the boy's stead.

Clustered about the garden gate, alarm and wonder reigned among the flock. The oldest could not remember such a delay, and nothing so disturbs the mind as the invasion of habit. The citizens of Maestricht themselves could not have felt more alarm at seeing the sun delay his rising than did the geese to see the garden gate still closed; and if the moon had appeared in the sun's stead, they would not have lifted their hands in greater astonishment than that with which the geese craned their necks to see Passe Rose behind them with the boy's staff. There was now no loitering to converse with their fellows by the way. The leader no longer regulated the march and its halts; for Passe Rose was quick of step, and many a joint ached, and many a throat was hoarse with remonstrance before the pasture was gained.

Beyond the town the way skirted the abbey hill to where the brook from the fish-ponds gained the plain; thence it followed the brook upward to an intervale hollowed out of the slope, like a man's hand. Here the stream lost all unity, running in separate noiseless rills about tufted islands of grass, or spreading itself to rest about all manner of water plants, such as the geese loved. Passe Rose, well acquainted with the place, knew that by ascending higher to where the brook crossed the road she might watch at her ease in the oak shade the flock on the meadow below. Thither, therefore, she went, and after washing her feet in the cool water and laying her sandals, which had been wet in passing through the meadow, on a stone in the sun, sat down near by under the trees.

Before her the narrow cleft where the brook ran widened out into the pasture, its water shimmering between the grasses and dotted with the bluish gray of the feeding flock. Farther on, where the stream gathered again to fall out of sight over the mead's edge, the plain covered with forest stretched into the dim distance, where we are fain to think lies all that is lacking in what is near. Passe Rose sat motionless under the oak, her chin on her knee; but no bird soaring over the plain roamed so fast or so free as her thought. It was now the third day, and she could scarcely wait for the night in order to tell to Friedgis the answer she had read in the gospels; for notwithstanding the consequences of her previous visit she was resolved at least to sing, as she had promised, the cuckoo's song without the wall. Then the recollection of her being mistaken for an evil spirit brought a smile to her lips, and — but why repeat the idle thoughts of an idle maid? Only be it said that behind them all was the image of the king's captain, riding through the forest, over the plain, among the geese, — in fact, wherever Passe Rose turned her eyes; while up from her heart welled the unsealed spring, filling her veins with an unknown pleasure. Thus rises sometimes the fragrance of a flower whose roots we cannot discover.

So distinct was the captain's image that at the sound of horses Passe Rose sprang to her feet

without a thought for her sandals, and ran bare-
footed to the fringe of shrubs and young shoots
which screened the road. The horsemen had
disappeared in the gully, and parting the sweet-
brier stems, Passe Rose made her way through
to watch for their reappearance on the farther
side.

It was then that Brother Dominic was passing
on his gray mule. Unaccustomed to such vio-
lent motion, drops of perspiration shone on his
round face ; but this he bore bravely, his dilated
nostrils drinking in the odors of field and wood,
and his hands clinging fast to the saddle-pouch,
both to insure his own safety and that of its
precious contents. From thinking how he
should bear himself at court, pleased also at his
good success in bestriding the mule, self-esteem
had gotten the upper-hand of humility ; and,
like many who perceive what they should have
said or done only after the occasion is past, he
devised imaginary perils wherein to exercise his
superfluous courage. " Fiend of hell ! " thought
he, " another time thou shalt not escape so
easily ; " and fortified by the bright sun and
pleasant air, he saw himself in Friedgis's cell,
advancing boldly on the demon, which trembled
at his approach. At this very moment, while
letting go his hold to wipe away the drops which
trickled from his forehead into his eyes, the

gray mule thrust forward its ears at the noise of crackling stems, and Brother Dominic saw the demon itself peering through the copse beside the road.

No sooner did Passe Rose perceive the monk than she sought to retreat, thinking her secret would be discovered. But in a thorn thicket advance is easier than retreat. Moreover, it was clear from Brother Dominic's face and movements that he still labored under his former misapprehension. His hand was raised with a show of courage, and his lips moved valiantly, but terror was gaining upon him fast, and the mule was apparently imbibing this emotion from its master. It is possible that it shook only because the latter was shaking, but Brother Dominic had heard marvelous stories of animal sagacity, and made no doubt that his mule smelt the fumes of hell. Passe Rose would willingly have sunk out of sight in the ground. It was no more to her purpose to be mistaken for a demon than to be recognized as honest flesh and blood. But the sight of the monk's countenance was too much for her prudence; laughter rose to her lips like the spring sap in a young tree; and at its sound, rolling from his mule, which he abandoned with the precious pouch to the protection of the saints, Brother Dominic fled with all his speed, in search of more substantial succor.

Neither Passe Rose nor the mule waited his return. The latter retraced complacently its steps, while the former struggled back with less deliberation through the thicket. If she thought to regain her flock unnoticed, it were better to have risked her sandals on the stone ; for Gui of Tours, to whom the monk had related with such breath as was left him what had occurred, and who, next to seeing Passe Rose, was fain to see a demon in a shape so pleasing as that the monk described, having given Brother Dominic into the care of his followers, and dispatched one of the latter after the mule, forced his way through the copse and came upon Passe Rose herself, tying her sandals and still struggling with suppressed laughter.

Passe Rose blushed neither for her short dress nor her bare legs, but for pleasure and surprise, and at the same time the laughter she could no longer restrain burst again from her lips ; for Gui of Tours, his head still full of the monk's story, could not utter a word, and the confusion of his thought was plainly to be seen in his blue eyes. He stood like a statue, looking at the girl sitting among the oak leaves, tying her sandal and laughing, he was sure, at him ; and if for a moment he himself doubted whether he had to do with flesh or spirit, Passe Rose might well have forgiven him in view of the merriment he afforded her, and the certainty she felt of her ability to set him right. But the sound ot voices in the road brought her thought to the matter in hand.

"Come thou with me," she said, springing to her feet and laying hold of his fur-lined cloak. "I have much to tell thee."

The captain was surprised enough to see Passe Rose, but to be pulled by the sleeve was wholly beyond expectation. Gone was all thought of the king's service; horses, followers, and monk were as if they never had been. He saw nothing but the hand which had pushed his away in the wood of Hesbaye, now leading him on, and the eyes, then brimming with mischief, now divided between pleasure and fear, as they glanced hurriedly from his to the place whence the sounds came. Down the slope beside the tumbling brook, between alder and hazel, he went in a sort of daze, recovering his wits but slowly, while those of Passe Rose, trained by early experience not to scatter at every emergency, were busy in her service. Knowing nothing of the captain's errand, she had to think only of herself, and every glance at his face settled her first impulse into resolve; for she saw there something hard to define, but which warrants confidence without other credentials than a manner of speech or expression of feature.

" Hark ! " she whispered, as they reached a shelter of black mulberry, where the stream dallied before spreading into the meadow. " Hark ! " she repeated, her hand on his arm, her finger at her red lips, and her ear turned to the road.

Meanwhile Brother Dominic, firmly persuaded that the captain had been carried off by the Evil One, having recovered his mule, argued it were better to proceed on their way. One bolder than the others, a swaggering fellow from Wasconia, but faithful of heart and daring of arm, swore he would spit the Devil himself on his sword rather than return to Immaburg without the captain, and drove his horse through the bushes, sword in hand. But devil there was none to spit, nor any trace of the captain save his horse browsing by the roadside ; so that after beating about in vain, reluctantly and but half convinced, he was forced to agree with the others that if the captain were alive he was well able to take care of himself ; and if not, it were a bootless search and far better to fulfill the king's service than to waste the king's time. Therefore at last they resumed their journey, leading their master's horse, Brother Dominic being well satisfied that he, a poor monk, had come out whole of soul and skin from a matter which had cost·the king a captain.

The sound of voices had ceased, and from the
click of retreating hoofs on the road Passe Rose
knew that all danger of pursuit was over. If she
had ventured alone at midnight into the cell of
the Saxon slave who had treated her so roughly,
certainly she had no reason in broad noonday
to fear one who had fastened her collar with
such trembling fingers; yet no sooner was all
risk of interruption past than she withdrew her
hand quickly from the sleeve where it rested,
and the warm blood under her skin rose without
leave, till her eyes swam and her ears were filled
with its murmur; and under pretense of making sure the others had indeed gone, she ran out
to drown her heart-beats in the brook's prattle,
and steady her thought in the fresh sunlight;
angry with herself, yet not forgetting to look in
the water mirror to see, not what was her outward appearance, but what secrets her rebel
face was betraying.

Satisfied with what she saw, yet she commenced to be afraid, exactly why, she knew not,
— only it seemed to her as if some stronger
spirit, having suddenly got lodgment in her
heart and driven her true self out, danced and
sang in its new abode, though too timid to show
itself. " What ails thee ? " she said, struggling
to get possession of her own self, and forcing
her feet forward as the juggler moved those of

the puppets at St. Denis's fair. Gui was just
on the point of following her to see where she
had gone, when the mulberry branches parted
and there she stood among their down-covered
leaves.

" What did the monk say to thee ? " she asked
almost in a whisper.

"That a demon appeared to him in the
thicket as he passed by," replied Gui.

" Hast thou no fear of evil spirits ? " said
Passe Rose provokingly, and seeking to break
the force of his gaze.

So serious was his gesture of scornful protest that she laughed aloud, and with her laugh
came back her courage.

" Sit down here, on this moss. Didst thou
hear aught of this demon at the abbey ? "

" Aye, indeed," said the captain, obeying her ;
and he began to relate what had been told him
of the abbot's recovery and of the demon's presence in Friedgis's lodging.

Standing above him as he sat on the moss
before her, Passe Rose imagined that she had
her enemy, as it were, under her feet, but so
great was her interest in what she heard that
before he had finished she was sitting beside
him, tying her loose sandal and listening intently
to every word.

" It is true," she said, when he had finished.

" I was there myself, but as for issuing from the abbot's body, that is impossible. I went in by the small gate that is north of the great court ; " then, looking into his face, " of all this thou art the cause and no other."

" I ! " exclaimed Gui of Tours.

" Thou," said Passe Rose, " because of the collar thou gavest me. I lost it in the press on the day of the elevation of the relics, but as I went out " — here Passe Rose frowned, remembering the manner of her exit — " I saw it in the hand of the porter. Give it me he would not, except I came at night ready to tell him whence I had it " —

" Dog of a slave ! " interrupted the captain.

" Wait," said Passe Rose. " Not that I cared for the collar," she continued, blushing, " but was vexed at the manner of losing it. So at midnight I knocked at the gate as the porter bade me, thinking to be gone before vigils."

" Alone ? " asked the astonished captain.

" Nay, my dagger was with me," pursued Passe Rose gravely. " The rest is as thou knowest. I had but entered when the monk opened the door. Dieu ! we frightened each other well."

" But afterwards — the doors were barred."

" The Saxon hath a hole in the wall : I scraped my elbow in passing through," said Passe Rose, showing her arm.

"The like of this was never heard before," murmured Gui, overcome with admiration for her courage, and pleased at the value she attached to the jewel.

Passe Rose, continuing her tale, related her consultation with the sorceress, her vigil in the chapel of St. Servais, and how she had gotten the clerk to read the verse in the gospels on the altar.

"Tell me now," she said in conclusion, " whence thou hadst the collar; for I have sworn to the Saxon, and will not fail in my promise."

" It came to me fairly by right of spoil in the division of Ehresberg," replied Gui. " More than this I know not."

" Then the Saxon spoke truly," said Passe Rose eagerly, her thought reverting to the verse the clerk had read her. " Is there no Saxon maiden in the king's household ? The gospels said ' In kings' houses.' "

Now Gui, who had been watching Passe Rose intently, although he heard her question, was thinking of other things.

" By St. Martin ! " she exclaimed, rising to her feet, " I have a mind to go and see."

The captain might well have laughed at this startling proposition, had not jealousy pictured consequences the mere thought of which pierced his heart.

" The king's house is no place for thee," he replied softly, although at that moment Passe Rose looked to him worthy to sit in the queen's seat.

" Why not?" said Passe Rose, turning quickly and fixing her eyes on his.

" Because " — stammered Gui, " because," — his eyes returned her gaze; she wished now she had not sought them, but withdraw her own she would not, — " because — the king's house is no place for maiden feet."

" I fear no height! " she exclaimed impetuously, suddenly conscious that what she said was of no importance and that her eyes, like his, were speaking mightier words.

" There are many who fain would never have climbed, and whom it were wiser to pity than to envy," said Gui.

" I pity no mountain top for the storms about its summit," retorted Passe Rose hotly, endeavoring in vain now to avert what she knew his eyes could no longer contain.

" And I swear if thou goest," cried the youth passionately, leaping to his feet as a sword flashes from the scabbard, " thou goest with me only."

They stood for a moment face to face, trembling, each afraid to take a step in the new world God had suddenly created. Passe Rose struggled hard to repress the flush of pleasure which rose to her cheeks, — pleasure, however, which the captain did not discover, for the girl frowned, and, fool that he was, he thought her vexed. So at this frown he hesitated, and in an instant that new world disappeared like the sun behind a passing cloud. One would say both were vexed now in earnest, for Passe Rose turned, saying she would go her own way and do her own errand. Gui followed her moodily out from under the mulberries into the meadow, finding no word to utter.

"What is thy business in Maestricht?" she said carelessly.

"My faith," answered the captain, faltering like a boy caught in wrong-doing, "I came on the king's business."

"On the king's business!" exclaimed Passe Rose.

"To inquire after the abbot's health."

"On the king's business!" repeated Passe Rose angrily, "and thou loiterest here with a flock of geese in a meadow!"

"Ah," — began the captain reproachfully, seizing her hand.

"Nay, nay, nay," cried Passe Rose, disengaging her hand, — for love will show itself unawares at the window of solicitude when it will not pass the door of its own pleasure, — "get thee gone — thy men are off — what will the king say?" Her alarm was unfeigned, and though it transformed the lover into the captain in a twinkling, the cloud was passed off from the sun. "Fire and blood! where were thy wits?" she exclaimed, as they scrambled up the slope together.

"If they have but left me my horse," said he, outrunning her.

But on breaking through the hedgerow they found the road deserted. Passe Rose was breathing hard, the slope being steep, and she made no effort to conceal either her anxiety or her vexation. But Gui had recovered the wits she taxed him with losing; for it was easier far to face the king in displeasure than a laughing maid who teased him.

"There is nothing to fret over," he said, as they hurried along the road to Maestricht. "A horse is always to be had in the king's name, and I will catch the monk's mule before it reaches the wood of Hesbaye. But listen," — stopping short at the thought which flashed upon him, — "the monk goes to the king with the tale of the demon in parchment."

"In parchment!" gasped Passe Rose.

"Aye, so the prior told me. Shall I stuff the scroll down his throat?" asked Gui eagerly.

"Nay," said Passe Rose, reflecting, "that will

avail nothing, — he hath it by heart;" then laughing aloud, "let the bird fly till it suits us to cast the lure."

"I will tell him I slew the fiend," suggested the captain, whose ideas multiplied.

"Aye," cried Passe Rose, clapping her hands, "and for a token show him the collar," and unfastening it from her neck she began to clasp it on his arm. It was loose enough at her throat, but it fitted the captain's arm closely, — so closely that she was forced to press the skin from between the clasps to adjust it firmly. "If thou art free to go among the queen's household," she said, bending her head over her task, "watch the eyes of her women, for the eye which recognizes this will answer its sparkle. Ask also among them for a Saxon maid whose name is Rothilde, and when thou hast aught to tell me, come this way again."

There was something so promising in these words that Gui was not only sure to come, but unable to go at all.

"Where shall I find thee?" he whispered.

"At the church of St. Sebastian, at vespers. Farewell, and hasten."

He was loath to part so abruptly, but Passe Rose shook both her hands forbiddingly, and seeing him hesitate, stamped her foot so imperatively that he was fain to obey. Half way down the hill, where the road curved, he turned to see her still standing watching him, and to catch her hand's signal, " Farewell, and hasten."

Thus it was that Passe Rose, in spite of the fay's injunction, parted voluntarily with her collar. As for the captain, it was not until after rejoining his companions in the wood of Hesbaye, as the towers of Immaburg appeared among the oak-trees, that in rehearsing for the twentieth time his interview with the demon he recollected there was any other maid in the world beside Passe Rose, or that he had been bidden to seek a Saxon whose name was Rothilde.

" Nay, that is impossible," he said to himself, thinking of Rothilde, the queen's favorite, whom the king had refused his father, Robert of Tours, in marriage. " Nay, that is impossible."

VIII.

Except the shepherds, who passed the summer nights abroad with the flocks, Friedgis, of all the abbey inmates, possessed most time to brood over his condition. The laborers returned from the fields to finish their evening tasks and seek their guerdon of sleep ; the monks, whose minutely regulated day left small loop-hole for

indolence, lay down without divesting themselves of hose or tunic; but Friedgis, when
night came, was neither overcome with labor
nor concerned with spiritual tasks. Indeed, the
prior, in assigning him to the care of the hospitaler, had greatly endangered the latter's soul.
For, having now a slave to assist him, this func-
tionary committed to Friedgis all the menial
share of his duties, and passed the time thus
ransomed in his little garden, which he dearly
loved, or in pretended offices for the guests. It
is probable that the abbot, had he not fallen
sick, would have perceived the temptations which
thus assailed the almoner — who, for that matter, was free of guile, liking only to sit on a
bench in the sun twirling his thumbs, or to watch
the savory growing in the plot without the vestibule. As for the prior, he was remarkable for
seeing everything and observing nothing, a trait
which endeared him to many.

Waiting the visit of Passe Rose with a sombre
impatience, long before complines Friedgis had
brought the materials for the morning baking of
sacramental bread to the small room adjoining
the sacristy, and, having prepared the oil for
lighting the church, when the service was over
and the priests had put off their vestments,
closed the sacristy and retired to his own chamber. Barring the door behind him, and hiding

the lamp in the embrasure, he withdrew carefully the stone from the wall, and, lying down
on the floor, listened for the cuckoo's call.

It were a curious, were it not an invariable
fact, that of all the representations within the
reach of memory those which afflict us are ever
uppermost. The heart treasures its losses, and
remembers best what it regrets. His eyes wide
open, Friedgis stared into the darkness, for the
light was so feeble that the walls of his room
were barely visible. Without the aperture could
be heard the plaintive sound of the wind;
within, the flicker of the flame set gigantic
shadows in motion ; and imagination, roused by
a subtle contagion, responded to these sense impressions, making the wind voices and moving
shadows the creatures of its own invention. The
walls of his narrow chamber receded altogether
from the dreamer's sight. He was no longer
lying on the stone floor, but under the swaying
branches of lofty trees, through which the stars
shone, — as when, a summer ago, defiling through
the great Hercynian forest, the army of Karle,
with its captives, had halted for the night at
the springs of the Lippe. Northward, the slopes
of the Teutoburger Wald, whence Hermann had
burst upon the legions of Varus, were studded
with camp-fires ; from the heights southward
they flared on the distant towers of Paderborn,

whither the king had gone to celebrate the feast of the Nativity of the Virgin; and in the valley between, where the bulk of the army lay encamped, thickly clustered along the river they formed a confused glare, which traversed the plain of sombre forest like the Milky Way above, ablaze with light and fringed with solitary stars.

The road, which, ascending the valley of the Alme, debouched on the plains of Sindfeld, had been thronged for days with fugitives. From the tower windows of Ehresberg, where, a score or more years before, the king had pillaged the heathen temple of Irminsul and overthrown its idol, the young Queen Liutgarde could see the bands of foot-sore exiles which, under Frankish escort, were being dispersed through Austrasia, Neustria, and Burgundy, — remnants of a people whose spirit fourteen ruthless campaigns had not broken. Despairing of destroying this nationality with fire and the sword, the king wished now to dissolve it by scattering its fragments throughout the Empire. The great roads leading to the Rhine were encumbered with soldiery returning to their homes, and colonists who passed on their way those whom they dispossessed. Paderborn was given over to rejoicing. Anthems of thanksgiving succeeded the solemn masses of the spring, when the favor of

Heaven had been implored upon the expedition. Those whom the clergy had then forbidden to indulge in meat or wine now feasted without restraint, and instead of paying their deniers into the treasury of the Church divided the spoils abandoned them from the share of their chiefs. The arrival of couriers from Pannonia, announcing the successful opening of the war against the Avars, contributed to the general joy; and the beloved daughters of the king, then in the splendor of their beauty, had hastened from Mainz to welcome their victorious father.

As the night waned the noises of the camp had gradually ceased. The horseman had tethered his steed; the foot-soldier had taken off his leathern corselet and helmet of bronze; and the captive, lying down with the oxen released from the yoke, among his own flocks, dreamed of the pastures of Bardengaw he should see no more. Having wasted the land of the Saxons from Frisia to the Elbe, this vast army, encumbered with hostages and booty, like some wild animal gorged with blood and heavy with drowsiness, had stretched itself upon the ground to sleep.

Through the midst of this slumbering host moved a monk, clad in the black robe of the Benedictines. The flickering fires, leaping mo-

mentarily into life, scarce lighted his face, thin
with fasting and worn by the fatigues of the
march, but the flame of a tireless zeal burned
in his eyes.   Passing like a shadow between the
tents of the guards, among the sleeping forms
of the Franks, alone, he still pursued his mission
of warning and comfort among those whom the
king had torn from their native land to trans-
plant to Frankish soil.   For him there was no
truce of peace, no night of rest.   In the midst
of these blood-stained warriors overcome with
toils, he was the incarnation of that sleepless
spirit of holy love, so strangely blended with the
fury of a war which had laid a province in ashes
in the name of the all-blessed Christ; and in
the stillness of the night, when the clang of
armor was hushed and the sword was in its
sheath, it seemed as if this divine spirit walked
abroad in his person on its errand of minister-
ing grace.

In an open space, made in the thick wood by
the spreading branches of an oak, a girl lay
asleep.   The smouldering fire, stirred at times
by the wind into flame, threw its red light upon
her face; then, subsiding with the breeze, left
it to the darkness.   Daughter of an Angrian
chief slain on the banks of the Weser, her dress,
though soiled by the dust of the march, betok-
ened her rank.   A fringe of gold bordered the

tunic, whose girdle was embroidered with silk and pearls. A gold collar engraved with Eastern characters, loot from the Huns of the Danube, encircled her neck, and an agraffe of enameled bronze fastened the cloak over her breast. Her yellow hair, whose braids had become loosened, fell unconfined over her shoulders, and a child lay asleep on her knees. Homeless and alone like herself, lost in the confusion of the camp, it had crept to her side at nightfall, and, touched with pity, she had wrapped it in the fold of her cloak. At a little distance, stretched at full length in the shadow, Friedgis watched the sleeper, lifting his head at every sound. So vivid now was his memory of the scene that, lying on his chamber floor, he drew his garment closer, as if the night air still chilled the wound which, then unhealed, burned under the tunic of otter-skin torn open on his breast. A soldier, stupid with wine, stumbled to the river to quench his thirst, and returned to his couch of leaves. The child opened its eyes; then, reassured by the girl's presence, fell asleep again.

Suddenly from out the shadows along the river-bank a tall form emerged into the firelight. The long hair escaping from the gorget indicated one of noble blood, and the helmet bore the crest of the king's guard. Followed by two men-at-arms, the Frank advanced into the open space, when he stopped, casting a quick look about him; then, motioning his companions to remain within call, approached softly over the turf of moss and stooped above the prostrate form of the sleeper, as if to assure himself that it was she whom he sought. The collar of gold shone as the flame leaped, but it was not its glitter which tempted the eye of the Frank. Friedgis, unobserved, raised himself upon his hands. His arms trembled; his lips were parted; his eye, seeking eagerly some weapon, glistened. The chain which had supported his shield hung broken about his neck; all else had been lost in the fight. As the Frank, signing to his followers to approach, laid his hand upon the woman's shoulder, the monk, coming out of the gloom of the wood, confronted him. Surprised, the warrior retreated a step, then, drawing himself up haughtily, waited till the monk should pass.

"Robert, Count of Tours," said the latter, "what errand of the king doest thou here?"

There was a cold irony in the monk's voice which brought the blood of shame and ill-suppressed anger to the soldier's face.

"And thou, shaven head, whose cursed race the king has banished from the camp, have a care for thy hood!" and, loosing his sword from its belt, he laid his hand on the hilt.

Undismayed, the monk stood between the captive and her assailant. Friedgis, crouching on his elbows in the shadow, watched and listened.

"Stand aside, dog of a priest! The maid is mine."

"She is God's," replied the monk calmly.

"I will send him thee in her stead," answered the count with an oath, drawing the blade from his cloak. But something of authority in the voice and mien of his opponent restrained his arm. "Who stands between me and mine?" he asked hoarsely before he struck.

"I!" said the monk, stepping forward into the light and throwing back his hood.

It was Rainal, friend and counselor of Karle.

Here in the night of the forest the two great powers of the age stood face to face. Force, insatiate and brutal, wandering over the Empire like a Fury with the torch of destruction, — driving the laborer from his field, the patrician from his villa, the king from his throne, and pursuing its victims to the foot of the altar, — and that perilous power of the priest, whose only authority was a moral one, received from an invisible Prince, whose riches excited envy, whose censure awoke wrath, and who, alone, defenseless, on the steps of the altar wet with the blood of the feeble, represented the principles of charity and justice amid the ruins of society.

Roused by the voices from dreams of the Weser, where her kindred had fallen and her Saxon home still smoked, the girl raised her head. Her assailant, trembling with a passion foiled, but fearful of the power he had evoked, quailed before the calm gaze of the priest. The naked sword in his grasp quivered like the hound in leash, but the strength of the hand on the haft was gone, and with a look of hate promising revenge the Frankish noble slunk away.

"Daughter, thy name?" asked the priest gently in her own tongue.

"Rothilde," she replied in a dull voice, lifting her eyes to his face.

"Rothilde," he repeated, drawing from his robe a silver flask enriched with gems, and laying his hand on her shining hair, " I baptize thee in the name of the one God, invisible, glorious, and eternal, and of his ever-blessed Son, and of the Holy Ghost, three in one Godhead of all power and perfection, reigning the same forever."

Immovable, her head thrown back, her eyes remained fixed upon the priest with the impassive look of the barbarian, indifferent to her captor and her fate. An expression of profound discouragement passed over Rainal's face. How often had these words of blessed benediction fallen fruitless from his lips, lost in the night of the heathen mind as the sparks which rose from the fire in short spiral flights were lost in the darkness overhead!

"The kings of Babylon carried their captives of old to a land of false gods, but ye are the captives of the true God. Through humiliation he opens the way of repentance, and in sorrow discovers the gates of life." Saying which, sighing, he made the sign of the cross above her head, and disappeared.

The sound of his footfall had not ceased when Friedgis, rising softly to his feet, stole to the girl's side. The latter turned her head at his approach, and smiled. Night after night during the long march she had closed her eyes in the consciousness of protection, and his presence now seemed to excite in her no surprise. Neither understood the conversation they had heard, nor knew the speakers. Neither needed to. The language and the forms of passion and charity are known of all.

"Some water," she whispered as he bent over her.

He went to the bank, gathered the cool water in the hollow of his hands, and offered it to her with a look of mingled solicitude and love. She drank eagerly, touching her lips to his hands. Taking the child from her lap, and laying it in a grassy hollow between the roots of the tree, he made a pillow of her cloak; and, as if soothed by his presence, unable to contend with fatigue, she laid her head upon it without a word, and closed her eyes. The smile still lingered on her face; it was a beautiful one, although the mouth was too round and small, the nose too pointed, the features too irregular; nevertheless it possessed that which charms the eye because it first gains the heart. Something of timidity, of sweetness, something of the irresponsibility and childishness with which certain natures defy time and invoke forbearance, was to be seen in her limpid but shrinking blue eye, in her fugitive smile, even in her attitudes and gestures. For a long time Friedgis sat looking into this face. The fire had gone out. The breeze had wandered away. The only sounds were the slumbrous flow of the river and the low breathing of the sleeper. More softly even than he came he returned at length to his place in the shadow. He also was overcome with weariness and the heavy summer night. For days he had walked beside her cart, shielding her from insult and sharing with her his food; for many a night he had watched while she slept. . . .

Suddenly there was the blast of a horn mingled with the neighing of steeds and the cries of hoarse voices. He woke with a start. The east was flushed with red, and the morning light filled the wood. The child was crying at the foot of the tree, but the girl was gone.

With the same quick cry which had burst from his lips on the banks of the Lippe, Friedgis started from his dream. There were neither horses, nor men, nor morning sun. He stood trembling in his narrow room. The lamp burned feebly in the embrasure, and the sound of the horn was the song of the cuckoo without the abbey wall.

IX.

For a moment Friedgis stood still, listening.

"He does not hear," thought Passe Rose, impatient, without, and again the cuckoo's late summer cry sounded plaintively, close under the wall.

Extinguishing the taper and drawing the bolt noiselessly, Friedgis crossed the inner court by the great gate through which Gui had entered, to the small door in the north wall. Pausing again to listen, but hearing no sound, he opened it cautiously the width of his body. The night was dark, and he could see nothing.

"Is it thou?" whispered Passe Rose.

"Enter," said Friedgis, drawing back.

"Nay; come thou out," replied Passe Rose decisively.

Friedgis stepped over the stone sill, closing the gate softly behind him. Not yet accustomed to the darkness, he stood peering about him.

"Here — where are thine eyes? Hush!" said Passe Rose, as a twig snapped under his foot. "Thou wilt have all the dogs in the yard a-baying. Follow me."

The dim outlines of her form moved before him down the path leading to the fish-ponds, where was a wooden bench at the edge of the water.

"They say fishes have no ears," she whispered, pulling him by the skirt to the seat beside her. "How fares the abbot? Hath the demon returned to vex him?" Unable to discern her face, Friedgis heard her laughing. "In my country," pursued she, "the little children have a pastime called 'the devil and the saints.' At a signal, one, being the devil, issues from a bush and seeks to catch the others, who run from tree to tree. These trees are the holy altars. There being more who play than there are trees, some soul is always lost. When the chase is hot and the devil runs well, it is very amusing. I have a mind to play this game yonder," nodding in the direction of the abbey. "What thinkest thou, — would they run or no, if I looked in at the dormitory door? If thou couldst but have seen the monk who set out for

Immaburg this morning ! He had a rare chance. The selfsame devil appeared to him by the roadside. By good luck I was there at the very instant." And Passe Rose was seized with uncontrollable laughter.

"One would say she is crazy," thought Friedgis. "Dost thou wander over the country both by day and by night?" he asked mockingly.

"By St. Martin!" rejoined Passe Rose angrily, "what is that to thee? Came I here for my pleasure? I had best minded mine own business, and left thine to thee." She rose quickly, as if going away, but Friedgis, remaining silent, heard her soon returning. "Are there sorceresses among thy people, father bear?" she asked, sitting down again beside him. "It is strange," she pursued, as if soliloquizing, — "certainly it is strange. Thou canst not see me who am under thy nose, yet this woman, albeit blind, perceives at a distance of twenty thousand paces." A star, appearing between the clouds, glistened in the pond. Passe Rose went to the water's edge and leaned over the low bank. "How deep it looks!" she said; "nevertheless the bottom is but the length of my arm." And as the clouds broke away Friedgis saw her, in the starlight, probing the water with a branch of willow. Indicating the depth by her finger, she held up the branch that he might see. " There are many things that cannot be explained," she said, shaking her head.

" Look," she whispered, after a silence, throwing back her cloak from her throat, " the collar is gone. Canst thou see? I once knew a Greek who worked in gold. He pretended to have made earrings for the Empress Irene, so delicately designed " — and Passe Rose half closed her eyes in a manner peculiar to her — " that one could not see the hook because of doves with spread wings. In truth he worked well, though he was a boaster. His hands were like mine, and his hair was perfumed. He asserted that his nation once governed the world," she said, with a scornful laugh. " What was I saying? — ah, yes. There are many things which cannot be explained." She moved the stick to and fro, watching the ripple rock the stars.

Approaching her suddenly with an abrupt exclamation of impatience, Friedgis tore the branch from her hand and threw it into the water. " What hast thou to tell me? " he said threateningly.

" They that wear soft clothing dwell in kings' houses," said Passe Rose.

" In truth she is mad," thought he, looking down into her eyes.

"In kings' houses," repeated Passe Rose significantly.

"Or foolish," he said to himself, turning away.

"Sit thee down here, by me. No? Well, then, have thine own way. In a strange land one mistrusts every one. That is not just. We are like other people, — the same as thine, — some are good, some are bad." Then, seeing he was indeed going, she called aloud to him. "Thou dost not trust me; but if I told thee the maid was found" — she let fall the words slowly one by one — " at Aix — in the king's household — Ah!" she cried, as he turned, his eyes glistening, "at last!"

"At Aix?" echoed Friedgis·doubtfully.

"Near by," said Passe Rose, indicating the direction with her head, "near by. But in the king's household — ah, in the king's household, near is far, like the star in the pond. I see very well thou dost not believe me," she continued, observing his face; "nevertheless it is true. The gospels said in the king's household."

"The gospels?" he said after her, advancing a step.

" Ay, the gospels; knowest thou not what are the gospels?" said Passe Rose disdainfully leaning over the water and recapturing the

branch. "The gospels lie on the holy altars.
There are the psalms, which are quite another
thing; also the gospels, — they are altogether
different. It is not easy to explain. But have
no fear, I speak truly; a clerk in the church of
St. Sebastian read me the words plainly, — in
kings' houses. Wait, we shall see." Observing, however, that these words made little impression upon him, she dropped another spark
upon his duller sense. "Certainly it is strange.
Thy collar follows thee from Ehresberg to the
shrine of St. Servais, and thou wilt not seek its
owner though I tell thee she is under thy hand
at Aix. It is wonderful that after being lost at
Ehresberg, where the spoil was divided, — scattered like beads spilled upon the ground, —
thy collar should be found in a great wood like
that of Hesbaye. That truly is hard to understand," and Passe Rose nodded her head slowly.
"Aix is so near."

While the girl was speaking Friedgis had sat
down on the bench. "Why not tell me all thou
knowest?" he said, searching her face wistfully.

"Dear Saxon," laughed Passe Rose, leaping
to her feet and seating herself beside him, "thou
hast such thirst thou wouldst empty the cup
at a draught. Have patience. Do the cruets in
thy country empty themselves at one turning?
Wait, I will tell thee all, — for that am I come.

And if I tell thee, it is because I trust thee indeed. I have a friend among the stars," she continued in a confiding tone. "Didst thou see the youth who came to inquire after the abbot's health? It is he who lost the collar in the wood, and it is he who will seek the maid among the queen's household. For me he will catch the wind in a net. He hath thy collar now, and will wear it in the eyes of all. Will not the maid recognize her own? Tell me, is she fair, — fairer than I?

> " Oh, as candles to a star,
>   Others to my lady are ! ' "

she sang, lifting her eyes and clasping her hands mockingly, after the manner of lovers. An angry frown appeared on his face, and in a twinkling her manner changed. " Tell me first truly all thou knowest, and I swear to thee that of all the maids in France I will put my finger on the one thou seekest. What happened at Ehresberg? Who took her from thee?" The confidence of the girl's manner possessed an irresistible fascination, and Friedgis began to relate what had taken place on the banks of the Lippe. So graphic were his narrative and gestures that Passe Rose, watching every word as it fell from his lips, seemed to see the actors in their places reënacting their parts before her eyes; and when the Frank, about to lay his hand on the sleeping girl, was disturbed by the monk, "Seigneur," she cried, divining what was to follow, "it was the abbot."

"The abbot!" exclaimed Friedgis, with a gesture towards the monastery.

"Ay, he was with the king in Saxony. Sawest thou his face?"

Friedgis shook his head. "Not well; his back was turned."

"Hast thou not seen him since his return?" she asked eagerly.

"Nay, as thou knowest, he came but lately. Thou rememberest the day. I was yonder in the tower ringing the bells, and saw the slaves going out to greet him, bearing boughs and chanting, and the young girls strewing flowers. He was already ill, and hath not appeared since. Believest thou the monk of the wood was he?"

Passe Rose nodded. "And the other — the soldier?"

"Him I saw well. Moreover, the monk named him. Knowest thou one among the king's leaders called Robert of Tours?"

Passe Rose drew herself up quickly, as if not believing her ears.

"Robert of Tours?" she repeated mechanically, her eyes dilating.

"So he named him."

Clasping her hands behind her head, Passe

Rose had the manner of one going over the list of her acquaintances, as if knowing every lord of the kingdom as well as she knew her ten fingers. But her heart was beating fast. "Robert of Tours," talking to herself, as it were; and then, quickly, "Well, afterwards?"

"When they were gone," continued Friedgis, "I fell asleep. My wound bled. For days I had not closed an eye — it may be that I swooned. In the morning she was gone," and he described his fruitless search in the confusion of the camp.

The organization of the army had been dissolved in a night. The German auxiliaries had been dismissed; the king's vassals, having feasted together in Paderborn till break of day, released from service, were gathering their followers in troops, and each, with his share of booty and convoy of captives, sought his own domain. The air was filled with sounds of lowing cattle, of axles creaking under their loads; the blast of horns and hoarser shouts of command echoed through the wood, above whose tree-tops columns of dust marked the windings of the road. Friedgis told how, frenzied with excitement and apprehension, he ran from place to place, questioning those who understood him not, jeered at for a madman, cursed for refusal to obey; till at last, faint from his bleeding wound and incapable of further resistance, he was tripped by an archer, and bound, trembling as a child, to the cross-bar of a baggage wagon, amid the laughter of the soldiery. "If thou sayest truly that she is found — though it were in the king's own chamber " — A spasm of grief and anger contracted his muscles, and he walked slowly into the shadow, beyond the girl's searching gaze.

Passe Rose had been more occupied with her own thoughts than with the Saxon's tale, but hearing his retreating footsteps, and believing that he was indeed going, an exclamation of impatience escaped her, and, leaping to her feet, she ran after him. "Whither now?" she said, standing in his path. "To Aix? Truly — I believe . . . Aix, Aix " — she cried, unable to find words with which to measure his folly. "As well seek the star in the pond!" She took him by the arm and led him back to the seat. For some minutes they sat beside each other in silence. A fragmentary sentence escaped now and then the girl's lips, as if she were endeavoring to reason with her companion while her own thought was elsewhere. "Plunge thine arm in to the shoulder — that were a child's folly! Patience." Her eyes, fixed on the star shining in the pond, shone also. "Have patience," she repeated abstractedly; and again, persuasively, "Have patience." Some deeper

emotion drove her hurrying thought before it ;
her eyes dilated, as if fascinated by expanding
horizons. With a rapid gesture she passed her
hand over her forehead, brushing back her hair.
" I know what thou thinkest. When I came for
the collar, thou saidst, A girl who has lost her
jewel, a fool seeking stars in the pond ! Look
at me, — I have wasted twenty summers. The
Queen Hildegarde was alive then, — twenty
summers lost ! Hast thou seen the late seed
shoot up in the harvest moon ? All the summer
it sleeps, and now it stirs and pushes, opening
its eye in a single summer night, to see its fellows grown and the season gone. Twenty seasons the blood stirred in my veins, and I knew
it not. I slept like the seed, in the moss un-
derfoot. Suddenly I opened my eyes : it was
in the wood of Hesbaye. When I told thee I
found the collar there, I lied ; *he* gave it me.
Till then I slept, ate, slept; played, like a child,
with the stars in the pond. But now ! " She
stood up, and stretched out her hands passionately to the sky with a short, exulting laugh.
" Being awake, do they think me content to
comb wool and make jelly of quince, — life being
short and twenty seasons gone ? By the saints !
I would like to know one thing : how happens
it that one star shines in the sky, and its fellow
in the pond ? We will see, — we will see."

" A king's captain, — that is not much," said Friedgis derisively.

She answered him with a quick glance of contempt, and turned away her head, with a scornful movement of her shoulders. Then sitting down beside him and looking up into his face, "Knowest thou not, dear porter, that were he the abbot's swineherd " — She paused. " Said I not there were some things hard to understand? So thou seekest thy maid Rothilde. Is it her jewels that thou covetest? Nay, nay, nay " — Her voice died away and her eyes filled with dreams. " Let him pass over this body with the wheels of his car — if he will — if he will " —

" What is that to me ? " said Friedgis, observing her attentively.

" What is that to thee ? " she repeated, breaking away from her thought with an effort. "Seigneur! it signifies that I wish thee well. When the heart is full, then it has the most room. Reason now a little. The king's captain — Peste! the name escapes me," she cried, beating her head with her hand : " it hath so long a Latin sound ; yet I know it well. Surely thou knowest."

Friedgis shook his head.

" He does not know," thought Passe Rose. " Never mind," she said aloud. " He will come

again shortly, and hath promised to bring me
word. Wait, and at the first chance observe
the abbot. He is sure now to recover his health.
I have the devil which tormented him safe in
hand. Hark ! " she whispered, grasping his
arm.

The sound of footsteps was heard on the path
near the gate. Friedgis pulled the girl into the
shadow, where, shielded from view, they saw
the prior emerge upon the walk bordering the
pond.

" Would I were a devil indeed," muttered
Passe Rose under her breath. " I would plague
his soul willingly."

With a gesture of silence, Friedgis covered
her mouth with his palm.

The prior stood for a moment looking at the
stars reflected in the basin ; then walked slowly
along the bank, like one who thinks himself
alone.

" Quick ! get thee gone," whispered Passe
Rose. " He saw nothing. Farewell, but speak
not to the abbot till I see thee again." And
pushing Friedgis by the shoulder, without waiting his reply, she turned in the direction the
prior had taken. He had stopped at the outlet
of the pond, where a thin sheet of water flowed
over a culvert of stone. His hood was thrown
back, and his pale face shone in the starlight

against the black background of verdure. " Here
is one not easily frightened by such demons as
I," thought Passe Rose.

As she stole cautiously by, the cry of the
cuckoo sounded down the road. " By St. Martin ! the wood is full of birds," she said to herself, sinking down behind a bush. " Never
heard I a cuckoo with so clear a song in the
month of winds." Crouching behind the leaves,
she distinguished footsteps on the road, and
presently low voices in earnest conversation.
She endeavored to part the screen of branches,
but every motion resulted in such rustling that
she was forced to sit still, through fear of betraying her presence. By dint of straining her
ears she made out two voices besides the prior's;
and hearing at intervals a metallic clank, "One
is armed," she said. For a full hour, cramped
in posture and wet with dew, Passe Rose fretted
and chafed at being able neither to hear a word
nor see a face. At last the voices ceased, steps
were heard retreating down the road; then the
gate was fastened, and everything was still.

" May the saints keep my bones from the
ague," she muttered, stretching her stiffened
limbs and issuing from her hiding-place. The
thought of her prolonged absence caused her to
hasten, but as she gained the road a small parchment scroll caught her eye. She picked it up

quickly, and while hurrying down the hill, her ear alert for those who preceded her, opened the roll sufficiently to perceive that its inner surface was covered with writing.

" Perhaps these are the new characters of which the clerk in the church of St. Sebastian spoke," she said, thrusting the parchment in her bosom with the dagger and the key.

While she lay concealed, the moon had risen, — not yet so high, however, but that its beams, grazing the hill's crest, threw long shadows down the descending slope, on which the girl glided till she reached the level below. Here the plain was flooded with light, and as she hesitated on the edge of the forest the flutter of a wood-dove above her head caused her to start. " There is no woman in Maestricht, having this place to cross at night," she said to herself, setting boldly forth, " who would not thank the saints for so comforting a moon." Her eyes were abroad to scan the smallest moving thing, but nothing was astir, and her thoughts were quickly occupied by the events of the day. " So, Robert of Tours, armed, and with two followers at thy back, thy sword becomes limp as a hempen strand at the sight of the abbot's face ! Had I been in the maid's stead — a monk's eye is no better than a maid's " — and hers glittered sharper than her dagger's point. Then came

Gui of Tours, leading the horse on which she rode in the wood of Hesbaye, or riding at the head of the troop across the market-place, or following close behind her, through the alders beside the foaming brook, driving away all power to deal with the plans half formed in her busy brain. For, intrigued as she was by the visitors whom the prior received at midnight, and whose parchment burned in her bosom; perplexed, too, at the thought of the demon, whose evil practices were, perhaps, already recited to the king; and alarmed, above all, at what might follow upon her lover's search for the Saxon maiden, — with all these thoughts her will was as limp to cope as the Frank's sword. In truth she was eager only to gain her quiet room, to give herself over to the dreams which border sleep, content to put over for the morrow all devices and plans; for all day long she had sipped a cup which never before had touched her lips, and never had Gui of Tours himself, after the banquet, more need of sleep to steady the pulse and clear the brain than she.

As she turned the corner into the street without the garden wall, a glimmer of light from her own window shone full in her face. Feeble though it was because of the moon, and blurred by the pane of horn, nevertheless there it twinkled, beyond dispute, like a wicked, winking

eye, and Passe Rose stopped short, one hand on
her beating heart, the other clasping the key.
An overmastering presentiment, beyond the war-
rant of reason, seized her like a hand that
clutches the throat and cannot be loosed. The
quick defense of innocence falsely accused, the
hot explanation of malign appearances, questions
which tore her heart and looks which struck at
pride, a sickening apprehension and rallying
rush of bravery, were all pressed into the second
she paused dismayed at the sight of the glimmering lamp in her chamber turret; and innocent as she declared herself to be, the key in
her fingers, stolen from its peg on the kitchen
wall, was heavier on her conscience than in her
hand. Being free of all guile, certainly it were
hard to enter the key warily in the grating lock,
like a thief or a culprit that may not look up
for shame. But this she had no need to do, for
the gate was ajar, and within stood the boy rubbing the wonder out of his eyes, and the two
maids (who loved her not overmuch), with looks
fitter than words to rouse wrath, and under the
kitchen eaves Jeanne herself, stupefied with the
dread of harm rather than the thought of evil.

Passe Rose had certainly thrown her arms
about Jeanne's neck and told her the whole
story, even to the fay's girdle, but for the scorn
on the maids' faces, which hardened her temper,

and turned her bearing from gentleness to boldness and defiance. Perhaps Jeanne guessed as much, for with a gesture she bade them and the boy retire. But before a word could be spoken Werdric came down the chamber stair, with the lamp in his hand.

For a moment the three stood silent in the full light of the moon.

It were strange indeed, were it not so common, that in one breathless second feeling can gather such headway that neither love nor reason can stay its course, though we know its end is folly, and desire nothing less than to follow its lead. The barriers which oppose its vent do but concentrate its power, and so it was that the very pleading of Jeanne's face and the challenge of innocence in Passe Rose's eye gathered Werdric's anger into one terrible word.

" Strumpet ! " he said, not believing his own ears.

A quick cry escaped Jeanne's heart, but Passe Rose only shivered, — so the bare flesh recoils under the first lash of the scourge. The blood ebbed from her cheeks, but the fire leaped to her eyes, and she made a step toward Werdric that seemed to dare him to strike again.

" Strumpet ! " he repeated, goaded now by madness and the defiance of her eye.

The word came like a blow full in the face,

but the girl neither spoke nor stirred. She stood for a moment like one dazed; then hung the key mechanically on its peg, and went slowly up the stair.

Jeanne sprang to follow her, but Werdric, sullen and ashamed, closed the door. "Shame!" cried Jeanne, all a-tremble, and clutching his arm. Then, all strength deserting her, she sank at his feet, tears of old age running free as a child's. "Who'd a thought it," she moaned between her sobs, rocking to and fro, — "the gift of God — who'd a thought it — from thee."

The moon traveled slowly across the turret window-pane, and its light began to blend with the coming dawn, and still Passe Rose sat on the bed's edge. Gone were the dream spirits that hide under maidens' pillows ; a cruel word was written across the floor on the spot where her eyes were fixed, and every pulse of the blood hurled it afresh in her aching ears. Now indeed might the garden sparrows have flown fearlessly to her shoulders, so like she seemed to the statue in the church porch, whose dull eyes stare always at the same place, and whose raiment of stone never yields to the breeze.

At last she rose, and in an absent way, as it were, unwound the veil from her head and shoulders, and unfastened her dress, broidered by Jeanne's own fingers, — the dress whose close-fitting sleeves leaving bare the lower arm, and girdle clasping her waist, was her especial delight and pride. She gave no heed to its broidered hem, nor to the clasp Werdric himself had wrought for her, and going to her chest lifted its heavy lid. There at the bottom lay the robe in which Werdric had found her in the wood. The edge was frayed and the color faded, and but one lacing-cord remained in the sleeves. As she lifted it from the chest, the silver sous clicked together in the purse which fell from its folds. She put on the dress, ill-fitting now as it was; then, stooping, loosed her sandals, for shoes she had none when she came. Having closed the lid, she opened the purse, and took therefrom one copper piece, the amount she had with her when she fled from the merchants at St. Denis's fair, and thrust it, with the dagger about which was rolled the prior's parchment, into her bodice. All this she did quickly, without deliberation; yet will not even the young shoot let go the soil without a wrench, and so Passe Rose, before she turned to go, struggled with tears, and kissed the golden sun blazoned on her pillow, hiding there her head. The purse was still in her hand when she rose, and an image of Mary the Blessed Mother looked down upon her as she lifted her head. A spasm of anger and pride drove the tears from her eyes, and she hurled the purse at the image in sudden scorn, as the words of the Saxon came to mind: "Of what avail the gods, since they do not hear! Henceforth they are nothing to me," and went down the kitchen stair.

It was unlucky for all that Jeanne, after sobbing the whole night through, had fallen asleep in the gray of morning, and that Werdric only was astir; for had Jeanne been there the girl had never crossed the garden unhindered. In vain had Werdric sought to justify the heat of his temper; but his pride was stubborn, and the greater one's own the less one allows for that of another. He had risen from bed to escape the presence of Jeanne, and was placing the fagots upon the hearth when Passe Rose came down the stair. He saw the dress she wore, and knew its import well, but the words of command he summoned failed him when he saw her face, for the spirit of the girl lorded his. She passed where he stood, paying him no more heed than the bundle of fagots in his hand, and his eyes followed her bare feet down the path and through the arch, gazing with a stupid stare at the place where she disappeared.

It was then that Jeanne, whose sleep was light, came from her room; and, although forbidden by Werdric to hold any converse with the girl, unable longer to restrain her desire, stole timidly up Passe Rose's stair. Before she had gained the chamber above, Werdric sprang to the gate. His heart was full of remorse, and he could not bide the issue of Jeanne's quest to that empty room. The street was vacant and still. He ran to the market-place. No one was yet abroad, save the rickety crone in the porch of the church of St. Sebastian, wondering to see a man at that hour running hither and thither, tearing his hair.

The wood of Hesbaye was still dark when Passe Rose left the high-road to follow the wood-cutters' path into its friendly screen. The little birds, shaking the night dew from their feathers in the branches above, called to her as she passed, turning their heads side-wise, but she paid them no heed. A hare loped down the path, paused a bow-shot beyond her, then, dropping its ears, plunged through the briers. Still Passe Rose went on, with only one thought in her mind: never again to pass Werdric's door, nor hear the sound of his voice. The path narrowed like a meadow rill, till, lost in the thicket, all ways seemed alike.

The day passed, the night came; still she went on. The night! Do you know what night is in the wood? Without, among the cabins on the plain, it approaches slowly, with manifold signs. The sun's edge becomes visible through the haze, touches the pine-tops on the horizon, blazes awhile between their branches, then disappears, as a beacon fire expires on the mountain. But it is not yet night. Saffron streamers shoot to the zenith; a cloud lies athwart them, like a lance dipped in blood; above, the wool-white clouds begin to glow; higher still a fleecy film of vapor throbs with rose. These are its heralds. In a moment they will float black as funeral garments upon the opal sky. And yet it is not night. A single star opens its eye; as at a signal, one by one, hundred by hundred, thousand by thousand, the hosts of heaven come forth. Now the lights twinkling in the cabins are extinguished, the tired lie down to sleep, and it is night. But in the forest there is no sun, no sky, no star. The light flees from its depths without warning, and swiftly, noiselessly, like the leap of the leopard, night is there. It enwraps the tall trees as the dead are enwrapped in their grave-clothes. High up only, the topmost leaves are free to flutter a little, so thick is the darkness. And oh, the sounds below! more ominous than the plain's silence — that stealthy footfall in the dry moss, that snapping twig, that rustle of leaves where no wind is. Here one is observed, yet sees nothing. Nay, look! two shining lights where no light is, — for the glow-worm is afar in the ploughed field, the fire-fly is abroad among the wheat-heads. These are the wood-stars that shine in the thicket, whether of timid doe or panther ready to spring, God knows! but the heart bounds, and the ear strains to catch the breath of the nostrils. Fly — but how, in this jungle? A night-bird fans the face with his wing. Oh for the clue that he follows! Hark! far off, hurling the living apart, a dead tree crashes, pauses, and falls in thunder. Wrap thy garment about thee, Passe Rose; draw it tightly over thy head and shut out this night; for to wait and watch and listen are beyond the endurance of reason. Hark again! is it the wind? — for within one cannot tell what is taking place without. It comes from afar, like a murmur of meadow waters; then nearer, a roar as of surf on the shore. The rain overhead! but below, for a long time all is still, as in the sea depths, till at last the bending branches drip, and every terrifying sound is drowned in a low, monotonous patter. Now dream, Passe Rose, if thou canst, while the wakeful ear is lulled to slumber. Surely this is the rain on the roof of thatch; thou art safe within the mud walls of the cabin; the night thrush sings in the bush, and the blessed stars look down upon thee.

X.

Buried from sight among the wooded spurs which prolonged the vast forest of Ardennes nearly to the Rhine, the castle of Immaburg seemed almost deserted; for the king, with the royal household, had set out for Aix, to await there the arrival of his son Pepin from Pannonia. So magnificent were the preparations made to receive the victorious young king of Italy, and so great was the curiosity to witness the triumphant entry of the army with its barbarian captives and hostages, that many of the permanent inmates of the villa had obtained permission to follow the court; only such servants as were necessary for the care of the kennels and stables, the orchards and gardens, remaining. A single company of guards was also left to act as escort for certain damsels of the princesses' household, who, while chatting over their needlework in the pleasance without the inclosure, were impatiently anticipating the morrow's ride to Aix and the festivities of the capital. Gui of Tours himself, the chief of the company, after yawning away a half hour under the gallery of the *préau*, strolled discontentedly across the silent court-yard through the gateway, where a few soldiers loitered, playing at dice or sleeping on the wooden benches in the shadow of the wall. A subdued sound of laughter from the terrace greeted the captain's appearance, for the company of women was well known to be his last resource. But the captain paid no more heed to the laughter than he had to the dice which the soldiers concealed at his approach, and disappeared among the outbuildings where were lodged the dogs and horses.

Shortly after, he was seen again on the road beyond the pleasance, gazing moodily over the cabins of the serfs, clustered about the paddocks and sheepfolds, towards the green wood which stretched unbroken to the horizon. It were no wonder if the women deemed the captain was searching for some flutter of the king's banner in the screen of leaves below, and the pout on the small lips of Agnes of Solier, as her eyes glanced from the valance spread over her knees to the distant figure of the soldier, betrayed the chagrin which his indifference caused her. So dense was the green curtain that the hare beneath was safe from the kite above; neither flash of spear nor gleam of flames on the king's standard rewarded the captain's gaze, and he wandered back to the court-yard gate like a restless hound left behind from the chase.

"Were I in thy stead," whispered young Heluiz of Hesbaye, bending to Agnes' ear, "I would ask the captain to replenish my reel. The silk is almost gone, and he chafes with nothing to do."

"If the captain chafes, he is best away," replied the girl, striving in vain to conceal the blush which rose to her cheek.

"Truly, I believe he is afraid of thy tongue's point, — it is sharper than thy needle," laughed her tormentor maliciously.

"What art thou saying, Heluiz?" asked an elderly dame, who, in the centre of the group, directed the work of the young girls.

"I was relating to Agnes of Solier, Mistress Chlodine, how Attila, king of the Huns, was slain by his wife with a golden needle on their marriage night."

"They say the Huns have the faces of apes," said a fair-haired girl, looking up from her embroidery; "like that which the Emir of Barcelona sent the king."

A sally of laughter greeted this statement, and the speaker, Gesualda, daughter of Leidulphe, Count of Arnay, bent her head over her work in confusion.

"What thou sayest is true, little dear," said Mistress Chlodine. "These people are pagans and sorcerers, fearing neither God nor man. Is it not so, Rothilde?" she asked, turning to the maiden nearest her.

The question was rude, for the girl was a barbarian, of that Saxon race whose perfidy had cost the kingdom such blood and treasure, and all knew that Mistress Chlodine bore with ill grace her presence among the princesses' women. Saxon and Hun were all one to Mistress Chlodine; she made no distinction between their abodes, putting them all together in the zone of heathendom, which girdled the land like the sea in the maps which the School of the Palace had made for the king.

Two limpid blue eyes looked up from the vignette border of the tapestry, and a faint blush overspread the girl's neck. At a passing glance, one would say she was the least beautiful of all present; yet there was that in the small face so attractive that he who looked into its quick-falling eyes waited till they should lift again, so trustful was their gaze, so timid their fall, so fraught with mute inquiry their slow return, — like a hand put confidingly into one's own. There was not a maid in the pleasance but deemed her sly and full of wiles, and not a man in the kingdom but would have scouted such talk for jealous slander, so gentle was her bearing. That the heart of Robert of Tours had become as wax in her presence was common gossip. It was said that he had seen her first among the captives at Ehresberg, and would

have had her, willing or unwilling, for himself
but for the Abbot Rainal, who had brought her
to the queen's notice. Every one knew that it
had been the abbot's design to send her back to
her own land to win her people to the service of
the true God, but whether the king had twice
refused her to Robert of Tours because he favored the abbot's design, or because he was
wroth that a great *leude* of the kingdom should
wed a Saxon rebel, was matter of dispute. Certain it was, however, that after the king's refusal
Robert of Tours went with Pepin to Hungary,
to vent his spleen on the Avars, and that Rothilde was sent from among the queen's women to
the school of the novices in the convent of Eicka.
If she remained at Eicka but a single month,
that was because of the favor of the young queen,
to whom, it was said, the king could refuse nothing. Be that as it may, she was back again
among the queen's women ; and one would have
sworn she was born in a palace, so apt was she
to learn, excelling the rest in all she did. Indeed, luxury suited her well, and she filled her
station as easily as water fills a jar.

As for the suit of Robert of Tours, if you
would know how it fared with the girl, in spite
of the king, ask Gesualda of Arnay. She
would bid you observe the fillet of black pearls
— the same which the count's wife wore when

she was alive — which Rothilde never loosed
from her hair. Not that Gesualda was wiser
than the others, — for the Saxon held her
tongue, — but was more friendly to the girl than
they; if not from affection, then from the love
of contrariety, which was so natural to her that
it often set her right hand against her left.

"We shall soon see for ourselves," she said,
parrying Chlodine's question for her friend.
"That the Huns resemble the Saracen's ape I
am sure. Ask the captain; he was with Theudoric on the Danube."

"He might as well be there now," replied
Heluiz of Hesbaye, with a sidelong glance at
Agnes.

"Jessé," said Agnes, calling to the page on
the terrace steps, "go say to the captain, Gui of
Tours, that Heluiz of Hesbaye is dying to put to
him a question about the monkeys of Barcelona."

A burst of laughter followed this retort, at
which Mistress Chlodine, not understanding its
import, frowned, and the fingers plied again between the silken floss and pearls in silence.

Agnes of Solier had long been betrothed to
Gui of Tours. Both her mother and her father
were dead, — unless, indeed, there were truth in
the rumor that the blood of Karle ran in her
veins. Certain it was that the king loved and
honored her next to his own daughters; and it

were strange that Robert of Tours should so set his heart on this betrothal if the girl were only an orphan dependent on the royal bounty. Certain also was it that on her mother's death the king had sent her to the abbey of Chelles, whereof his sister Gisèle was abbess, but neither his commands nor the abbess's entreaties had been able to dry her tears or stem her protest; so that after the lapse of a year the girl had her way, and exchanged the modest dress of the cloister for court attire. It were no new thing, surely, for a girl to brave the will of a king, but that the king should take the rebel into his favor lent strength to current rumors; for so he did, and even the Queen Fastrade had received her without jealousy in her household, exercising her mind by various devices and her fingers in every skillful work. If there were little in her voice and features which resembled Karle, she possessed his courageous spirit. It leaped to her eye in anger, it burned like a coal beneath her silence, to flash forth again between her parted lips and white teeth in the merry laugh which gladdened the king's heart. Not one in the company would dare to provoke her as had Heluiz, who withal teased without malice and loved without envy. What from her lips was only a sallying breeze from a rose thicket, from another would have been a biting, worrying wind

that stings the blood like a wild nettle. If she
teased, it was from curiosity to know what she
could not otherwise discover ; for at times her
friend matched Gui's indifference with scant
words, and again the black lashes quivered over
swimming eyes, — whether for love, or pride, or
anger, Heluiz of Hesbaye was sore in doubt, not
yet dreaming with what sorry company love will
sometimes abide. Waiting for the captain's
coming, she stole a glance now and then at
Agnes' face, and seeing the fine lines of pride
quiver said to herself, "So the covert of leaves
stirs when the fawn within trembles."

A slope of broad steps led up from the roadside to the terrace. Elsewhere the latter was
circled by an open balustrade, and so pressed
about by the wood that at high noon its marble
floor was dark with the leaf shadows. The
frown had scarce left Mistress Chlodine's face
when Gesualda, sighing that she should be at
work when butterflies were abroad, chanced to
follow one with her eyes in its flight over the
balusters, and gave a quick cry.

"Mother of God!" she said, her hand on
her swelling bosom, "I thought it was a wood
spirit."

The occasion of this exclamation was a young
girl, who, emerging suddenly from the copse
surrounding the pleasance, and surprised at the

scene before her, hesitated whether to advance or retreat, fixing her large eyes in succession upon the faces turned towards her. She stood holding the branch which had barred her passage, her uplifted arm bare to the view, for the lacing-cord of the sleeve was gone and the braided wrist unfastened. A border of silver lace, tarnished and frayed, encircled the low neck of her dress, and, continuing down between the spiral pleats of the bosom, terminated in a broad band, which accentuated her slender form, and from which hung innumerable tiny trinkets and bells. Worn and dusty as was this dress, it served only to enhance the wearer's vigorous beauty, which burst through her outgrown garment as the ripe fruit bursts its sheath.

Judging from her attire and appearance that she was some wandering dancer, who, separated from her companions, had become lost in the forest, Mistress Chlodine addressed her kindly, bidding her approach and rest on the terrace steps. Releasing the branch, the girl advanced slowly to the opening, where she stood scrutinizing the rich apparel of those about her.

"What is thy name?" asked Agnes of Solier, on whose amice of seed pearls and ermine kirtle the stranger's gaze was riveted.

The girl lifted her eyes, without replying, to Agnes' face, where they rested with so frank an

admiration that the latter forgave their beauty
and daring.

"Either she is dumb or does not understand!" exclaimed Gesualda, whose earnest
lisping voice was always the signal for laughter.

"Nay," said Heluiz of Hesbaye gently, offering her a small tray on which were bean cakes
and almond pasties; "she is tired and hungry."

The girl took the tray, and, sitting down on
the step, began to eat without ceremony.

"Any one can understand that language,"
lisped Gesualda.

Lifting her large eyes to the speaker's face,
the stranger smiled; whereupon all laughed
aloud, even Mistress Chlodine. "It is good,
pretty dear," said the latter, condescendingly.

"The captain, the captain!" cried Gesualda,
clapping her hands. "Have ready thy question, Heluiz."

The girl, from whom attention was momentarily diverted, looked up from her tray. Down
the path came Gui of Tours, twirling the empty
strap of his baldric and followed by the page.
His head was uncovered, and the sun shone on
the metal band confining the brown hair above
his forehead. As he drew near, his eyes sought
Agnes' face, where was clearly to be seen pride
at his manly grace, mingled with a nervous
apprehension as to how he might bear himself
towards her.

" Captain " — said Heluiz of Hesbaye.

But in turning his eyes from Agnes to Heluiz, they got no farther than midway from one to the other, for there between them on the step sat Passe Rose.

Passe Rose it undoubtedly was, but in such guise that the captain's cap fell from his hand for wonder and surprise. Her hair was powdered with the red dust, and her dress so torn and stained that if ever he had been in doubt of his heart's desire, the plight of the girl made it plain. There she sat, eating her cake, apparently unconcerned, her eyes upon the wicker tray between her knees, — she of whom he dreamed by night and thought by day, the light of whose eye was dearer than the king's oriflamme, and whose laugh was sweeter than all other of God's sounds.

" Captain," said Heluiz, " we have fallen into words over the Avars " —

" Whether they have the faces of apes or of men," interrupted Gesualda. " Hast thou not heard the song about Sigebert, how his army took flight at the mere sight of the Huns ? My mother told it me when I was young."

A chorus of laughter greeted this evidence of the little maid's age ; but still the captain could not tear his gaze away from Passe Rose, in whom, it was now evident to all, he took more interest than in the Avars.

Although quietly eating her bean cake, a storm of emotions tore Passe Rose's heart: shame at the contrast between her and the laughing girls, and a burning dread lest Gui should deem she had sought him out; envy of all the joyous ease and rich attire about her, and scorn for it all in comparison with what she herself could give; a bitter anger against injustice, and a sense of loss made doubly keen at the sight of things beyond her reach; but most of all the consciousness of the captain's gaze, for its open eloquence caused her both fear and exultation. It was to measure the effect of this gaze that she lifted her eyes, and saw the curious glances fixed upon the captain and herself. Even Gesualda had forgotten the Avars.

With an effort Passe Rose stood up, confused before so many eyes.

"Art thou rested?" said Heluiz kindly. But the girl could make no answer.

"Bid the captain give her shelter for the night, Mistress Chlodine," said Agnes; but the tone of the voice was at such variance with the meaning of the word that a sudden fire blazed on Passe Rose's face, and the eyes of the two met with a shock as when flint strikes flint and the fire flashes between. Neither knew cause for enmity; but as often one feels more than is perceived, so a secret foreboding filled their hearts with mistrust and defiance. It seemed as if each forgot her own beauty at the sight of the other's, and it were hard to tell what had happened (for the rest looked on in wonder) had not Gui stepped boldly forward, taking Passe Rose's hand, and saying, "Were the king here, shelter and food were surely thine, and in his name I offer them." With this, delaying for no reply, he led her down the step to where the page stood in waiting, and, being still observed of all, gave her into his charge without further words, and returned to answer Gesualda's question.

"I have followed the Count Theudoric from the Kamp to the Vaag," he said, pushing back the hair from his forehead, "but have seen more apes in France than in all the land of the Avars."

"By what sign dost thou know them?" asked Gesualda, in doubt whether he was in jest or earnest.

"By a certain chattering speech, — without meaning or purpose," replied the captain.

"I think thine hath overmuch of both," said the girl, hot with vexation. It was evident to all that things were not as they had been before the stranger's coming, and Gesualda, losing all interest in the Huns and eager to repay the captain's thrust, divined the point of attack in spite of his nonchalant manner. " Mistress Chlodine," she said innocently, and plying fast her needle, "after working on the queen's valance, I am sure the king would grudge us no pastime at supper. Here is this girl, who doubtless hath tales of adventure, or can otherwise divert us with jugglers' tricks or even rope-dancing "—

" Nay," interposed Gui abruptly, " let the girl rest ; she hath walked from Maestricht "—

" From Maestricht ! " exclaimed Gesualda, lifting her eyebrows. " Hath she taught thee her conjurer's art ? She said no word, and yet thou knowest whence she came."

" I saw her in the abbey of St. Servais," stammered the captain, getting nearer the truth than would have many another in like vexation.

Gesualda contented herself with a glance at Agnes and a subdued laugh, indicating vast amusement over something she chose not to utter.

" For my part," said Heluiz of Hesbaye, " I had far rather ride to Aix this very evening. The moon is full, and I love dearly to see the wood by night."

" Aye, let us have all," chimed in Gesualda : " dances at supper, the moon on the plain, and torches for the wood."

So lively a murmur of approbation greeted this proposition that Mistress Chlodine smiled assent, and at the same time took the cover of gilded leather from the needle-case on her knees as a signal that work was over. The embroidery was quickly folded in its silken cover; there was rustling of robes, flashing of beads, and chatter of loosened voices; a score of light feet pattered over the terrace floor, a half score gowns swept the steps, and the pleasance was left to the birds and the leaf shadows.

"Who is she,— the one with the ermine kirtle?" Passe Rose had asked of the page, as she followed him down the path.

"With the ermine kirtle?" said the page, turning to see whom the girl designated. "Oh, that is Agnes of Solier. She is betrothed to the captain who commands the guard;" and half closing his eye with an expressive glance at Passe Rose, "They say she is a king's daughter."

XI.

A bat sweeping from the night gloom into a blaze of candles would be no more dazed than was Passe Rose when, from the silence and twilight of the wood, she stepped into the maidens' chatter and the light of her lover's eye.

Fascinated by the scene before her, and gladdened at heart in the midst of her misery by the sight of Gui, yet through all the maze of her feeling ran a single thought like a leading-string, — to escape again, and free herself from suspicion of seeking aught at his hand. But when she heard the page's answer, the design she had formed to outwit the boy between the terrace and the gate passed clean from her mind. She followed him now willingly, the image of Agnes of Solier in her ermine kirtle before her eyes, heeding so little whither she went that she neither saw the soldiers about the gate nor observed the woman to whom the page committed her; and when her thoughts returned, there she was — like one who, waking from sleep, sits up in bed — alone, on a bench in a sort of alcove, curtained off from view. A mat of reeds covered the floor, and a bed of moss and dry leaves was spread in the corner. Pushing aside the curtain, she saw a large room, with seats ranged along the wall, and a table before the fireplace, at which a woman was cooking. The light fell full in her face from the door opposite, so that at first she could distinguish nothing clearly at the farther end of the vast apartment; but on shielding her eyes from the sun, she perceived a monk seated at the table. He had apparently just finished his afternoon meal, for, taking a cloth from his bag and wiping his mouth, he pushed his seat to the wall, near the fireplace, where, with hands locked over his paunch, he composed himself to slumber.

Having cleared the table of its cup and platter, the attendant raked the unburnt sticks from the fire, and disappeared in the shadows beyond. Passe Rose was about to let fall the curtain, when a woman whom she recognized as one she had seen on the terrace entered the doorway. Casting a quick glance behind her, the latter traversed the room with a rapid but timid step, as if seeking some one, and seeing the monk dozing near the fire hastened towards him. So light was her footfall that the monk knew nothing of her approach till he felt her hand upon his shoulder.

"Dost thou return to Maestricht to-night?" she asked, checking his surprise by her question.

Passe Rose listened.

"I am told," continued the speaker, "thou art a holy man, much esteemed by the Prior Sergius."

Passe Rose could not hear the monk's reply, for his voice was thick, but its tones betrayed satisfaction.

"I have a message to send him, and lest thy memory should be overtaxed I have committed it to writing. Where is thy money-bag?"

The monk showed the bag whence he had taken the napkin.

"Is it secure?" asked the woman, testing its cord, and at the same time putting within it something she drew from her bosom. "Deliver it into the prior's own hand without fail, and may God keep thee."

Followed by the monk, the speaker retraced her steps, and Passe Rose, fearing to be seen, let go the curtain.

"Remember thou givest the parchment into the prior's own hand. Thou shouldst have heard the queen praise thy work; it was marvelous."

"Honey-tongue!" thought Passe Rose. They were now close by, and she could not resist the temptation to part the curtain again the width of her eye; and there, beaming with self-complacency, stood the monk who rode the gray mule.

"From whom shall I say — should the prior ask" — he stammered, under the woman's soft eyes.

The latter hesitated, balancing something in her mind. Then, after a moment, "Rothilde," she whispered.

"By St. Martin," thought Passe Rose, "the gospel was right."

"Here comes thy mule. God speed thee,"

said the woman to the monk, and, retreating from the doorway to escape the observation of those who brought the mule, she glided down the room and disappeared in the obscurity.

Brother Dominic, little thinking that only a hempen curtain separated him from the demon, smiled in the doorway. He had expected to win the queen's praise, but it was news to him that he stood high in the prior's favor. As for the woman's voice, it was sweeter than the king's wine.

"If the sight of me were not too much for thee, dear monk," said Passe Rose, thinking of Friedgis, "I also would intrust thee with a message."

The mule was at the door, and Brother Dominic was preparing to mount. "Hold thyself steady till I am firmly on," he said coaxingly. "So — there, now, by God's grace we will reach Visé to-night, and to-morrow" —

"Good father" — said a voice within the door, from behind the curtain. The monk turned in his seat as best he could, but discovered no one. "As thou goest from the square of St. Sebastian by the house of Werdric the goldsmith, knock at the garden gate, and say to Jeanne, his wife, that I am well, and send her greeting."

Partly from surprise and partly because of

the mule's impatience, Brother Dominic found no reply at hand. To tell the truth, he had fully recovered from neither the wine taken at supper nor the nap so suddenly interrupted.

" My voice is not so sweet as the other's," continued Passe Rose, " but if thou givest my message I will thank thee none the less; and if it tax not thy memory overmuch, say the sender is Passe Rose."

By this time Brother Dominic had lost all hope of checking the mule's ardor. It was enough for him if he were able to guide the beast through the gateway, through which, however, he passed in safety, but with sorely confused ideas of his messages, their mysterious senders, and those to whom he was to deliver them.

Having watched the monk through the gate, and waited till all was silent again, Passe Rose, satisfied that she was alone, unlaced her sleeve, loosed the band about her hair, and, kneeling down beside the shallow basin on the floor, near the bed, began to bathe her face and neck in the cool water. While she was thus occupied came Gesualda with Heluiz of Hesbaye, — the former having sought permission to bring the girl to supper, the latter accompanying her at the command of Mistress Chlodine, who would as soon have trusted a filly in the open field as

Gesualda with liberty. Passe Rose had taken her dagger from her bosom, and, bending above the basin, was parting her long hair with the blade's point, so that she neither saw nor heard anything till, throwing back the hair from before her eyes, she looked up, and perceived the two standing hand in hand without the parted curtain. Gesualda's face was pretty enough; what it lacked the queen's toilet chest could not furnish, — a certain depth of expression beyond her years; yet Passe Rose passed it by to rest her gaze upon Heluiz, who looked neither upon her soiled feet nor her disheveled hair, but steadfastly, with a kindly promise of amity, into her eyes.

"Thou hast a stout comb," said Gesualda, who had watched the dagger's passage through the shining hair.

"It hath served many a purpose," replied Passe Rose, seeking to fasten the neck-band over her bosom, while still looking at Heluiz.

Nothing daunted, Gesualda advanced and sat down on the bench's edge.

"I have an ivory one, white as a dog's tooth, I will give thee, for a tale or a dance at supper," she said, scrutinizing the bells which bordered Passe Rose's dress.

Little had the latter thought, when boasting to Friedgis beside the abbey pond, that she was

to dance like the water stars for those that shine
in the sky; but her pride was numbed with the
dread of leaving the place. Had the servants
driven her from the gate, she would have hovered about the skirt of wood. Her thought was
no more of silk or pearls; she had lost all memory of Jeanne's tears, the shame of their parting,
and the weary journey in the forest; a single
face barred every way to which her thought
turned, the face of Agnes of Solier, and the bitterness and loneliness of her heart uprose in a
single hate against this face which stood between
her and her soul's desire. For the love which
unawares had consoled her in her wandering,
self-confessed and unrebuked, now mastered
every other desire.

"Wilt thou come?" persisted Gesualda.

"I am ready," replied Passe Rose, rising from
her knees.

The three crossed the room to the doorway
through which Rothilde had passed, Gesualda
leading. This door led to a flight of stairs,
which they ascended to the floor above, where a
corridor with openings upon the court conducted
to a spacious vestibule. Between its pillars
hung white cloths fringed with purple, and, as
they entered, sounds of approaching voices were
heard between the curtains. Whispering a word
to Gesualda, Heluiz drew Passe Rose aside.

The voices grew louder, two pages held back the swaying drapery, and a merry company came forth from the room beyond. It was the women of the princesses' service passing to supper.

"Come with me," said Heluiz, taking Passe Rose by the hand, and drawing her into the apartment whence the women had issued. Hurrying across it to one of the smaller rooms surrounding its three sides, she called to a serving-maid loitering by the water-tank, and, putting into Passe Rose's fingers the key she took from her girdle, said, "Take what thou wilt from the chest within; thou canst return it when supper is ended;" and to the maid, "Bring water for her feet, give her sandals, and wait upon her;" saying which, she hastened back to join the others at supper.

The maid, filling her basin from the pool, regarded Passe Rose with curiosity. Passe Rose, alone with the maid, looked about her in no less wonder. Sitting where she was bidden, she gave herself over to the girl's service, gazing down at her own feet in the limpid water which curled about her ankles, giving forth a scent of roses under the maid's hand. Having finished her task, with a sulky face at having to serve one whom she took to be of no dignity or degree, the maid stood by, waiting to see what orders Passe Rose dared to give. But Passe Rose did not

observe her. The warm colors on the walls, the
soft cushions of brilliant hues, the lustre of enameled tiles strewn with sweet-smelling herbs,
delighted her senses, and, refreshed by the cool-
ing water, she sat gazing about her, holding tho
key in her hand. The girl brought her sandals,
finished with soft leather reaching half-way to
the knee, and, suiting her motions to the maid's
endeavor, Passe Rose was watching the fitting
of the hooks in the silver eyelets, when the wind
lifted the curtain of the vestibule, bringing the
sound of voices from those at supper.

She rose quickly to her feet, saying "Enough!"
to her curious attendant, and entered the side
room which Heluiz had designated. A couch
covered with a serge cloth occupied one angle;
in the other stood the chest whose key she held;
between these a square window, high up, admitted the light from the corridor. Below the window was a recess in the wall, containing a mirror
of polished metal mounted on a bronze stand,
with other articles of toilet. From among these
Passe Rose took a comb and a long silken band,
and began to braid her hair, still hanging over
her shoulders, weaving the band in and out deftly
between the braids. Having finished, she fitted
the key to the chest's clasp and raised the lid.
On the top lay a mantle, covered with the finest
plumage of the peacock's neck and bordered

with swan's down, and above her shone the mirror, with the lines of her sloping shoulders in its dark face. She smoothed the mantle with her finger-tips, lifted it cautiously to feel its weight, held it high in the beam of light, then spread it about her neck. To slip the pin in the double clasp at the throat was the work of a moment; the touch of the plumage upon her down-bent chin was soft to feel, but to observe the garment well she must needs turn her head with a side-wise glance over her shoulders, and there, in the doorway, stood Jessé, the page, his eye sparkling with admiration, and his message sticking fast in his throat.

Thinking he summoned her to supper, Passe Rose laid the mantle quickly in the chest, turning the key, and, taking the boy's hand, crossed the room. But on reaching the vestibule the youth found his tongue.

"The captain, Gui of Tours," he stammered, holding out her collar of gold, "bade me bring thee this token that he waits in the strangers' court to speak with thee."

Passe Rose took the jewel from his outstretched hand.

"Dost thou know the place where they are at supper?" she asked, smiling upon him.

"Surely," replied the boy; "it is there, straight on," pointing the way.

"Go tell the captain," said Passe Rose, "that I am gone to dance before Agnes of Solier, his betrothed, having a fancy to see her so strong that I cannot come." Saying which she left the page gazing after her, and disappeared in the direction he had indicated.

XII.

Not since she saw the candle burning in her chamber window, on her return from the abbey of St. Servais, had Passe Rose felt so light of heart as now, entering the supper-room of Immaburg. In its doorway she stood on the threshold of her ambition, and Jeanne's garden seemed far away. Have you seen the bright edge of clouds piled high against the sun's disk at dusk? The passage of the Lady Adelhaïde with her train in the streets of Maestricht had been nothing less to Passe Rose than that glimpse of splendor lying on the farther side of the cloud, where the sun is; and here she was, passing into the glory of the king's court, where, come what might, she was resolved to stay.

As she entered, servants were removing from the dresser a quarter of roe-deer garnished with flowers and jelly of loach; others were bringing wine and spices, and Passe Rose, who lived to

the full each passing moment, while searching
for Agnes of Solier among those at table, saw
these and many other things, enjoying all as
they were her own. She took no notice of the
surprise occasioned by her coming before she
was bidden, turning her eyes slowly from face to
face till they fell upon Agnes, sitting in the
chief seat, Mistress Chlodine being in chapel at
prayers for the safety of the night journey.

"Come hither; have no fear," said Gesualda,
who, although the youngest, was the readiest
with her tongue.

Advancing slowly to the centre of the room,
Passe Rose stopped, her gaze still fixed upon
Agnes of Solier.

"What is thy name?" asked the latter, washing her hands in the basin offered by a page.

"Passe Rose," replied the girl, returning the
curious glances directed upon her, and observing
Rothilde at Agnes' side.

"Passe Rose?" repeated Gesualda. "That
is a strange name.   Whence dost thou come?"

"From whence the swallows come at night,"
replied Passe Rose.

"Hast thou no master, no kin?" asked Agnes
of Solier.

"Nay; I am free."

"Thou saidst thou wouldst dance for us,"
said Gesualda. "Thou hast a pretty foot, since
it goes into the sandals of Heluiz."

"I danced once before the Queen Hildegarde, and I have made a vow to dance no more except before a queen," replied Passe Rose.

Gesualda opened wide her eyes. "Before Queen Hildegarde! Pray what is thine age?"

At this moment Passe Rose caught Rothilde's eye, and, without heeding Gesualda's question, began to fasten about her neck the collar Gui had sent by the page, exposing it full to view. The Saxon uttered a cry of surprise.

"Whence hadst thou my collar?" she exclaimed, spilling her cup as she leaned forward over the table.

"By St. Martin," replied Passe Rose carelessly, "that is the question which Friedgis, the Saxon serf who keeps the gate for the monks of the blessed St. Servais, asked me, and I am tired of answering it."

At the mention of Friedgis' name Rothilde fell back in her seat, turning pale.

"What ails thee?" asked Agnes, observing her pallor. "If the jewel is thine" —

"Give it her to see!" exclaimed Gesualda. "Bid her give it, Agnes!" she said excitedly, rising from the table, with a glance of suspicion at Passe Rose.

As she spoke Gui appeared in the doorway, and at the sound of his step an insolent light gleamed in Passe Rose's eyes. The message she had sent her lover by the page, seasoned though it was with bitterness and cold with seeming indifference, was little else than the call of the wounded bird to its mate ; and when first her ear caught his step she knew for whom he came.

"The jewel was given me by my lover," she said, looking straight into Agnes' face, "and I swore at the time to give it into no hand but his."

"Let it pass," whispered Heluiz to Agnes, pressing her hand beneath the table. But the words on the latter's lips were beyond restraint. Gui's first glance had been for Passe Rose. Agnes had noted it well. "Captain," she said haughtily, "bring me, I pray thee, the girl's collar, that I may show it to Rothilde."

"Thou hast chosen well," said Passe Rose, turning for the first time to Gui. "It was the captain who gave it me, and he may have it if he will."

Between differences of wealth and station, where no love is, a man may waver ; but for Gui to be at Passe Rose's side was station enough, and the message in her eyes more than gold. "To this girl," he said, taking her hand, "I gave the protection of the king. Since that is not ample to cover her, henceforth she is under mine."

There was not one present who, at these words, did not expect from the king's favorite some angry retort or harsh command, and not one, remembering afterwards how she bore herself, doubted the story of her birth; for she only laughed, fondling the hound beside her chair, and, rising from table, bade the others follow her, saying to Gui, as she passed, that the girl was safe now, and she felt at ease to prepare for the journey, — just as often the king himself, when vexed or even insulted, had been seen to put the occasion by with a jest, and bide his time.

"If the girl has not the chance to dance in truth before a queen, and a king also, ere her oath is a week older, then am I no prophet," thought Gesualda, as they left the room.

Scarcely were they gone, whispering together, with backward glances, than Passe Rose began to speak, as if she would give the captain no chance to utter a word.

"I fell on the Saxon maid at the first cast," she said, struggling to command her voice; but her bravery was over, and she retreated towards the table, facing Gui, who followed her. "Thou shouldst have seen her face. When I put on the collar she cried out, asking whence I had it. Did I not tell thee, in the field? I said to her the serf" —

"I heard thine answer,—that thy lover gave it thee."

"Nay," said Passe Rose hurriedly. Her eyes shone and her voice faltered. "I said the serf Friedgis put me the same question. Thereupon the Saxon turned white. Does a woman wax pale and swoon on finding her lover?" Gui, advancing, smiled, and Passe Rose knew the color on her cheek was answer to her question. Still receding, she found her retreat cut off by Agnes' chair. The collar bound her swelling throat, and the words fell nervously from her lips. "She sent a message to the prior by the monk. Her voice is like honey and wine. The monk was drunk with it. She hath soft eyes, looking down. I hate such"—

Gui took both her hands. "I love thee," he said.

Passe Rose trembled from head to foot.

"I love thee," repeated the captain. His words enveloped her like a mist. In an instant his arms were about her. Power to speak, to stand, strength of will and limb alike, were failing her, when suddenly, like a spark out of the dark, came the thought of Agnes of Solier. A quiver ran through her body, and she slid from his arms into the chair, hiding her face with her hands.

Seizing them by the wrists, the captain drew them away, and uncovered her eyes.

“ How happens it, being betrothed to ” — the words died on her lips — “ that thou lovest me ? ” She had twisted her wrists from his grasp, and, shrinking back in the chair, trembled.

“ I swear ” — cried Gui passionately, seeking her hands.

“ Sh ! ” said Passe Rose, leaning forward suddenly, and covering his mouth with her fingers.

It was Mistress Chlodine returning from prayers. Her eye glanced down the deserted table, and she had certainly discovered Passe Rose, crouching breathless in the chair, had not the captain come boldly forward between the two.

“ Countess,” said he courteously, but chafing inwardly, “ the sixth hour is just called, and time presses. To a man on a good horse an hour is nothing, but with baggage and women’s litters ” —

“ Have no fear,” she replied. “ In an hour’s time all will be ready,” and she passed out whither the others had gone, observing nothing, for the room, dimly lighted from without, was growing dark.

Now it happened that Brother Dominic, whether because of the wine he had at supper or the conversation he had with Rothilde, whose presence lingered with him like odor of musk, had gotten no farther than the outer gate, when he began to query whether the written message in his pouch or the spoken one of Passe Rose was for the prior. In vain did he cudgel both his wits and the mule; and having so excellent a reason for hearing that sweet voice again, he turned back to the room where he had supped. Finding it empty, he left the mule at the door, making inquiries of all he met for two women, — though his thoughts were of one only, — till at last, full of misgivings, and so bewildered by many turnings that he began to think of nothing but to find his mule again, he came up the private stair from the oratory to the supper-room just as Mistress Chlodine finished speaking, to find himself face to face with the captain, furious at this second interruption. It was enough for Brother Dominic to be thus confronted by one whom he thought beyond redemption in the grasp of the demon; for he had not seen the captain since they parted on the abbey road. What then was his terror on seeing the demon also advancing upon him from behind the captain. With no thought but of flight, the monk retreated precipitately into the corridor; but before he had passed the door Passe Rose had him by the sleeve.

Holding him fast, — an easy task, — "Go thou," she said to Gui, who looked on in amazement.　"Nay, listen," for the captain advanced towards her: "go thou and prepare a litter for me also, and come again quickly to the chapel." An exclamation of love and remonstrance burst from the captain's lips.　"Nay," cried Passe Rose, stretching out her arm forbiddingly.　"As thou lovest me, go; and, as thou lovest me, come shortly."　Saying which, she drew the monk with her into the passage, leaving the astonished captain as she had left him in the wood of Hesbaye, and on the road which descends to Maestricht, consumed with love, yet loath to disobey.

Deserted by the captain, and alone with the girl in an obscure corridor, Brother Dominic planted his feet as firmly as ever his mule had done, making the sign of the cross above his tormentor's head.

"Blood and death!" cried Passe Rose, in no mood to trifle with his terror, "art thou mad? Only show me the way to the chapel.　Do demons seek the altars of God?"　Somewhat assured by this reflection, Brother Dominic ceased his gesticulations, but still stood, obstinate, his back against the wall.　"Feel my arm," said Passe Rose, thrusting it under his nose; "hath a devil flesh and blood?　Do thou pass first, and I will follow."　By no means convinced, but persuaded that compliance was the door of his safety, the monk shuffled down the corridor, taking by good luck the stair to the chapel, for he had no recollection of the way he had come. The private stair by which they descended opened directly into the porch in front of the curtain. " May the blessed St. Servais reward thee," said Passe Rose, as they emerged into the air. A few penitents, who had been listening to the service within, were still prostrated before the curtain. " Hast thou the message safe which I gave thee?" she whispered in his ear. " I thought by this time thou wouldst be well on thy way."

" The message " — stammered the monk, bewildered, and fumbling in his bag.

" Aye, for the prior — quick — let me see."

" Here it is," replied the monk, drawing it forth ; " but surely it was the other gave it me."

" What other?" said Passe Rose, taking it quickly. " Tut, tut, dear monk, thou art bewitched. Say to the prior I have more to add to it, and will send it by the captain when next he goes to inquire for the abbot's health. Farewell." With this she wrapped the parchment about her dagger, with the other found by the abbey pond, and lifting the curtain disappeared within.

The torches which had been lighted during

the vesper service were extinguished, and for
a moment Passe Rose could see nothing but the
candle of yellow wax burning under the cupola
of the altar. As she went down the nave she
put out her hand instinctively before her, till,
becoming accustomed to the gloom, she perceived the reading-desks in front of the chancel
and the iron gates leading into the choir.
Opening one of these gates, she passed in, and
stood contemplating the altar. The curtains
between the columns supporting the canopy
were drawn aside, and the dove containing the
Eucharist, hanging by four silver chains between
the pillars, was visible. Behind the altar, on
the screen, stood two angels collecting in a cup
the blood flowing from the feet of the Christ on
a cross above them. Below the angels was a
manger, within which was represented an in-
fant wrapped in swaddling-clothes. Passe Rose
gazed in silence at these things, which seemed
profoundly to affect her. Her face shone, and
one hand rested on her bosom. If she thought
of the image lying broken on the floor of her
chamber where she had hurled it, she made no
effort to reconcile that act of anger with her
present purpose, One thing she knew, — she
loved ; and this love, unutterably precious, in
which she exulted and for which she trembled,
she had brought to the protecting shelter of the

power so mysteriously symbolized in the emblems before her. Absorbed in contemplation, she remained motionless, scarcely breathing, when a voice close beside her said : —

" Woman, what seekest thou ? "

Passe Rose turned her head, and saw a priest. Hearing the clang of the chancel gate, he had come out from the vestry, where he was disrobing, and perceiving a woman within the railing, whose upturned face he scrutinized in vain, and whose strange dress proclaimed her no ordinary inmate of the villa, had hastened to ask her errand. Passe Rose seemed in no wise surprised by his presence. She stood smiling, her hand still resting on her bosom.

" Whom seekest thou ? " repeated the priest.

Passe Rose turned her ear to the porch and listened. The neighing of horses in the court could be heard, but the church was silent. " Father," she said, " we have need of thy blessing. Come." Descending the chancel stair, she opened the gate, and listened again. It was evident that she expected some one, and the priest, following her motions, peered into the darkness which enveloped them. " Have patience," whispered Passe Rose, " he will come; let us wait in the porch," and she extended her hand.

" For whom dost thou wait ? " asked the priest, observing the girl suspiciously.

A quick blush overran her face. " Knowest thou the captain, Gui of Tours?" The priest assented. "It is he — we seek thy blessing." The captain was well known to the priest, and, seeing the girl color, he doubted not into what manner of adventure she had fallen. " Come," she stammered. Chilled by the expression on his face, she began to tremble.

" Thou hast sinned," he said gravely, eying her steadfastly.

Passe Rose looked up quickly. " Nay, to love — that is no sin " — She stopped, her confusion increasing. " Is it not in the porch that they who love receive thy blessing? Said I not we seek it?" Her voice faltered. She read on his face the expression she had seen on that of Friedgis, by the pond.

" Is she mad or foolish ? " the priest was saying to himself.

" Knowest thou not that Gui of Tours is betrothed? The king himself was present at the espousals. Who art thou? Tell me all," he said gently, for he saw her limbs tremble as with cold.

But Passe Rose, retreating through the gate, shook her head. " He will come," she murmured ; " he hath promised."

" To marry thee ? " Passe Rose, holding fast to the gate, nodded. So astonished was the priest that he smiled incredulously. At this smile the girl quivered like a tree when the lance strikes fast in its heart. "Daughter," he said gently, "the blessing thou seekest were of no avail" —

"Thou refusest!" interrupted Passe Rose hoarsely. The priest sighed. The girl had turned away her eyes, and was gazing at the altar. Beside the screen were two nuptial crowns. Suddenly she drew herself erect. "It is well — thy blessings are for the great — Because I come to thy porch with no train of damsels nor sponsors" — Her throat swelled. "If I brought thee my shame, thou wouldst receive it. I have come with my love, and thou wilt have none of it. So be it, — so be it," she repeated to herself, casting a scornful glance at the altar. "The Saxon spoke well; henceforth thy king and thy God are nothing to me."

Hot with passion, she had scarce passed the chancel gate when she saw the captain, who, entranced by her promise to accompany him that night to Aix, advanced eagerly from the porch to meet her. She stopped short, her feet rooted to the flagstone like a tree to the soil. The blood ran from her face and neck; with a convulsive effort to reach the priest's side, she cried, "Father, save me!" Then the walls rocked before her eyes, as the walls of the house before the eyes of the revelers, when Samson laid hold of the pillars.

When she awoke, she felt the cool autumn air upon her face. Was she still in the wood of Hesbaye? Nay, she thought, raising herself on her elbows. She was in a cart, and her limbs were sore with the jolting. Crawling to the opening, she looked out from under the cover of skins. A long cavalcade of wagons and horsemen stretched before her. Through the smoke of the torches she saw stars and waving branches. The red flames streamed in the wind, and shone on the metal plates of the harness. Returning to her rough bed, she endeavored to collect her thoughts, watching the reflections dancing on the covering over her head. All at once these reflections disappeared in a man's shadow. She lifted her head. "Hush!" said a voice which made her blood quicken. "Art thou well? There is wine beside thee. Reach hither thy hand." She put forth her hand. "I swore to the priest by the sacred books, and thou hast his blessing. Art thou satisfied?" A hand pressed hers to the lips which spoke. "Sleep on, and fear nothing."

Passe Rose lay down again. The jolting cart pained her no longer. She had no need of wine or sleep. An ecstasy of joy possessed her, and she smiled, alone, in the darkness.

If one has not seen in midwinter a gray birch copse filled quickly with such a wealth of sun that the very buds seem to swell, though the ice-drops hang from the tips of the twigs ; if one has not seen a dull waste of sea under a rack of low cloud answer a random slant of sun with a play of such colors as fire the stone in the brooch of the king's mantle ; nay, if one has not felt within his own breast, though for no longer a time than the passing of a bird's shadow, the presentiment of an endless joy, one would never understand how Passe Rose should so smile and dream on her bed of skins in the king's baggage-wagon. Fears enough were ready to assail her, pressing close as the night without on the torches, yet held aloof, as it were, by that smile ; and just as the torches' flame flared brighter and their fiery sparks leaped higher for the very thickness of the shadows, so was her joy sharpened by her heart's hunger.

Suddenly the wagon stopped ; there was neighing of frightened horses and stamping of hoofs on the loose stones, for they had come to the ford of the Wurm, and the water was high because of the rains. Rising on her hands and knees, Passe Rose peered between the loosely sewed covering. Blocked by those in advance, the wagons stood three abreast at the edge of the shoal. She could see horsemen sounding

the river shallows with their lances, the glare of
uplifted torches reflected in their armor plates
and dancing on the swollen waters. The foremost wagon was already midway in the stream;
its horses, snorting with fear, pricked forward
their ears, scattering the spray at every hesitating step upon the leather pleatings of their
riders' tunics.

"Is there danger?" cried Mistress Chlodine,
from the wagon in front.

"Nay," replied a horseman, "the bottom is
firm; have no fear."

Passe Rose, widening the crevice between the
skins with her fingers, searched for the captain.
As she looked, a low, familiar voice issuing from
the adjoining wagon caught her ear. The axle-
ends touched each other, and the words came
distinctly: —

"Tell me, then, dear Rothilde, what it is that
wins a man's fancy. If to be a king's daughter,
and to possess beauty" — Then the words were
lost amid the shoutings.

Passe Rose pressed her ear to the opening.

"Which thinkest thou hast the greater beauty?" said the voice of Gesualda again.

"It is plain what the captain thought," replied the other; then a horse shook himself, and
the voice was drowned in the rattle of the harness.

"One would say she thought to wed him on the spot," laughed Gesualda.

"He will have her no other way, mark me."

"Saints of God! a dancing-girl"—

"Moreover, the captain will do her bidding," pursued the other. "I noted them both well. She hath his heart, and the king himself cannot buy it from her with the treasure of the Huns, though for his own daughter."

"What a king cannot possess he destroys," said Gesualda, significantly; "thou shouldst know that well, being a Saxon."

There was a moment of silence.

"If Agnes will let him. Dost thou not remember what the priest read yestermorning: how, when Solomon would have divided the child between the mothers"—

"The case is far different," interrupted Gesualda. "Which is easier,— for a dancing-girl to give herself to a captain, or for a king's daughter to forget an injury? For if he had Agnes' heart, he gave it back to her in presence of us all. Mark well what I tell thee,— this business will cost him dear. One hath his heart; the other will have his head"—

"Heu, heu! forward!" cried a horseman, brandishing his torch. The voices ceased, the horses strained to the task, and the wagon whence the voices proceeded entered the river.

Like the dazed hound, mute under the scourge of its master, so, on her knees, dazed and powerless to reason, Passe Rose remained motionless. " The other will have his head ; " and then, like the cut of a whip's lash, " Strumpet ! " cried the voice of Werdric. Her own wagon began to move. A hand thrust aside the covering in front, and she saw the captain.

" Art thou afraid ? "

" Nay."

He made a movement as if to enter. She held up her hand. He smiled, his eyes shining under the steel rim of his helmet, then disappeared. Crawling like a cat over the skins to the rear of the wagon, Passe Rose drew her dagger from her bosom and made a rent in the covering. She could hear the gurgle of running waters, the wagon swayed on the rolling stones, then the wheels sank in the yielding sand, — they were over. The leather thong fastening the curtain was knotted tightly. She took her dagger again, and widened the rent clean to the bottom. The edge was keen, and in her haste to thrust the weapon back in her garment she cut her wrist. Lifting the flap, she put out her head. The night was dark, there were none behind her, — the way was open. About to leap, yet she could not stir ; it seemed to her that her heart was in a vise, that it was not beating. Looking down, she saw the blood upon her wrist. Wetting her finger in the spot, she drew on the covering of the wagon a large heart transfixed by a dagger, — such as she had seen of marchpane and sugared sweets at the fair of St. Denis. The sight of this heart seemed to give her pleasure as she contemplated it. "Heu, heu!" cried a driver. With a rapid twist of her dagger she cut out the heart, hid it with the blade in her bosom, and leaped.

The entire train had crossed the ford, and the momentary disorder caused by the passage was repaired. The foremost wagons, having waited for those which followed, had begun to move again ; the escort were taking their places ; and the horsemen, appointed to close the march, galloping down the line, wheeled into position almost on the spot where Passe Rose had leaped.

"By the mass !" exclaimed one, leaning forward on his horse's neck and examining the rent covering, "one would say the claws of a wild-cat."

The other — that Gascon who would have saved the captain from the demon on the road to Maestricht, and who, having seen the captain return sound of body, but indisposed to answer the questions put to him, and having, moreover, assisted in secretly carrying Passe Rose to this very wagon as the train drew out from the court at Immaburg, was ready to swear there was more flesh than spirit in the business — thrust his torch eagerly through the rent. "The cage is empty," he said, withdrawing his torch, and, beginning to believe that the monk was right, he put spurs to his horse, and hastened to tell the captain.

XIII.

It had been felt by all the inmates of the Abbey of St. Servais, after Brother Dominic's return from Immaburg, that his journey had wrought in him some strange transformation. He who used to labor at his desk with such patience, content to spend an entire day on a single gigantic capital (though able to copy in that time an entire epistle of the blessed St. Peter in Tironian characters), now sighed at his window like a longing girl, or paced the garden walks in restless self-communion. Brother Dominic was himself aware of this change, although he would have strenuously denied it, had it been brought to his charge; for at times, in the oval of the capital he was tracing, a face looked out upon him, his pen was entangled in a tress of yellow hair, and a mist of blue eyes hid the page altogether.

Reflecting upon his experiences at Immaburg,

he was at least ready to admit there was that
in the world he had not suspected, and that the
wine of a king is sometimes stronger than that
of an abbot. He endeavored in vain, however,
to retrace in sequence the events of his journey.
At whichever end he began, he came always to
that fatal cup on the eve of his departure from
the villa, — a cup in which the strands of memory had dissolved away. Certain he was that
before setting out from the abbey he was no
favorite of the prior. How then should the
woman know that he had the prior's esteem?
It was equally true that before his journey he
gave no thought to the coarseness of his frock,
which now irritated and displeased him as he recalled the *cendal* of soft texture about the neck
of the woman who roused him from his nap in
the strangers' hall at Immaburg. So dear to
him had been his copying-desk, its parchment
and inks of vermilion and gold, that when he
fell asleep he was dreaming of nothing more
than to be seated at it again ; and now he gazed
listless at the manuscript spread before him, and
his former pursuit afforded him no satisfaction.
More than this, a fragrance other than that of
the holy spices mingled with the smoke of the
censer, and a voice not the reader's ravished his
ear in the very midst of the sacred offices.

Exactly what had happened while the fumes

of the wine were upon him he could not tell.
A confused recollection of messages given and
taken ; of seeing the captain with the demon ;
of the demon itself, which nevertheless had
thrust an arm of honest flesh under his nose,
and had entered the house of God freely without signs of terror ; and above all, of a face and
voice sweeter and more potent than even the
king's wine, was all he could recover from memory. He felt conscious of having committed
some grievous error, but whether it consisted in
holding converse with the woman or the demon,
in receiving the message or in surrendering it,
he could not determine. On his homeward way
he had reflected upon what he should say to the
prior when he rendered an account of his journey, and after much misgiving had purposed to
tell in all sincerity how a woman of the princesses' household had given him letters for a
certain goldsmith of Maestricht, but had taken
them again, saying she would dispatch them by
another messenger ; also, how another, whether
woman or devil he knew not, had bidden him
tell the prior she was well. Less than this he
dared not utter, more he could not. But when,
after relating the issue of his mission to the
king and the queen's reception of the missal,
the prior questioned him of other matters, between his own confusion and the chill of the

prior's eye, his courage failed him, and he held his peace altogether.

Had any one deemed it worthy of notice, a change as great as that which had befallen Brother Dominic might also have been observed in Friedgis, after the last visit of Passe Rose to the abbey. Upon the apathy and dejection into which misfortune had plunged him she had blazed like a star. Suspicious as he had been of her sincerity, it was only when she failed to reappear that he realized what credit he had attached to her promises. As the days passed, his suspicions had deepened. But a hope once kindled is hard to kill. The monotony of the abbey life jarred with this hope and irritated his expectancy. As he lay awake at night, listening for the song of the cuckoo, balancing the girl's promise against her long delay, those mysterious words of the gospels, "in kings' houses," came to him with all the assured conviction of Passe Rose's utterance, and he followed the courses of awakened hope and desire as the Northman's bark follows the rising wind. Did the girl indeed speak truly? He would verify her words in person. Being a slave, to flee was to steal, and to steal was to lose, for the first offense, an eye; for the second, the nose; for the third, life. Beyond the instant when, outside the abbey walls, he should set his face

in the direction Passe Rose had so vaguely indicated as that of Aix, he had no plan. But to
plan was not his nature; he would meet what
the future brought as the bark's prow meets the
waves. Surely the collar was an omen from
the gods, — the gods, always forgotten in pros-
perity, denied in misfortune, and remembered
again at the first gleam of hope! Of a truth
the gods lived; for on the very eve of his projected flight Brother Dominic came to his cell,
bidding him prepare to accompany the Prior
Sergius on the morrow to Aix as his servant.
Aye, surely, the gods lived!

Upon Brother Dominic, whom the prior also
took with him, the announcement of this second
journey produced a strange exhilaration. Inas-
much as Sergius, the abbot being still weak,
went to represent the latter on the occasion of
the return of Pepin, victor in the campaign
against the Avars, it was natural that Brother
Dominic should argue that he was certain to
share with the prior the king's hospitality, — a
thought well calculated to excite pride. And it
was thus he sought to explain the elation which
the anticipations of this journey caused him, as
he rode one morning of the harvest month from
the abbey yard, just as the sun rose out of the
wood of Hesbaye. "I have served God these
many years," thought he, drawing himself erect

on his mule; " the saints forbid I should now
serve the devil!" If it pleased him to go to
Aix, certainly that was because he should mingle there with great people and witness a great
pageant. Vassals of the king from the Marches
of Spain to the land of the Obodrites, nobles
from Brittany and Carinthia, prelates of the
Church and dignitaries of the State, the king
himself, his young queen and fair daughters,
women of the royal household, — when Brother
Dominic reached this point in his enumeration,
the beatings of his heart forced him to grasp
the mule tightly, till the vision had passed.
Surely the woman was right ; he had the prior's
favor, else why was he now his companion ? It
was strange ; who had told her ? Yet the very
sweetness of truth was in her voice, and her
eyes — Here Brother Dominic's heart was
seized with such new tremors that the Saxon
Friedgis, who walked behind with the servants
and beasts of burden, looked to see him lose his
hold altogether.

Mounted upon a fiery horse whose restive
movements he controlled without seeming to
heed them, the Prior Sergius rode alone in advance of Brother Dominic's gray mule. At a
little distance he might have been mistaken for
some *fidèle* of the king, on his way to the Champ
de Mai to fulfill the service of the ban ; or, if

one observed his Roman dress, prescribed for
the clergy, for one of those Frankish prelates in
whose veins ran the blood of a conquering race,
and whose instincts of enterprise and audacity
often led them to exchange the solitude and
idleness of the cloister for the excitement of war
or the adventuresome life of missionary conquest. As he drew near, one observed a certain grace and elegance of carriage, betraying
his Italian descent, and announcing, in spite of
his dress, a courtier of the Eastern Empire rather
than a prelate of the West. On closer inspection, one saw the pale face of the scholar, pos-
sessing the magic and reserve of learning, and
forgot in its dreamy gaze both the courtier and
the warrior-priest.

These contradictions in the external appearance of the prior were paralleled by the differences of opinion in which he was held. The
monks of St. Servais, being forbidden to speak
ill one of another, would have testified that he
was fair of speech, just in government, and nice
in the discharge of his duties as in the care of
his person. Yet his glance begot in them all
an uneasy self-examination. When a rule was
broken, one thought of the prior first, of God
afterwards. The guests at the monastery table,
on the other hand, won by his manner and cheer,
were loud in his praise; except it were some

surly fellow who, while the rest fed on the
prior's smile, growled in his beard over his
cups, "Such a smile never fattened man nor
The children, playing in the court as the
rode out on the road to Aix, ceased their
at his approach. For them he was so
black shadow, chilling their laughter as
assing cloud dulled the crimson mist of
buds on the hill slope beyond the ponds
ring. More sensitive than their elders,
esponded more quickly to the iron string
vibrated under the pleasantest tones of
ior's voice.
hepherd of the abbey had once found a
the woods at a she-wolf's teats, and en-
it back on his return at night. None had
suffered from its bite, yet all who saw it,
now and well favored, asleep in the gate,
bered that it had wintered with the wolf.
ior constrained the same deference.
as the woman of Immaburg had said,
er Dominic enjoyed the prior's favor, it
vident that he did not possess his confi-

made who has not seen it break, nor loves it well who does not greet its first approach, when flowers are bedewed and birds sing. For what man, if he delights in the face of his mistress, will not go before her coming to see her countenance when joy is fresh upon it? Brother Dominic was no poet to feed upon dew and larks' songs, and it was not long before the cravings of his stomach, stimulated by the morning air, carried his hand to his wallet. Yet a poet's thoughts, unformed and unuttered, stirred in his simple soul.

The road which the prior had taken, traversing the luxuriant meadows about the Meuse, soon entered the narrowing valley, following close now to the river's dancing waters, and now to the oak-crowned cliffs, whose bastions, like a mighty fortress, overtopped the deep moat of the stream. Alive to new impressions, his lips moving softly to a bubbling stream of pleasure, Brother Dominic saw all that passed before his eyes: the corn-flag whence the blackbird shook the dew in his sudden flight; the hamlets hidden among the trees; the villages nestling to the water; the barges floating by; and above, the bluffs of towering rock, out of whose heart the Roman stronghold overhanging the valley had long ago been hewn, and whose quarries now furnished the material for the royal edifices of Aix.

It was clear that in taking the longer road to his destination the prior purposed to spend the night at Visé, a royal bourg where the king had established one of those hospitable houses which afforded free shelter and security to travelers, and which were designed to facilitate commerce and intercourse throughout the kingdom. Brother Dominic remembered the place well, for he had passed this way on his return from Immaburg; and it was not long before the rude movements of his mule and the exhaustion of his wallet combined to render it a very haven of rest and fruition to his quickened imagination. It was with no little satisfaction, then, that he saw at last its outlying farm-buildings, and detected, as he approached, the savory odors of roasting flesh and steaming stews.

The sound of a horn woke the valley echoes as they entered the inclosure. The prior, well known at Visé, was received with ceremony; one hastening to take his horse as he dismounted, another running to fill a copper bowl with water for his ablutions. Brother Dominic, content to mingle with the throng gathered about the fountain, finished his toilet quickly, not failing to observe, meanwhile, among the trees, the smoking dome of the kitchen, which, like an immense beehive, swarmed with servants running to and fro, and gave forth sounds and scents most agreeable to his senses.

"Sir," said a voice, suddenly, at his side, "tell me if, by the grace of God" —

Brother Dominic turned to see who it was thus plucking him by the sleeve, but, the press being great, he discovered no one, and passed with the rest into the room where the tables were spread. Scarcely, however, had he seated himself when he felt his sleeve pulled again, and heard a plaintive voice in his ear : —

"Tell me, in the name of the good God, if by his grace thou hast seen anywhere my dear daughter" — And then came the servants bearing covered dishes, and once more his interlocutor disappeared before he could discover who it was thus addressing him.

After the repast was over, accustomed as he was to the hour of meditation prescribed by the rules of the monastery, and bewildered by the songs and tales of those who lingered at table, he betook himself to a quiet, sunny seat in the open air, where, finding his lids growing heavy, he began to repeat the five canticles whose first letters form the name of the Blessed Mother; and while thus engaged he thought himself transported, by some magical power, to the strangers' hall at Immaburg, and that a voice, sweeter than honey, took as it were the very words of the canticle out of his mouth. Rousing himself with an effort, he perceived that in fact a woman sat be-

side him, but resembling in no wise the woman
of the princesses' household. Her hand shook,
whether from age or palsy he could not tell ; her
voice, sweet though feeble, trembled ; her eyes,
vacant of intelligence, were yet restless and full
of lights.

"Sir, I beseech thee — she was the gift of
God. Never did she suck these breasts, yet was
she mine. See, this was her girdle. Sawest
thou ever one so small? I keep it here, warm,
within my bosom. Surely thou wouldst know
her by this girdle. Well, then, who hath taken
her from me? Listen. I have a house in Maestricht — In Maestricht, did I say? Yes, that
was right, — a house with a garden. Loriots
sing there every morning, but she sings there no
longer. Tell me, I pray thee, why the loriots
sing there, when she is gone ; it is not fitting."
Troubled by her incoherency, Brother Dominic
made a motion to rise. "Nay, I beseech thee,
tell me first where she is ; the world is so very
large, — never before did I conceive it was so
large. How is it possible I should find her?
Every one must search. Thou wilt know her by
her mouth, — a little mouth, like a red rose. No
one has so sweet a mouth. Ah, my God, the
rose-leaves are not softer nor so fragrant! If
one followed the bees, surely one would discover
her," — her face brightened ; then, relapsing

into her monotone, — "but they fly so fast! Who can follow the bees? That is impossible."

"Good mother" — interposed Brother Dominic.

"Aye, good mother, — that is what she used to say, — good little mother. I remember it well, when she said this, standing beside me: her breast reached to my shoulder, — she was obliged to stoop to kiss me. Oh, I remember it well! I have a long memory, for it is a long while. Let us see how long it is. My husband began on that day a silver image of the Virgin. It is said that the king has forbidden that one should prostrate one's self before an image, but to make an image of silver, delicately carven, for God's altar, that is quite different" —

"Is thy husband, then, a goldsmith?" interrupted Brother Dominic, remembering suddenly the message with which Passe Rose had charged him.

"Does not every one in Maestricht know Werdric the goldsmith?" replied the woman. "But it is only I who know why he works day and night on the Virgin's image. That is because he struck the gift of God. Did I say he struck her? It seems to me that he struck her." She passed her hands over her eyes, in the endeavor to recollect. "When a blow is given the blood runs to the spot. That is what I saw.

Where the grass is trampled, there the wild boar
has passed.   Is it not so?"

"Good woman," said Brother Dominic, "me-
thinks thy daughter is well. When I was at"—

"Oh, she is well, never fear. Every night
she comes to my bed. Only that cursed collar
which the fay gave her has cast a spell about
her. Hast thou heard how the fay lost its girdle? My child found its comb by a pool in the
wood of Hesbaye. Who would not pick up a
comb of gold? I do not blame her. But when
she laid hold of it, the fay gave forth such sobs
and wailings that her heart was touched, — her
heart is so tender!" Brother Dominic could but
be interested in this narration. The great pagan
gods were indeed gone forever, but a host of
lesser divinities, like the skirmishers of a retiring army, still lingered in the sacred places and
haunted the popular imagination. "So she gave
back the comb, receiving in its stead a collar of
gold, — cursed collar! It has bewitched my
child"—

"Wait a little, my good mother," interposed
the monk. "Listen a moment. When I was
at Immaburg, at the king's villa, a girl like the
one thou tellest of bade me say to the goldsmith"—

"Aye, aye, the goldsmith, — that is my husband. He is making an image for the Virgin

Mother because he struck a virgin. That is just.
It is very easy to appease the Blessed Mother.
Her heart is like the good God's. She will for-
give. But my child will not forgive so easily.
The blow cut her heart in twain."

"I tell thee I have seen thy daughter!" cried
Brother Dominic; "that is to say, I have no
doubt of it. When I was at Immaburg, a woman
came to me after supper— Wait a little,—there
were two. One gave me letters, the other bade
me say she was well. Certainly the message
must have been for thee. One of the two I saw
not, but heard her voice only. Either she gave
me the letters for the prior, which is clearly impossible, since I did not see her; or she took the
letters who did not give them, which is contrary
to reason ; or the demon — God defend us !"
said the monk, scratching his head in perplexity,
"would I had told the prior the whole truth!
Only, not knowing the truth, how could I utter
it ?" And pleased at the sudden discovery of
this balm to his troubled conscience, Brother
Dominic smiled on his companion.

His words had made no impression upon her
mind. Even the announcement that he had
seen her daughter passed unnoticed, and as he
spoke she continued muttering to herself with
that incoherency of a mind hurried on by the
torrent of its own disordered thoughts, and pow-

erless to fix its attention upon even the objects of its desire. But her senses, reveling like hounds escaped from the leash while the master is abroad, were alive to sights and sounds beyond the knowledge of others, and she raised her head suddenly at the rustle of leaves in the thicket behind her to see the prior disappearing softly; and, leaving the monk bewildered by his strange interview and the misgivings which it had aroused, she plunged into the bushes, crying, " Seigneur, listen in the name of Christ " —

" The blessed St. Servais preserve us ! " thought Brother Dominic, doubly troubled with pity for the woman and concern for himself. Renouncing at last the effort to reconcile the contradictions of memory, he entered the house to inquire of the king's vidame if the woman were indeed the wife of the goldsmith of Maestricht.

" Aye," replied the vidame, " her husband cannot restrain her ; " and tapping his forehead, " God hath taken her wits from her. They say at Maestricht that she hath housed a demon these ten years."

Remembering his experience with the demon, Brother Dominic trembled. Many were his prayers and brief was his sleep that night at Visé ; and riding behind the prior on his mule the next morning, it seemed to him that Sergius read his thoughts whenever he turned to speak with him, and that the very birds, fluttering from the boughs as they passed underneath, laughed aloud at his trouble. But gradually the morning sun cleared his brain of bodings, as it had cleared the fog from the valleys. The wood was fresh and cool. At the crossing of the Geule he saw the road which branched to Immaburg. Soon the ford of the Wurm was passed, and then the towers of Aix rose up unexpectedly on the skirt of the forest.

At the city gate their entrance was blocked by a passing troop. Sounds of laughter and women's voices filled the echoing archway, and the prior, checking his horse to observe the riders as they went by, smiled when his eye fell upon the Saxon Rothilde, between Gesualda and Agnes of Solier. Her face was bright and her laughter gay. "Robert of Tours returns with Pepin from Hungary," thought the prior. Then, as he looked, the girl's face grew white, and the smile left it. "So," thought the prior, "am I then come amiss? Nay, little one, I will give thee thy lover over the king's will — and body."

Behind the others, Friedgis, on foot, and Brother Dominic, on his mule, could see nothing, and the troop was soon gone, like a flight of swallows. Then the three rode in, — prior, monk, and slave, — little dreaming that each was thinking of the same woman.

XIV.

It had been a day of delights for Brother
Dominic.   He had sat at table with the abbot of
Fontenelle, director of the royal buildings, with
whom the Prior Sergius lodged; and though his
place was with those of less degree, it was enough
for him that the meats were well seasoned and
garnished with flowers, that the wine in his gob-
let was interdicted by no vow, and that the crystal jar of honey stood at his elbow.   Free to
come and go, he had passed the morning hours
in viewing the imperial city, whose growing
splendors he doubted not would eclipse those of
Rome itself.   He had wandered at will through
its streets and squares, stood on the foundations
of the vast theatre which the king was building
beyond the northern gate, marveled at the mighty
columns transported so great a distance for the
new basilica, dipped his hands in the springs
whose heat proclaimed the reality of regions in-
fernal, and braved the guards at the palace gate
to gaze at the king's abode.   But more than all
these things, at the evening hour, while sitting,
fatigued with wonder, on one of the marble
benches of the palace court, he had seen the
woman of Immaburg.   Ah, fool that he was!
to be so overcome that he must needs stare, with-

out the wit to speak or move, as at a were-wolf issuing from a cavern! His back was turned to the place whence she came, but as she passed a smell of sweet ointment carried him in a twinkling to the strangers' hall at Immaburg; and then strength fled from his limbs, so that when he would have risen the damsel was already far from him. Worst of all, when he would have followed her, — for what purpose God knows, — a devil of a soldier at the gate beset him with questions, jesting at his haste, and charging him with evil intent, so that for very shame he forced himself to go another way than that the woman had taken.

Rothilde had not so much as noticed the monk. Her face was covered as she crossed the court, though it was late twilight. One would have sworn her to be only some servant of the palace, — as indeed the soldier had thought, — for her head-cloth was of coarse serge, and her shoe-nails sounded on the stones as she walked. Paying no heed to any she met, she went her way by the street which skirted the eastern side of the palace to the church of St. Marcellus, into which she disappeared. If it was dusk without, it was night within, and she stood inside the door till her eyes were accustomed to the darkness; then, following the wall, entered one of the side chapels, where the obscurity was almost complete. Against the pier hung a small votive casket, inclosing a sweet gum, from which the smoke curled upward in spirals. In the centre of the chapel was a sarcophagus of Parian marble, executed in Italy for the king. Upon this the girl seated herself, gathering one foot beneath her, and waited. A verger came down the nave, and lighted four candles before an altar in the opposite aisle. The taper in his hand hovered a moment about the candles, was effaced by a pillar, reappeared again, then vanished altogether. Silent and immobile, the girl watched the retreating light. It was evident that she did not wish to be observed, yet in her attitude there was an insolent unconcern. Her hood had fallen from her hair, where the black pearls of Robert of Tours shone with a dull lustre in the candle-light reflected from the pavement.

Yesterday, at the Liege gate, she had seen Friedgis, her Saxon lover. Till the dancing-girl spoke his name in the supper-room at Immaburg, she had forgotten him. Yet she had loved him — once. He stood with the asses behind the monk to whom she had given the papers for the prior. Had he seen her? How her heart had leaped! "What ails thee?" Gesualda had said, observing her pallor. Certainly it was her collar the dancing-girl wore at Immaburg. At the sight of it the past had come back like the memory of a dream, — her Saxon home and lover. She changed her posture mechanically, shrugging her shoulders with a movement of disdain. How was it possible she had ever loved him? Her eyes followed the smoke ascending from the casket along the rough surface of the wall to the carven capital, where, curling outward, it crept along the curve of the arch to the keystone. Did he know where she was? Had he come seeking her? She remembered the look the dancing-girl, had given her when uttering his name. Did she perchance come from him? The smoke, escaping from under the arch of the chapel, floated higher into the vaultings of the aisle. "Come up hither," it seemed to say, "above the pavement where the multitude kneel, into the tribune of the king." Rothilde leaned forward to watch its ascending spiral. She had sought the dancing-girl after supper, and from the gallery had seen her conversing with the monk at the door of the chapel. But when she descended to speak with her, she found no one, and seeing the captain approaching had retreated hastily. "Friedgis, the Saxon slave who keeps the gate for the monks of St. Servais," — that was what the girl had said. A slave, leading the asses! how could it be that she had ever loved him! — and her blue eyes followed the smoke-wreaths, stealing ever upward softly, as if fearful of hindrance or surprise, into the great dome.

A sound caused her to turn her head and draw her cloak about her. In the shadow of the pillar near the font something moved. Slipping from her seat, she removed her shoes, and gliding obliquely in her noiseless sandals towards the black figure beside the font, paused, as if to dip her finger in the holy water ; then, with a quick motion, threw back her head-cloth and revealed her face.

" Enough," said the prior softly ; " cover thyself." Without doubt he remembered the monk Fardolphus, who, secreted beneath one of the altars, had overheard the conspirators of Pepin the Bastard, and had hastened to tell the king. With a gesture the girl led the way into the recess of the chapel, where she seated herself again on the lid of the sarcophagus. The distant candles shone on her face, still uncovered ; the fillet of pearls gleamed in her hair ; her teeth glistened between her parted lips. " Cover thyself," repeated the prior authoritatively. She obeyed but in part, and reluctantly. It seemed to give her pleasure to reveal a little of the beauty concealed behind the coarseness of her garment. Standing between her and the light, the prior looked at her attentively, struck anew

by this beauty which the Abbot Rainal had
thought to consecrate to the service of God.
Keener in his perceptions than the abbot, the
prior had seen in this convert, destined for the
Saxon mission, a tool of another temper, fitted
for other ends. More learned, too, than his superior, the prior was acquainted with the writ-
ings of certain Greek authors, who maintained
that moral character may be discovered in the
expression of the face, even in the forms of the
members ; that the shape of the extremities in-
dicates the fineness or coarseness of the intelligence ; and that in the movements of the body
are revealed those of the soul. Looking about
among the king's household for an accomplice,
when his eye fell upon Rothilde, it had rested on
her face with satisfaction. In truth, the Greek
was right. Does the habitual state of the soul
leave no trace upon its dwelling? See how she
has decked her body. Is not that eye which delights in the things of sense the eye also of the
soul? Those fingers, so frail, yet so full of nervous energy, are fingers to clutch at a crown.
That mouth, so small, what passions tremble on
its fine lines, what desire sleeps in the hollow of
its lips ! "It is she I seek," the prior had said,
looking into her eye. It was a blue eye, trustful, but not trusty ; in repose clear as a shallow
pool in an open field, — then filling with sudden

lights ; one saw there what one would, — stars
or flames.   When he first saw her, she wore, as
now, the black pearls of Robert of Tours, to
whom the king had refused her in marriage.
Should he win her to his purpose by playing on
her love of kindred and home, fill her soul with
the desire of vengeance?   " Nay," said the prior
to himself, observing her more closely : " to such
an one a nation is less than a man; she will do
greater things for her lover than for her country."   On inquiry, he learned that Robert of
Tours had won the young queen to his suit.
The king, however, remained obstinate, and to
rid himself of further importunity sent the girl
to the convent of Eicka, to take the veil.   So
chance threw her into the prior's hands; for the
convent of Eicka belonged by royal diploma to
the abbot's domain, and during the latter's sick-
ness its oversight, both as to internal order and
external affairs, fell to the prior's charge.   Having thus become director of the girl's conscience,
he had opportunity to study her character, and,
by mitigation of the rules in her favor, to estab-
lish himself in her confidence.   He knew how to
render worldly pleasures attractive in condemn-
ing them, and to deepen the sullen rage of her
disappointed ambition by dwelling upon the ir-
revocableness of her lot.   To strip her arms of
their jewels and her dress of its silver fringes, to

break her garnet girdle and lay it on the altar, to give herself over to the austerities of fasts, vigils, and macerations, to abandon her passionate love for the mystical substitute offered her, — all this the prior knew how to paint in words fit to quicken her terror and disgust for the tomb to which she saw herself destined in the very plenitude of life and ambition. Meanwhile, he had obtained, through the young queen's intercession, the king's permission for her return to court, on condition that she renounced all hopes of marriage.

On the eve of her consecration Sergius entered her room. Sleepless with rage and fear, she saw him leaning above her bed, shading his face from the taper in his hand.

"What wilt thou of me?" she stammered, pressed against the wall.

"To leave this grave, and take thy place in the queen's household."

She raised herself on her elbow, still gazing at him fiercely from her blue eyes.

"Rise and dress thyself. The horses are at the gate."

"The king relents?" she said, dazed.

The prior smiled.

"What wilt thou of me?" she asked again, sitting up in bed, and searching his face.

"Obedience."

" And afterwards? "

" Obedience."

" Afterwards? " she insisted.

" On the night I bid thee, to open the door of the king's apartment, and lead him thou findest without to the king's bed. Afterwards," said the prior softly, " I will give thee to Robert of Tours in marriage."

That night Rothilde set out for the court, wearing her girdle and pearls.

Not a little vain of his perspicacity in having divined what lay beneath the innocent expression of her blue eyes, the prior had often smiled at the abbot's naive projects for Rothilde; but after her return among the queen's women, he had often also experienced a nervous apprehension of what he had discovered. Having, as it were, been unmasked by his penetrating eye, the girl made no further effort at concealment from him, seeming rather to take an insolent satisfaction in revealing more than he had perceived. On several occasions, trembling for her discretion, he had been on the point of saying, " Cover thyself! " as just now, when she threw off her disguise in the church of St. Marcellus, despite the candle-light shining in her face. Moreover, if in discovering the weakness of another one acquires a sense of superiority, in profiting by it one falls into bondage; and Rothilde, sitting on

the lid of marble, was more at ease than the
prior, walking irresolutely to and fro between
the chapel walls, as if dreading to make use of
the instrument which he had chosen.

"The king is still obdurate," he said at length,
pausing before her, and approaching the subject
in hand indirectly.

"Thou art not come to tell me that!" replied
the girl, returning his gaze.

"Nay," he said quickly, "but to remind thee
of thy promise" —

"I remember," she interrupted. "Is the
time come?"

"Within a month's time I will wed thee in
this very place with Robert of Tours — if thou
darest."

"Why ask?" she replied dryly, leaning forward and resting her chin in her hand.

"I have here the abbot's ring," continued the
prior, drawing it from his pouch; "with this
ring one may enter the palace at all hours, even
to the king's chamber. Only, to reach the king's
chamber, one must know the way" —

"Especially when it is night," interposed
Rothilde.

"It is for thee to show the way. Thou wilt
wait at the stair by the door of the audience
hall." The prior spoke rapidly, and the girl
listened intently. "He who wears this ring" —

"Who?" she interrupted again.

Sergius made a gesture of impatience — "will come after matins, at the eighth hour of night. He will show thee the ring, and will follow thee."

"I will be there." She reached forth her hand. "Give me the ring, that I may know it when I see it again. Is the night fixed?" she asked, examining the ring attentively.

"Not yet. He who" — The prior hesitated.

The girl looked up. "Strikes," she said, observing his repugnance.

— "is not yet come."

"Who is he?" she whispered.

"A Greek from Pavia. His arm is sure. When — when it is over " — He paused, feeling his way softly, and seeking fitting words.

"Well?" said the girl.

He laid his hand on her arm, and, grasping her robe, drew her palm from her chin. "Such a secret is for two only, — thee and me." She seemed not to comprehend, but her eyes dilated. "This man cannot live. If he escapes, gold will buy his tongue as it hath bought his hand; if he is taken, if there should be an outcry, torture will loosen it. Escape he must not, and if taken — dead — the dead keep their secrets, and ours."

For a moment neither spoke nor moved.

" Yes," murmured the girl absently, " that were better." She sat motionless, like a figure sculptured on the lid of the sarcophagus.

The prior drew a poniard from his cloak, and laid it softly beside her. Her eyes, half closed, looked beyond him, and he could see her bosom rise and fall under the *cendal.*

" He — the Greek — is not yet come ? " she said almost inaudibly.

"Not yet. He who came with him is here. They parted company for greater surety." He was going to say more, but saw she was no longer listening to him. Her eyes were fixed on the blade lying beside her. The head-cloth had fallen again upon her shoulders, but the prior paid no heed to it. He seemed fearful of disturbing her, watching her as a fox watches a pheasant approaching.

" I would see him, the Greek, first," she said at length, lifting her eyes.

" It shall be as thou wilt, when he comes," he replied eagerly, unable to repress his joy.

" And if he fails ? "

" He will not fail."

As he spoke, footsteps echoed in the vaultings. The girl snatched the blade from the stone, and drew the cloth over her face.

" Dost thou know the tower by the ford of the Wurm, on the road to Immaburg ? — to the

east, beside the river, a hundred paces. Bring
thy Greek thither at night, the third day. Here
— the ring — quick " — and slipping from her
seat, the girl glided from the chapel, and disappeared in the darkness.

In the street she threw back her hood, and
filled her lungs with the cool night air. Absorbed by her thoughts, she was not conscious of
the dagger in her hand till she emerged into the
open space before the baths, where a torch flared
in the wind. Secreting the weapon in her
cloak, and covering her face quickly, she crossed
to the opposite side, to avoid those going in and
out, and in her agitation stumbled against a
passer-by. She recoiled, holding herself flat
against the wall, — it was Friedgis! Dieu!
how coarse he was! She followed him at a little distance, cautiously. He walked carelessly,
looking from side to side, the cord of his tunic
swinging against his bare legs. Notwithstanding her emotions, the girl laughed, it was so
droll. What would he do if he knew? At the
gate of the palace he stopped, scrutinizing its
massive walls, and moving from place to place,
like a spy observing the camp of an enemy.
The girl's heart beat heavily. Did he know?
At last he went slowly away. She could see him
looking back from time to time, till his form
grew indistinct in the darkness. As if possessed

by a sudden idea, she took a few quick steps after
him; then paused a moment, undecided, and
finally turning back entered the gate. Within the
court the lights shone on the pavement, and she
followed the encircling gallery in the shadow of
the pillars. At the stairs in the angle, some one
sitting on the lower step rose at her approach, and
between the folds of her head-cloth she recognized
the monk of Immaburg. Unable to resist the
promptings of his imagination, Brother Dominic had lingered the entire evening in the vicinity of the palace. Now that the vague hope he
cherished was so unexpectedly realized, timidity
paralyzed him, and, ill at ease under the glance
of those eyes which fascinated him, he would
have fled, had not the girl laid hold of his
sleeve.

"Art thou not he to whom I gave the papers
at Immaburg?" she asked, peering into his
face.

"Aye," replied Brother Dominic, trembling.

"I saw thee yesterday at the gate with the
prior of St. Servais;" and in spite of his trouble,
this mark of interest was not without its effect.
Seeing his tremor, Rothilde smiled assuringly,
as one encourages a child. "There was another
with thee, — he who held the asses."

"Aye, the porter."

"Stand not here; the night is cold," said the

girl, pulling him by the robe along the gallery.
Brother Dominic's courage began to return in
the obscurity.

"What porter?" she asked.

"Of the abbey; a Saxon serf whom the king
gave the abbot."

"The good abbot! It was he who baptized
me in the wood at Ehresberg." They were passing under the gallery towards the gate. "Does
he lodge with thee, this porter?"

"At the abbot of Fontenelle's," replied
Brother Dominic proudly.

"This way," said the girl, drawing him after
her. He felt her hand in his, warm as the
spring waters in the king's baths, but it suggested to the poor monk no place of torment.
"Thou gavest the papers to the prior?" Brother
Dominic trembled again. "He has much faith
in thee, therefore I trust thee." Her hand
pressed his, and Brother Dominic passed from
apprehension to ecstasy. "Hast thou lodgings
of thine own at the abbot's?"

"Aye, a goodly chamber in the court, with a
Damascus carpet."

The girl could but laugh. "Truly, a Damascus carpet!"

The laugh smote his heart like the ripple of
soft fingers on a lute's strings.

"Aye, I will show it thee," he stammered,
amazed at his own daring.

"What said the dancing-girl to thee at Immaburg?" asked Rothilde abruptly.

But Brother Dominic could articulate nothing. As to many others, so it happened to him that, having often thought to see demons, now that one assailed him he did not recognize it. At the archway of the court where he lodged he paused. He heard behind him the girl's breathing, and, observing no one, entered softly, hugging the wall's shadow, suddenly full of resources.

Before the narrow door of his room he hesitated, terrified at what he was doing. The girl pushed him aside, and entered.

A taper burned on the table. Uncovering her face, she glanced rapidly about her. Brother Dominic stood in the door. "Listen," she said, approaching him and pulling him within. "I would see this Saxon. Bring him here to me, and leave us a little space." Brother Dominic, a moment before ready to abandon this adventure, perceiving now that it was to see another she had come, stood stubbornly his ground. She laid her hand on his sleeve and smiled reassuringly. "Then come again." For such a smile the monk would certainly have gone to fetch Cerberus from the Acheron. "Hasten," she said, pushing him gently.

When he had gone, the girl threw off her

hood, removed her shoes, and surveyed herself
eagerly. Her under-skirt was short, closely fitted,
and its points were tied with silver cords. Her
neck was visible under a veil of tissue, fastened
behind to her hair. Between the draperies of
her outer tunic shone her girdle, set with garnets,
and the silver lacings of her sandals, binding
the stamped leather above her ankles. Satisfied
with the result of her inspection, she stood waiting, her back against the door. Presently the
door was pushed open, and Friedgis entered.
As he crossed the sill, the girl, leaning against
the door, closed it deftly and slid forward the
bolt. Friedgis had at first seen no one; then
he uttered a suppressed cry of joy and surprise,
and caught her in his arms.

XV.

Is there any one who, in years of ripeness,
does not look back with wonder upon the things
which charmed his childish fancy? And if,
perchance, for any reason, he must needs feign
an outgrown pleasure, what more vapid and
wearisome than a former delight outlived and
dispossessed of power? The shining flint contents no longer the eye which has seen the dia-
mond's lustre; the softest fleece chafes the limbs

that have felt the touch of spun-silk raiment;
and the heart that has fed in a king's palace
from the golden dishes of vanity and ambition,
what palate hath it for things which once satisfied its unwhetted appetite? Far away, indeed,
for Rothilde, were the wooden huts and sheep
pastures of Bardengau. In Friedgis' clasp, so
strong with sudden, unfeigned joy, a thrill of
revolt ran through her, as her body had shrunk
from the touch of her serge garment. Yet she
let him have his way, and clung to his neck, her
head upon his breast, her blue eyes smiling under the pearl chaplet. It was a long journey
from the camp at Ehresberg to this chamber at
Aix, and she must needs go over it all with her
lover, recounting, between his kisses, what had
befallen her. There were questions to ask
and to answer, a story to tell and to hear, and,
after the first thirst of his heart was slaked,
questions hard to parry; and while he gave her
lips scarce time to speak, fearing to utter a
sound, lest joy, like a frail vase, should break
at a murmur, she smiled through her half-shut
eyes and held her shrinking body still, with no
thought but of Robert of Tours, no anxiety but
to know how long a time the poor fool of a
monk without would give her to accomplish her
purpose.

"How knewest thou I was here?" he whispered.

"I saw thee with the monk at the gate."

"And thou camest at once?" He stooped and kissed her. "I knew thou wert here. There came a girl to the abbey wearing thy collar. It was she who bade me seek in the king's house."

"The captain's dancing-girl," thought Rothilde; then aloud, "It was to seek me thou camest?"

"Aye, indeed. But for this journey of the prior's I had come alone. The girl spoke like a seer." Then he bent to her lips again. What mattered these things? Why waste time in speech? Silence and kisses were better.

The minutes slipped away, he not heeding them, she counting them. At last, sighing, she unclasped his arms and stood up. "I must be gone; it is time," she said.

"Go?" he stammered, bewildered. "Whither?"

She touched her lips to his forehead. He saw now for the first time her silver-corded dress, the girdle and pearls, and a shadow of jealous fear crossed his face.

She saw it, and smiled sadly. "Why am I here?" she said reproachfully.

"Because thou lovest me," he replied, springing to her side.

"And thou?"

"Thou knowest I would die for thee."

She freed herself gently from his clasp. Why did she look at him so pitifully? What was she going to say to him? She made an effort to speak, smiled helplessly, and turned away, her eyes bright with tears. A terrible fear began to oppress him. Suddenly she turned again, standing before him. Her eyes shone dry as fire; her very body, rigid with purpose, seemed changed. "Whither do I go?" she said, in a hard voice. "Whither, indeed, but to the king's palace! The girl spoke truly. See," — she loosed the pearls from her hair, — "here are the proofs. Where will a maid find such but in a king's palace?" Friedgis stared at her in silence. "For what end should a king take a captive from the dust of the road to put sandals on her feet and deck her hair with pearls?" She watched the poison work in his veins. "He hath slain her kindred and laid her roof in ashes. One thing yet remains undone, — to waste her heart with fire as he hath wasted her land. Hush! The monk is at the door." Friedgis was advancing towards her. She put out her hand to stay him, gathering her cloak from the floor, where it had fallen when she entered, and drawing it about her.

"Thou shalt not go," he said hoarsely, seizing her arm.

Her eyes softened with pity. " Art thou able to contend with a king ? "

He still held her arm. In her fingers were the pearls of Robert of Tours. " Give me the gems; " and taking them from her hand, he ground them under foot. " Thou goest back willingly to thy king ? "

" And if I go," — she loosed her dress, and drew forth the prior's poniard, — " what dost thou fear? Tell me, when thou strikest, when the foe's arms are locked about thy neck and thine eyes swim with mist, when time presses, where dost thou push the blade home? Is it not here? " She laid her hand on his breast. " Fear nothing. I am strong — and I am thine. "

" Give me the blade," he demanded. " When the eyes are thick with mist it is too late. I am stronger than thou. "

She trembled now, recoiling · before him. " Thou — the king " — she murmured, retreating as he advanced. " Nay, not thou " —

" Give it me," he repeated sullenly.

" Nay, nay," she pleaded. " They will slay thee. Let me go. Thou art mad — they will slay thee — it is not possible." Her back was against the wall, his hand on her wrist; his fingers loosed hers from the handle. With a sudden gesture she let go, and tore the veil from her throat and bosom. " Strike here, then ; that were better. If thou lovest, strike. It is I who lead thee to death. If I had not come! — but I loved thee! Strike, I tell thee, now, while I love thee!"

The blade fell from his grasp, his frame shook, and he sank at her feet, hiding his face in his hands.

She stooped quickly, picked up the fallen poniard, and adjusted her dress. " Listen," she said, between her breathing, and forcing his hands from his face. " Death is not sweet to those who love, but it is sweet to those who hate. Dost thou remember the dead we left to the vultures by the Weser? In the night their wounds cry out to me. If I lead thee to his chamber," — she lowered her voice, — "the king's, that were a thing worth dying for; I and thee together."

She raised her head. Brother Dominic was tapping irresolutely at the door.

"To die!" she whispered passionately in his ear. " Nay, I will not have it so! I love thee — we will fly. Leave it only to me — I have a way. For him, death and justice; for us, life and love." He had caught her again in his arms. " Nay, nay." She struggled. " Loose thy hold. Let me go. The monk will rouse the house. My shoes!" She slipped her sandaled feet into them, drew back the bolt, cast a quick look of promise and triumph at her lover, and closed the door behind her.

Brother Dominic, waiting impatiently without, had at first laid his ear to the door and listened. Then, fearful of discovery, he hid himself in an angle, squatting in the shadow. He had forgotten the five canticles, upon whose efficacy he relied in hours of peril, but had resolved to put an end to this mystery, when the girl opened the door suddenly upon him.

" Dear monk," she said, pressing his hand in her own, " I have seen thy carpet; another time I will see thee. Thou hast done me service, and when I come again I will pay thee in what coin thou wilt; only be discreet. Farewell."

Enveloped in her cloak, she hurried through the arch into the street. She had done well to come! Friedgis was seeking her. She had felt sure of it. He knew where to look, too ; the girl had told him. Who was this girl? Aye, she had done well to come. What wax men were in soft hands! That was a happy thought, to say the king loved her; if it were only so indeed! Just now she might have slain Friedgis, when he lay at her feet, and, again, when he held his lips to hers. The temptation was strong, though the monk was at the door, — she loathed him so. But this was better. The idea came to her when the prior said the Greek had not come. Pray

God he might not come!   As she hurried on, she met the prior returning home.   There was another with him, and the two were laughing. "Fool!" she said to herself, turning to gaze after them.   "Fret not over thy Greek.   I have one to take his place, one whom I fear not to use thy blade upon, — only, by thy God, dear prior, I will use it before he goes in to the king, and I will waken the king myself.   If he gave the monk Fardolphus an abbey for revealing the Hunchback's plot, he will give me my lover. Nay, what will he not give, if I have but the wit to ask aright?"   And in her exultation a cry of triumph burst from her lips.

XVI.

It was one of those mornings such as come only in the early autumn.   The air was crisp, sonorous, and still.   On inhaling this air, so pure, so invigorating, one thought of the wood, its odors and lights, its leaves and birds.   The king had gone to Frankenburg to hunt, and no wonder.   For some other day, less alluring, the sordid suit, the pitiful complaint, the accounts of the vidame; for some other day, less fair, the disputations of the school, those terrible questions, What is man, what is life, what is death?

and those terrible answers, A guest in his own abode, the expectation of death, a doubtful journey. To-day, a spear, a horse, and the wood!

On his way to the service of the first hour, Brother Dominic inhaled this air with delight. On rising from his bed, his foot had encountered the girl's fillet of pearls. Some were missing, their fragments scattered on the floor; the rest were whole. What a sweet odor they exhaled! But he thrust them quickly out of sight into his pouch, for shame afflicted him sorely, and never does an evil action appear so shameful as in the gray light of dawn. He wished to flee from himself, and hastened out into the street, already full of people, with whom he mingled gladly, listening to their conversation, greetings, and laughter. When conscience convicts, one feels one's self an outcast; so it comforted Brother Dominic to join this stream of life, to enter the church with the congregation, to raise his voice with others in the anthem, and to listen to the clerks reciting the psalms. Fortified by all these things, he said to himself that he was not so bad, after all. Having breakfasted, he felt still easier, and found nothing better to do than to go to the service of the third hour, also. Yet he was conscious that he was no longer the same man. Ordinary sights and sounds had acquired a new significance; a veil had been torn away

from life. As he returned, a band of singers
and players, issuing from the church of St. Marcellus, descended the steps of the parvis strewn
with flowers; and following the instruments
came the newly married, hand in hand. The
pair possessed for him a strange fascination.
They walked erect, knowing all observed them,
blushing and hiding their joy. Dieu! how
beautiful it was! As he went his way, two
maids preceded him; they had baskets, and
pruning-knives to cut the grapes from the
vines. They chatted gayly, and one said, "If he
comes to-day, do thou walk beside me in the
same row;" then they laughed, one with pleasure, the other with envy. Was the world then
so full of love? It suddenly occurred to him
that he ought to restore the pearls; and he began to imagine with what dignity he would com-
port himself.

"Here — thy pearls."

"Heaven bless thee," she would say. "I had
feared " —

"Heaven bless *thee*, and save thee indeed,"
he would answer, and go his way.

Rehearsing this scene, he took the broken fillet from his pouch.

"Sawest thou the queen as she passed to the
chase?" said one girl to the other.

"Aye; she is fairer than the last one."

" And all the women with her? One had a girdle of dragons and lions."

" The images of those who will one day devour her."

" I would I had one like it, nevertheless," sighed the other. Then they laughed together.

" How still the palace is! There is not a soul left," observed one, as they passed before the gate.

Brother Dominic paused. Surely, since all were at the chase, it were no harm to enter. He crossed the court, and stopped under the balcony. It was here he had seen her. He might sit down now in tranquillity ; there was no danger she would come. Within, a maid talked with a page over the stair-rail. " When wilt thou come again ? " asked the page in a low voice.

" How can I tell ? " she replied, leaning on the balustrade.

" Adieu," said the page reluctantly.

" Adieu," answered the girl. The boy lingered.

" If perchance thou wishest a kiss — take one," said the girl. He took three ; then light feet ran up the stairs.

" What a world ! " thought Brother Dominic, as if he formed no part of it, and contemplated it as he would contemplate an object held in his hand. " After all, it must be so," he added reflectively. The sun, rising above the roofs, began to shine in his face ; so he left his seat and walked along the gallery. At the angle was an open space separating the main from the lateral buildings. A stairway, ascending from the gallery, led to an elevated platform, uncovered to the sky. A woman servant, bearing a jar on her head, coming down the steps, gazed at the monk curiously. What was he doing there? Was he perchance going into the gynæceum? At the foot of the steps she turned to observe him. Fatigued by the ascent, Brother Dominic was sitting in the shade. "Yes, certainly, it must be so," he was repeating to himself, turning over the pearls in his hand. A second stairway, covered by an arch, led down to the level of the court on the other side. The gate at its bottom step was open. He could see shrubbery and hear birds. "There must be a garden there," he thought. Holding his robe in his hand, he went down the passage steps leisurely. How still it was! As the girl had said, every one was at the chase. Aïe! that were fine, — to gallop in the wood, spear in hand, after the deer ; and he began to imagine himself in full pursuit, the flanks of his horse white with foam. It must be easier to ride a horse than a mule, it appeared so simple ; he would throw the rein on the neck, and leave his companions far behind.

How they sped! like an arrow from the bow,
horse and rider as one.   And now, entangled in
the thick copse, the stag was at bay, its horns
were lowered, it was about to charge.   The
spear flew.   "Dieu! what a fine blow!" said a
voice from behind, — hers, whose purple hair-
band fluttered at the head of his lance, dyed
deeper now in the jet of blood.   Agitated and
perspiring at the thought of this scene, Brother
Dominic started back.   Where was he?   God
preserve him! the garden was full of women.
It resembled the cloister at Maestricht, only
more spacious, more beautiful, and with women
for monks.   He turned precipitately to retrace
his steps, when, under the trees close to the spot
where he had come, he saw a maid looking full
upon him.   Her spindle trembled with her
laughter; her eyes shone with merriment, as
only Agnes of Solier's could.   He must have
passed her as he entered, and there she sat,
more terrible in her beauty and her laughter
than the dragon at the gate of the garden of
Hesperus.   Every woman in the place ceased
her work to stare at him: this he knew well,
though his back was turned.   Had God then de-
livered him, like Job, into the power of Satan?

In his confusion he made the sign of the cross
with the girl's fillet of pearls.   Seigneur, what a
rosary for a monk!

At the sight of the black gems in his hand Agnes ceased her laughter. Rothilde's pearls!

"Whence hast thou the pearls?" she called to him, making a sign that he should draw near.

"The pearls?" stammered Brother Dominic, assailed in an unexpected quarter. "I found them hard by."

"Hard by?"

"Aye. Some one hath dropped them in the court. I was seeking her to whom they should belong."

"Give them here," said Agnes, reaching out her hand. The monk obeyed with alacrity, ready to profit by any way of escape. "Some one hath set his foot upon them," she said, examining them.

"It was not I. I found them so when I rose from bed." Ah, cursed tongue! What was he saying?

"From bed?" said Agnes of Solier, looking up with surprise. "Thou saidst hard by, in the court."

"In the abbot's court," stammered Brother Dominic, sinking deeper in the mire, — "the abbot of Fontenelle's, where I lodge."

"Is thy bed then in the court?" asked Agnes of Solier, marking his confusion and observing him sharply.

"Nay," gasped Brother Dominic, seeking to

extricate himself, " said I in the court ? In my
chamber." Seigneur! his tongue would prove
his ruin; and the girl had said, " Be discreet!"

"In thy chamber?" said Agnes of Solier,
pricked with curiosity.

"It was not to me she came, but the Saxon,
— the porter." Brother Dominic perceived that
he was no longer responsible for what he was
saying. It was the devil that spoke, not he.
If ever a man was possessed of a demon bent on
his ruin, and the girl's too, it was he. He heard
himself speak with terror ; he endeavored to arrest his tongue, — impossible. There was but
one thing to do, — to fly. Never would he betray the girl! He cast a despairing look about
him, and called the saints to his succor for a desperate effort.

" Wait!" cried Agnes, rising from her seat.
" I would speak with thee."

But Brother Dominic's foot was on the stair,
and naught but a wall or a barred gate could
arrest him. "Blessed St. Servais, aid me!" he
ejaculated, taking two steps at a time. Ah! if
ever he got back to his desk again, he would
serve God indeed.

Many a good resolution is conceived in fear,
and a nightmare serves sometimes to wake one
from moral lethargy. In the heat of his igno-
minious retreat Brother Dominic formed a pious

resolve. To his excited imagination, the garden
into which he had unwittingly penetrated, with
its flowers, fountains, and maidens, became a
symbol of that paradise whence our first parents
were driven, and before the reproaches of his
conscience he fled as they had fled before the
sword of the angel. He would go back to that
quiet cell whose window overlooked a world
with which he could not cope, a paradise whose
trees bore such sweet but terrible fruits of
knowledge, and with whose realities he was
unfit to wrestle. God had provided that cell for
such as he, and he had known no peace since he
left it. The world was too vast a scene for his
activities; it entangled him in matters whose
issue threatened soul and body. Every step involved a peril. He would go back to that solitude where he could hear the voice of God.
The mirth of the abbot's table, its wine and
flowers; this woman whose smiles entranced
him, whose garments shed forth perfumes;
these hours of idleness breeding dreams of forbidden pleasures; this great capital whose
splendors allured and overwhelmed him, — how
should a simple monk contend with such
things! Danger? It was the very fragrance
of the flower, the sparkle of the wine, the glitter
of the girdle and the beauty which it zoned.
Doubtless others to whom God gave his grace

might walk in safety amid such perils, as the three holy ones had stood in the flames of the furnace clothed in the dew of purity. But as for him, he would that very day gain the prior's permission to return to Maestricht. This resolution was taken before he reached the palace gate, and in passing from under the portal the air seemed fresher, his step more buoyant, and he experienced the charm of that cloister garth he had forsaken with so foolish a pride, desirous of seeing the world from whose vortex he was now escaping with his soul in his hand.

The prior was abroad when he returned. Evidently God would try his purpose. He would fast that day, and observe the hours. Firm in his resolve, he recited his prayers incessantly, keeping his room, and rising even at midnight to attend the service in the king's oratory.

XVII.

It was the harvest month, and the leaves were beginning to strew the windy lanes of the wood. All the day long the hillsides resounded with the baying of hounds, baffled by the water of the marsh where the boar had fled. One could hear the heavy flight of the heron scared from his haunt, and the quick beat of the wild duck's

wings skimming the surface of the pond. The
quail, listening with head erect, ran through the
thick reeds as the tumult drew near. But their
fear was vain; it was not these the hunter
sought. Twice the long, monotonous bay of
the pack changed to the sharp, quick cry whose
meaning the hunter knows so well — when the
trail grows fresh, and more than water to the
dripping tongue is the sight of his prey to the
eager hound. Twice had those foremost in the
chase found a spot where the trampled grass was
matted with blood and torn from the mould by
the struggling feet; where the flags were pressed
into the moist earth, and the boar on his
haunches had waited his pursuers — and here,
ah, poor Brochart, the leader of the pack, slit
from breast to flank by the tusk! — what, thou
canst still lick the hand? Brave dog! And
here another has crawled into the thicket, leaving a red track. Is it thou, Biche, thy mistress's favorite? Seigneur, what a struggle
was here! The dog moans pitifully, feeling the
hand's caress. But hark! the beast is at bay
again. The hand strokes the ears gently once
more, then lifts the horn to the lips, and the
dog is left alone to die.

At last, for the third time, the boar turned.
It was at the very spot where, startled from its
sleep, it had first heard the distant cry of the

pack, and, rising on its fore feet from the moss, had crashed through the reeds bordering the swamp. Hound and hunter were scattered now. The race had been hot, and there were dogs in the wood that never would answer cry again. Its bristles erect on its neck, its small eyes twinkling with rage, blood and foam dripping from its yellow tusks, the boar waited on its haunches. A hound, springing out of the thicket, leaped upon one of these tusks to receive its death-wound before the cry on its tongue was finished. Its fellow, following close behind, stood at a little distance, howling piteously, its flanks smeared with blood. At the sound of its master breaking through the flags it began to run to and fro, yelping furiously. The boar paid it no heed, watching the place whence came the sound of breaking stems; *there* was the enemy to be feared — Gui of Tours.

Gui stopped at the edge of the opening to get his breath. His horse had been long since abandoned; his spear was lost; he had a wooden javelin shod with iron in his hand, and a knife in his belt; the broken cord of his horn hung from its ring. For a moment man and beast confronted each other. Cowed by the silence, the dog began to whine. The boar was still unhurt, though lacerated by the dog's teeth. It was an old one, as could be seen by the curved tusks. Gui drew his knife and looked into its eyes. He would have risked death a thousand times to find Passe Rose — but why should he risk life to slay a boar? When the blood is up one does not think of such things. He wiped the perspiration from his eyes, planted his feet firmly, drew back his arm, and launched his weapon.

A heavy weight had crushed him to the earth. He struck out blindly with his knife; it was in his right hand — how had he changed it? His hip burned as with fire — was it the tusk, or the hoof, he wondered. Ah, he had struck the dog — A warm stream ran down his arm, then a shower of sparks danced before his eyes, and the weight on his chest grew heavier. He made an effort with both hands to cast it off — there was nothing there; yet it grew heavier — was he bound? He endeavored to cry out — what had he said in that moment of involuntary terror when the fear, not of death, but of ceasing to think, to feel, to love, seized him? — Passe Rose!

The sun was already low, a cold fog was beginning to rise from the marshes, and the queen had resolved to return to the hunting-seat of Frankenburg to await the king. The day had not passed as had been planned. Everything

had been arranged as for a battle; actor and
spectator had each been assigned his post and
duty; but the ambuscades had failed, the
would-be actor had heard the noise of the pursuit drift away, and the spectator had found
himself in the thick of the fray without warning; twice the *cortège* of the queen had been
scattered — the battle had become a *mêlée*. Followed by a numerous train, the queen advanced
slowly through the wood. Where was the
king? God only knew. From far away came
the cry of baffled dogs, a solitary shout, the
echo of a horn. The queen rode in silence, surrounded by her escort; from time to time she
turned her head to listen, or to address some
question to those at her side. In advance went
the royal equerries, alert, their javelins in their
hands. With such a beast it was necessary to
be cautious, even though the vine-clad tower of
Frankenburg was in sight. The waters of the
lake shone through the trees like an amethyst
— it was said that these colors were due to the
fires of Fastrade's magic ring, hidden in its
depths. Behind the queen, among the king's
daughters, there was laughter and whispering.
All were there, Rothrude, Bertrade, and the
timid Gisèle, their robes double-dyed with
purple and sewn with flowers of gold; and last
of all, Rothaïde, the eldest, grave and stately

between the young children of Fastrade. In proportion as the distance from the queen increased, the laughter was more merry and the conversation less restrained. They recounted the day's adventures, conjectured its issue, and discussed what should have been done.

" Do they chase the boar with thee ? " cried Gesualda to Rothilde, leaning back on her horse.

" If I had had a net, when the beast halted, perceiving us, and the dogs were upon him," — a page was saying.

" Thou would'st have attacked it single-handed," laughed Heluiz of Hesbaye, patting the blonde head at her stirrup.

" Ho, there ! " cried the page to a greyhound, which, leaving the boy's heel, sniffed in the bushes.

" It is a hare," said Rothilde.

" Ho ! " cried the page, tugging at the thong, and raising his whip. The dog, straining at the collar, tore the strap from the boy's hand. " By the King of Heaven ! " exclaimed the latter, disappearing after the hound in the thicket.

" He hath the king's oath by heart," laughed Heluiz of Hesbaye.

A furious barking, succeeded by a shout, came from the copse. At the sound of this cry

Heluiz's laughter ceased. Two men-at-arms ran into the bush, followed by Gesualda and Rothilde. "What is it ?" cried those in advance. "A dog hath started a hare," said one. But a sort of terror spread through the troop. Some ran back, others waited, listening. Beyond, among the king's daughters, they turned their heads, asking what had happened. Her heart beating, Heluiz urged her horse in the direction whence the cry had come. At a little distance the copse grew thin; there was an opening, and a crowd about something in its centre. "Water, — run to the lake !" cried a voice from its midst.

Heluiz slipped from her horse and ran forward. Stretched on the ground were a man and a dog. "Agnes ! Agnes !" she cried involuntarily. The man's body was straight, the hands by the side; but the dog, lying on its back, seemed still defending itself, its mouth full of hair and bristles, and a dagger buried to the hilt in its neck.

"Ho, here ! the boar, the boar !" cried one from the edge of the opening. Those on the skirts of the group ran to see.

Heluiz pressed forward to where Gui lay. "Is he dead ?"

"Nay, a scratch," said the page, unfastening the tunic, and wishing it were he who was thus

watched by such eyes and lifted by such hands.
For Heluiz had taken Gui's head in her lap.
She tore the wet moss from its roots to lay it on
his brow — it was wet indeed, but with blood.
"Loosen the belt," she said to the page.

As he obeyed, Rothilde, leaning over the
captain, uttered a cry of terror. Between the
leather pleatings, next his heart, she saw the
sealed packet of papers she had given the monk
at Immaburg for the prior. They were those
which Passe Rose had gotten from Brother
Dominic, together with that other she had found
in the road by the abbey the night of her last
visit to Friedgis. They had fallen from her
bosom when the captain bore her in his arms
from the chapel at Immaburg to the wagon, and
he had thrust them in his tunic, where they had
remained to this day. Rothilde, paler than
Gui, reached forth her hand to take them, when
a rough arm pushed her aside, and a voice of
command said, —

"Away with these women! Here, you fellows, think ye a dead boar will run away?
Make a litter of lances and boughs." And the
speaker lifted Gui in his vigorous arms.

On every side they were discussing, questioning. Each related how the affair had taken
place. He must have closed with the boar knife
in hand, — there were six thrusts behind the

shoulder within the space of two palms, from below upward, — therefore the beast was above ; the dog had leaped on its back, and received the knife by hazard.

" I would I had been there," said the page.

Rothilde was not listening. She wished to follow the litter, but dared not. At the sight of the papers, a multitude of pictures, hitherto distinct in her mind, blended into one, — Passe Rose, wearing her collar in the supper-room at Immaburg, with Friedgis' name on her lips ; her whisperings with the monk at the chapel porch, and Gui's defense of her on the terrace and at supper. " Cursed girl ! " she muttered, following at a little distance her companions.

Heluiz thought only of Agnes, who, vexed with her lover, had refused to join in the chase. " In the morning one pouts, and at night sheds bitter tears," Heluiz said to herself. " My heart bleeds for her," she whispered to Gesualda as they left the place together.

" Nay," answered Gesualda, knowing well of whom Heluiz spoke, " the wound is not deep, only when blood is lost " —

" I would some one told her gently," interrupted Heluiz.

Rothilde, walking behind the two, stooped suddenly to the page's ear. " Wilt thou ride with me to Aix to-night ? "

"Aye, truly, mistress," said the boy wonderingly.

"Run, then, quickly to the queen, and say
that I have gone to soften the tidings to Agnes
of Solier. Here, take my horse; I will find
another."

The night was near when the two left the
wood. On reaching the road Rothilde gave her
horse the rein. "Hold firm," she said. The
boy laughed scornfully to think a woman should
so address him, and drove his horse to her side.
But the girl was mounted on a long-limbed mare
she had gotten from one of the escort, while
he had but her palfrey; and stride by stride, to
his rage and mortification, she drew away, till
naught but a cloud of dust was before him, and
a distant beat of hoofs borne backward by the
wind.

Fleet as her own shadow, leaping from stone
to hedge, and from hedge to meadow, leaped the
girl's thought from conjecture to plan. She was
ignorant of the contents of the papers. A clerk
from Beneventum — one of those sent by the
Pope to teach the plain chant — had given them
to her at Immaburg for the prior, and the latter had bidden her send such by the hand of
Brother Dominic. "Cursed monk!" she repeated under her breath as the lights of Aix
came in view. The strings of the net had been

in her grasp, the life of the king in her hand,
wherewith to buy of his gratitude her heart's
desires. A few days more — and now, perhaps,
the sword and the cord. She did not fear them,
but to lose her soul's desires. And with her
rage mingled a fierce indignation, the indignation of a virtue balked. For was she not pur-
posing to save the king's life? and this lovesick
monk would ruin all. The distance was scarce
two thousand paces, but the steed breathed hard
and hung its head as the girl drew up before
the abbot of Fontenelle's. Sliding from her
seat, she patted the warm neck, bidding the
mare stand, and went boldly in the gate. Her
mind was made up. She would know the contents of the papers, and if it proved as she
feared, she would go that very night to Frankenburg and tell the king. By the fountain on the
side of the stables men were watering horses,
and among them she saw with joy the prior's
asses. Raising one hand to her lips she uttered
a low, peculiar cry. Instantly one of the men
turned and ran towards her. It was Friedgis.

"Hush," she whispered, laying hold of his
hand. "Is thy master, the prior, within?"

Seeing her white face he nodded speechless.

"Go to him and say, 'To-night, this very
hour, at the ford of the Wurm, without fail.'
Repeat the words after me." He repeated

them. " Aye, without fail. And do thou," — she
pressed his hand and drew nearer to him, — " do
thou take the horse thou wilt find without, and
wait for me at the west gate, the gate by which
thou camest." She raised herself on her feet till
her lips touched his. " Go," she said.

She stroked the mare's neck again as she
passed in the street, hurrying to the palace on
foot. The square was crowded with those waiting to see the king's return. She threaded the
throng as a young quail threads the rye, slipped
between the pillars under the gallery, and ran
up the stairs. At the threshold of Agnes' room
she hesitated. It was not for this she had come,
and words failed her. Agnes was sitting before
her toilet-table preparing for the supper await-
ing the king's return. She would not ride that
day with her lover to the chase, but she was
making ready, nevertheless, for his coming, and
was looking at herself in the metal disk when
she saw there the face of Rothilde. She turned,
penetrated with a sudden fear.

" He is not much hurt," stammered Rothilde.

" Who ? " said Agnes, striving to conceal her
own wound, but seeing the walls reel.

" A mere scratch," said Rothilde, remembering what some one had said in the wood. Then
she saw Agnes put out her hands and totter.

She sprang to the table for the cruet, and there
beside the flasks of rose-water lay her pearls!
For a moment she stood aghast, then, grasping
them in her hand, ran out, calling aid. "Thy
mistress is ill," she said to the women who answered her cry. "Gui of Tours is hurt by the
boar — go to her — and you, Marcent, run for
the king's leech," saying which, she disappeared
down the stair.

In the court the page was dismounting from
her palfrey. She laughed at his rueful face.

"Give me thy knee," she said.

"Where art thou going?" he asked, aiding
her to the saddle.

"To meet the queen."

"Another time, mistress," said the boy, clench-
ing his fist, "I will ride with thee " —

She laughed over her shoulder as she went
out of the gate, and put the palfrey to a gallop
on the road to Immaburg.

XVIII.

On leaping from the wagon at the edge of the
ford, Passe Rose fell; but, springing quickly to
her feet, ran with all her speed, giving no backward glance till she came to the waters. Every
eddy and muddy cloud which the wheels had

made was gone, and the stars shone placid in
the smooth-flowing current; but so deep were
they set, and so forbidding was the stream, that
for all her haste she turned along the bank, still
running, nor stopped for breath till the wood
had hidden the distant glare of the torches.
The moon was behind the trees, but she saw by
the narrow lane of stars overhead that another
road branched from the ford, and this she took
without debate, now running, now walking, and
so pressed by the fear of pursuit that all her
thought was fixed on the sounds she could scarce
separate from her own flying footsteps. Suddenly the star-track above widened and a dark
mass, distinguishable only by reason of its denser
blackness, detached itself from the gloom of the
forest. She stopped, spent and terrified, when
a low familiar sound of cooing doves, crowding
each other on their perch, came as it were from
the treetops. Reassured, she advanced step by
step till the thatch of a roof stood out against
the sky line, then stopped again, listening.
Heated by her long run, the night air made her
shiver. As she debated whether to seek shelter
in this hut, thinking how those within might receive her and whether, if any pursued, to tarry
here were not certain discovery, a distant shout
caused her to start forward again; but being
out of the road she stumbled and fell, and on

regaining her feet found her passage blocked by a low outbuilding. Her outstretched hand touched the door-post — an odor of trodden hay and steaming bodies came from within. Stooping to avoid the thatch, she stepped over the threshold, groping in the darkness. It was the sheepfold. "So, so," she said softly, for the sheep, huddled together, began to press toward the opening. "So, so," she repeated. But the flock crowded the more, and knowing well that to argue or threaten were folly, she dropped on the floor among them. The space was small, and they pressed about her, she lying still as if one of them till their alarm had subsided. One had its nose against her neck, and the murmur of its breathing filled her ear. She lifted her head and listened — without, also, all was still; then she rested her cheek on the soft shoulder next her, her face deep in the fleece, the smell of the wool in her nostrils, the hot breath on her throat. The warmth and shelter of the place filled her with a sense of safety and comfort, and no longer shivering, she closed her eyes.

It is strange that the mind, having such power to torture us, should be so readily set aside by a little bodily discomfort. The scratch of a pin or an aching nerve is enough to make it loose its hold; the lesser pain routs the greater, and thought and feeling must wait till the body hath ease again. But no sooner did Passe Rose close her eyes in warmth and safety than thick-coming thoughts forced them open, and there they stared in the dark as if the fold were lighted by a thousand candles, and her mind's pictures painted on its clay walls. Little the sheep knew what splendors and miseries of love and passion God and the Devil there showed her; and it would have puzzled the abbot, or even Alcuin, the king's chief scholar, to separate on the right hand and on the left the motives which kept her to her first resolve. Mixed with the clay and dross as they were, they filled the secret deeps of her heart with a sweet satisfaction, like the calm below a wind-tossed ocean. Often she was ready to rise up and go to claim her own. Was it not hers by right? What if she should possess it for but a moment — that moment of possession in the eyes of them all, of Agnes? Oh, Mother of God! Was this not hers in justice? Why should she hide like a felon in a sheep-pen while another laughed in the sun? Her blood boiled, and, lying the while motionless among the sheep, she braved, in thought, the guards at the king's gate, and stood before them all. Jewels and dresses were not her quest, but he, her lover. The king would frown, the women stare, and Agnes of Solier —

there she stood, insolent, as in the supper-hall
of Immaburg. What mattered it? She would
put her hand in her lover's, — its grasp was like
iron, — it was hers and none other's. If the
king smote her, — nay, let God himself smite
her, — the greater the despoiler, the greater the
wrong. He was hers by right. The world
might grind her to dust — what mattered it? —
and him also — ah, no! And like the river, the
rush of whose waters the rock, mid-stream, hurls
back and scatters, her thought recoiled, and she
began to tremble. Why throw away everything
just to lie on his breast? She could wait, oh,
for ages; and a vision of some far-away place
rose before her. When? Where? She did not
ask, but some time, somewhere — God would
not permit it to be otherwise — her lover would
come. She saw him afar — at every step she
quivered — now he was come, and stood above
her; his touch made her cry out; then she lay
still in his arms, trembling. Cramped between
the sheep, she slid down lower at full length.
Her foot pained her. She must have hurt it
when she leaped. What had he thought when
he looked in the wagon and found her gone?
By this time they must have reached the city.
Would he turn back to find her? If he came
she would lie still, and if he found her, that
would be a sign that God would have it so. She

would arise; they would go forth together; and a sudden childish memory of a blue sea shimmering in the sunlight passed before her eyes. She recollected the Greek jeweler whom she had met when she was with the merchants. He had told her of isles in a sea where no rain fell. Bah, how she loathed him and his jewels! "Oh my Gui, my Gui!" she whispered. Her thought grew more confused. The murmur of the breathing sheep sounded louder. Now it was the oft-heard roar of the river next the wall at Maestricht, of the leaves in the wood of Hesbaye, and now the lapping of the blue sea waves on isles where no rain falls. Her eyes struggled to open. It was true! Nightingales were, indeed, singing in the myrtles, and she had thought herself pursued and hiding in a sheep-pen! She opened her eyes wide now. The ugly dream was over. Her lover bent over her; above his head was the sky. "Oh, my Gui, my Gui!" she murmured, and so fell asleep.

It was fortunate for Passe Rose that the master of the grange was with Pepin in the marshes of the Theiss, for his soul was small with the greed of gain; and another mouth to fill, though it were that of the babe that came the last Easter night, made him cry out against God's injustice. But the wife was tender of every living thing, even to the hare which fled from the kite to her door. The children had found the girl still asleep in the gray of the dawn, and had brought her within, gaping with wonder at her strange dress, the tinkling bells, and the anklets about her feet. " Give me only shelter from the wolves," had said Passe Rose, " till my foot is at ease," — for she limped with pain, — " and I will gather thy fagots and grind thy wheat."

" Whence art thou ? " asked the woman, astonished at her beauty.

" I am from the South," said Passe Rose ; and seeing the woman observing her hair, " In my country a girl may braid her hair if she will."

" Hast thou no kin ? "

" Aye," said Passe Rose, thinking how Agnes of Solier had asked her the same question at Immaburg, " I have a mother who loves me well."

" Poor soul," replied the woman, " thy foot is bruised."

" Give me the babe while thou stirrest the stew," said Passe Rose. The woman hesitated. Her babe was christened, yet if by chance the girl were a witch — " I will guard the pot myself," laughed Passe Rose.

If the mother feared, as well she might, her doubts scarce lived till night. Never in the prime of her strength, before her children taxed her care, had she accomplished what Passe Rose

did that day ; and when they were all together
in bed Passe Rose had the babe in her arms
while the wife was planning what she should
say to her husband that he should grant the girl
to stay; for, if by God's grace the Huns had not
slain him, he must now be well on his way home.

Within a week's time Passe Rose was no
more to be spared than the thumb of one's
hand. She drew the water from the spring
which ran into the Wurm, and made a cape of
lamb's wool for the boy who watched the sheep
in the meadow below the spring; she ground
the corn and gathered the wood, and put such
savor into the pot that to smell the steam was to
long for what was within. Her foot was well-
nigh healed, though she spared it not, and the
goodwife feared each day to see her go.

" How happens it," she asked, "that thou
leavest thy mother if she loves thee well ? "

" Never fear," replied Passe Rose, whose
hand was on the mill ; " it is as I say."

Then once again : " Is thy father in the expedition with the king's son ? "

" I have no father," said Passe Rose, winding
the yarn.

At another time : " Is thy mother far ? Perchance thou returnest where she is ? "

" Between them that love there is no space,"
said Passe Rose.

So the woman bridled her tongue lest her questions should drive the girl away.

Behind the house a path led to the spring, for all the world like the fay's pool in the wood of Hesbaye. Overrunning the hollow whence it flowed, it slid between the stones to the river just below the ford, and where it left the stones for the rushes stood a black tower which the Romans had built before the ford shifted its place. Its stones were still firm, and a stairway led to the top, whence one could see the river up and down, and a glint from its surface across the meadow beyond the bend till the wood barred the view. The woman of the grange indeed had no desire to climb its stair, for the walls of her hut, or at most the circling forest, bounded her world, and little she cared to see what was beyond. Her husband would come soon enough without spying him out from afar. Moreover, the tower was of heathen construction, and the children were warned against looking even in its door for fear of some evil imp that might dwell within. But all the thoughts of Passe Rose were of that beyond the wood horizon, and it eased her heart to stand on the tower's top and follow the river's flow as far as she could see.

Having filled, one evening, her jar at the pool, she followed the rill to the stream, and entered

the door, dark as a wolf's mouth, for the arch
was low, and, because of the winding stair, no
light came from above. The sun was behind the
trees shooting beams of red light, like the fingers
of a mighty hand, through the openings, and a
thin mist lay on the water beneath. As she
looked a company of travelers came to the ford,
and halted on the farther side. Presently one
pricked his horse forward into the Wurm and
passed over, but the second, a monk, following
after on his mule, got no farther than mid-
stream, for there the beast stopped, and neither
blows nor coaxings would prevail upon it to advance or retreat. The robe of its rider trailed
in the water, the current foamed about its legs,
when a third person strode into the stream, and
lifting the monk in his arms bore him safely
over. Passe Rose, watching this scene, sprang
suddenly to her feet. If the arms which grasped
so fat a monk thus easily were not those which
had borne her from the press at the exposure
of the relics, then her eyes deceived her. Descending the stairs in leaps, she ran along the
bank, and reached the ford in time to see Friedgis wading the river with the beasts of burden,
the monk of Immaburg mounting his mule,
and the prior of St. Servais chafing at the
delay. Then the three resumed their journey.
Passe Rose waited till they had gone, then stole

from her hiding-place. There they were, on the
road to Aix, already indistinct in the shadows,
and now beyond sight and hearing. An over-
whelming desire to follow them seized her. She
walked slowly along the road under the mastery
of a presentiment she could not resist. Why
try to? What had she to do with those behind,
— with the water-jar at the pool? Her business
was with these, at the end of that road stretching before her. It were better to go on — nay,
she must. The very certainty of it was a satisfaction. She stopped suddenly, and ran back
with all her speed. The time was not yet come.
Some day she should follow that road to its end.
When that time came it would be in vain to
resist. "Yes, certainly, it will come," she said,
lifting the jar to her shoulder.

After this encounter an uneasy feeling ha-
rassed her. Death itself was not so certain as
this *something* near at hand. The sense of it
made her heart stand still and the spindle drop
from her fingers; it struck her like a chill in
the middle of the night, in broad day. "Oh,
my Gui," she repeated under her breath, terrified. Yet never once did she imagine that her
lover had forgotten her. There were times
when she was happier than she had ever been
before. The bitterness with which she had
thrown down the holy image in her chamber and

cursed the altar in the chapel of Immaburg had left her; sometimes it seemed as if God were in her heart. She went now often to the ford, to gaze at that road she was one day so sure to follow. She stopped midway in the wood path, as often too she started from her sleep — did any one call her? No, the time was not yet come.

One day she sat in the doorway combing the washed wool. Behind her the woman of the house was hanging the rovings on a stick suspended at either end from the rafters. The odor of the fleece filled the room, so that Passe Rose had seated herself where the air was fresh. The woman was talking of the approaching *fête* at Aix. "Of what use to us are all these treasures," she was saying, "since they serve only to increase the price of everything? It were better to leave them to the Huns. More than a thousand horses, they say, were left down there in the marshes. My husband was forced to furnish one, a fine colt that is now doubtless food for vultures, and he will come back empty-handed, for this treasure is not for us. They will make pictures of little stones in the church the king is building. Hast thou seen these pictures? I saw one in the church of St. Marcellus. The mantle of the martyr is of little stones, of gold and silver and red garnet. But what avails it to shed blood for treasures if a silver

sou is worth no more than twenty deniers? Let
us keep our husbands and our horses, and leave
the Huns their gold."

"In my country they have many such pictures," said Passe Rose with an air of superiority.

"And all the young girls in thy country wear
collars of gold," rejoined the woman, vexed.

"Nay," said Passe Rose, the color mounting
to her cheeks. "The collar is not mine own.
But if thou wilt thou mayst have my anklet,"
unfastening it as she spoke and offering it to the
woman; for in divesting herself of all Werdric
had given her, she had forgotten her anklets.
"It is of beaten gold; my father gave it me."

"If thy father gave it thee," said the latter,
ashamed, but weighing it in her hand, "it were
certainly dear to thee."

"Thou mayst have it and welcome," replied
Passe Rose.

"Nay," said the woman, giving it back, "if
thou lovest it " —

"I love it not," said Passe Rose.

The woman looked at her curiously. The
anklet shone in the wool where she had placed
it. "If thou wilt not wear it, I will put it in my
chest, the daws are such thieves," she said, opening the lid. "The key is at my girdle and thou
mayst have it when thou wilt."

Passe Rose made no reply. The daws peeped
from the rabbit-burrows in the hedge, their
gray ear-coverts and black plumage shining in
the sun. The comb flashed back and forth in
the white wool. Suddenly it fell from Passe
Rose's hand to the floor, and she rose to her feet
with a suppressed cry. Over the hedge, far
down the road, the form of a woman appeared.
Passe Rose stood still, only trembling, the wool
about her feet. A fire seemed burning in her
breast. She walked slowly down the slope to
the hedge, then she began to run, her eyes fixed
on the short, thick figure advancing with the
uncertain gait she knew so well. As she approached, the woman stopped, gazing at her suspiciously. Passe Rose ceased running and began
to walk again, then stopped also. The fire in her
breast had become like ice. It was Jeanne —
yet it was not Jeanne. The latter still eyed her
uneasily. Passe Rose advanced a step; she endeavored to speak, but could not.

" Hail, little dove," said Jeanne timidly.

At the sound of this voice Passe Rose trembled again. One would say these two feared
each other. " Mother — little mother," whispered Passe Rose.

A momentary gleam of recollection flashed in
Jeanne's sunken eyes. " Hush," she said, glancing nervously about her, "I am no mother. If

I were a mother I should find my child — my
bowels yearn for her, but being no mother I cannot see where she is. She was of thy height.
They say that if a string be stretched before the
door at night-fall — I have the string here in my
wallet," — her fingers fumbled at the pouch, —
" but the door is lost."

" Come," said Passe Rose, drawing her by the
hand which still held hers. Some stranger soul
which knew her not seemed to tenant this body
so familiar and so dear to her. She wished to
clasp it against her breast, but dared not.
" Come," she repeated irresolutely.

" Willingly. Thou hast a good face," said
Jeanne, looking wistfully into her eyes. " Is
there perchance a little cake in the oven ? "

Passe Rose did not reply ; the words filled her
throat. Her mother was hungry.

They walked together side by side, Passe Rose
looking straight before her. Jeanne, who had
not yet withdrawn her hand, stole from time to
time a timid glance at the girl's face. It seemed
as if the hand lying so passive in that of Passe
Rose recognized what the spirit could not, as if
the touch of the girl's fingers awakened sense-
impressions to which the mind could not respond,
yet which soothed it, producing a feeling of contentment and ease.

" It is my mother," said Passe Rose to the

woman who stood in the doorway watching them.

Jeanne's face shone with pleasure. " Foolish little one," she said in a supplicating voice, "let her think so if she will; it can do no harm." She hesitated. " I am no beggar. If ever thou shouldst pass by Maestricht, ask for the gold-smith of St. Servais. I will give thee a little cheese such as the abbot loves, — four every year I send to the abbot, and six to the king."

" Enter," said Passe Rose. It was more hu-miliating to her to see Jeanne receiving succor than to have asked for it herself. She drew her to the table and set before her some wheaten cakes and a cup of goat's milk, of which Jeanne partook eagerly. In the satisfaction of her hun-ger she lost all sense of the presence of others, bending over the platter and munching the dry cakes from which she could not take her eyes. When she had finished, she glanced nervously about the room till she found Passe Rose ; then she smiled.

" Come," said Passe Rose, " it is time to rest." Forcing her gently to the bed, she made her lie down and threw over her a coverlet of wool. Jeanne submitted without remonstrance, but kept her eyes fixed upon Passe Rose, who sat down beside her.

" To sleep one must close one's eyes," said the

latter. Jeanne shut her eyes. Presently she opened them again, and, reaching out her hand, drew Passe Rose's face to hers.

" To-morrow we will search — for her — together," she whispered.

" Aye, to-morrow," replied Passe Rose.

Satisfied, Jeanne closed her eyes again, holding the girl's dress fast in her hand. Gradually the tired body asserted its claims; the mouth opened, the lids parted and ceased to tremble, the smile disappeared from the face. Sleep seemed to increase its age and despair. But Passe Rose saw in it only the work of her own hand: *she* had furrowed those wrinkles and filled them with tears; *she* had blanched those cheeks and driven recollection from those eyes. Releasing herself from the hand which still held her, she crossed the room on tiptoe to the woman, who looked in silent wonder.

" She shall have my place this night in the bed," said Passe Rose, pointing to Jeanne. " To-morrow we will go hence."

" Thy mother is " — The woman tapped her forehead with her finger.

A gleam of anger shone in Passe Rose's eyes. " Nay," she replied, struggling with her tears, " her heart grieves her."

" Be at ease," said the woman, assuringly. " She shall rest here till my husband comes."

"Thou shalt keep the anklet, and I will give thee its mate."

"Nay," remonstrated the woman indignantly, "that were"—

"'Sh," said Passe Rose; and she went to the bedside and sat down again. She thought no more of the road to Aix. All those forms which had filled her imagination — Gui, Agnes of Solier, the prior, Friedgis, and the rest — had become as dreams. She saw nothing but Jeanne.

All the afternoon Jeanne slept, and Passe Rose sat motionless beside her. Night came, the firelight danced on the smoke-stained rafters, and she had not moved. "I have brewed for thy mother some wine of mulberry," whispered the woman. "Do thou hold my babe while I fetch the water from the spring." Passe Rose started. Her thoughts were far away in the garden at Maestricht. It seemed to her that once within its walls Jeanne would be well again.

"I will fetch the water, lest the child cry," she replied, taking the jar and lifting it to her shoulder. The night was soft and clear. As she went down the path she calculated the distance to Maestricht. "If her strength does not fail her, we will go to-morrow," she said to herself, thinking of Jeanne. She dipped the jar to its brim in the pool — "To-morrow, to-morrow," the gurgling water repeated. Would the day be fine? She set the jar on the moss, ran to the river and up the tower stair. Above the forest the sky glittered with stars. "To-morrow," she said, half aloud.

Passe Rose had scarcely crossed the threshold with her jar when Jeanne opened her eyes. She looked straight upward, vacantly, for a moment, then raised herself on her elbow. The woman, seeing her awake, laid her babe on the bed and brought the wine. "Drink," she said; "it will refresh thee. Art thou better?" Jeanne, sitting on the edge of the bed, took the bowl in both hands and drank. The child, alone on the bed, began to cry. At this cry Jeanne seemed to recollect. "Where is she — thy daughter?" she asked, looking about the room anxiously.

"She hath gone to the spring for water," replied the woman. "In a moment she will come."

Jeanne eyed her suspiciously. The woman took the bowl from her hand, then, loosening her robe, gave the child her breast. This sight seemed to affect Jeanne profoundly. Her hand wandered over her bosom, and her lips trembled.

"Lie down; she will come presently."

Jeanne obeyed, but, only half closing her eyes, watched through the lashes. The child, satisfied, slept in its mother's arms. The latter rose gently and laid it on the bed. "She sleeps again," thought she, looking at Jeanne. No sooner was her back turned than Jeanne arose softly, stealing to the door.

"Where art thou going?" exclaimed the woman, hearing her footsteps and hastening to intercept her.

"Stand aside!" cried Jeanne. Her eyes gleamed, and her hands were hooked like a tiger's claws.

"Saints of God!" gasped the woman, recoiling, terrified. Whether by chance or instinct, Jeanne, spying the path from the door into the wood, followed it without question. "Saints of God!" ejaculated the woman as she disappeared.

Passe Rose was issuing from the tower's arch when she heard the sound of some one coming through the wood, and suddenly Jeanne stood before her. A look so glad greeted her from Jeanne's eyes that she reached out both her hands. "Mother, my mother," she cried, straining the trembling form to her bosom and searching the eyes passionately. It seemed to her that Jeanne made a mighty effort; she pressed her closer. "O God, a little help for my mother." No, the task was too great. She felt the body in her arms relax, as one who, straining at a burden he may not lift, gives over exhausted, and, burying her face in Jeanne's neck, she gave way to uncontrollable sobbings.

"Hush," said Jeanne, shaken with their violence. "Hush," she repeated, caressing the girl's hair and striving to lift her face. "I had just now a dream. Listen while I tell it thee." She raised the head from her shoulder and kissed the eyes as she spoke. Passe Rose experienced a strange sensation in contemplating Jeanne's pale face — its eyes so bright but haggard, its cheeks so sunken, in feeling herself the object of such pity from a creature so pitiful. "I dreamed that I returned to my garden in Maestricht. I went in by the little door close to the square, and there, under the plum-trees which hug the wall, was my daughter." Passe Rose began to smile; that was her dream also. "She rose up to meet me. Come, let us go back. I will show her to thee — she is like thee — when thou seest her thou wilt love her also."

"Yes, let us go," murmured Passe Rose.

"I am strong," continued Jeanne eagerly, "if only thou knowest the way" —

"I know it. Is there not a little walk in thy garden between the grass and the shallot?"

"True," said Jeanne, listening intently, "the grass is on the left hand."

"Set with wild-cherry trees, and on the right the plums" —

"It is there she sat," interrupted Jeanne, "come. But how knowest thou the place so well?"

"Hear me," said Passe Rose earnestly. "I will lead thee to the very place. Trust me, for I know it well. But the night is now come, and thou hast need of more rest. See, how thy limbs tremble. To-morrow" —

Jeanne was troubled. "Show me the way, since thou knowest it so well," she said.

"How can I tell it thee? But to-morrow" —

"Nay, if thou knowest it, surely" —

"And if I show it thee, wilt thou wait till the morrow?" cried Passe Rose.

"Aye, if thou showest it truly."

"Come," said Passe Rose. She took Jeanne by the hand and led her within the arch. "Hold fast to my hand — now — there is a stair — so, I will help thee; it is not far. There, dost thou see the river where the stones make the ripple? The ford is there. Beyond the ford is the road we shall take. Art thou satisfied?"

"Truly," said Jeanne, following with her eyes Passe Rose's outstretched finger, "I believe thee."

Passe Rose threw her arms about her and drew her close. "Thou mayst indeed. I know the way well. We will start with the sun. We shall find her. She will rise to greet thee, for she loves thee."

"Nay, it is I who loved."

"Did not thy daughter love thee?" stammered Passe Rose.

"Aye, but a fay bewitched her."

" The spell is broken," said Passe Rose. " She will love thee, — I swear to thee she will love thee. She will hold thee as I do in her arms; she will leave thee no more; the birds will sing in the garden; we will sit there in the sun, and listen to the chant in the church of St. Sebastian. Dost thou not remember that she loved thee? Though she said it not, yet she loved thee; when thou findest her again, she will tell thee, — her tongue will be loosed."

Jeanne, feeling the heart beating next her cheek and the arms fast about her, watching now the eyes, now the stars bending above her, listened in silent delight to the words murmured in her ear. Dim recollections came back like the snatches of familiar songs. As a child lulled to slumber she sighed from time to time, · and when Passe Rose ceased and stooped to kiss her, she was asleep.

And when the child sleeps on its mother's breast, does not the mother dream of the stature to which those tiny limbs shall grow, of the deeds they shall do? Oh, of so many things! So Passe Rose began to dream, to merge her life in that of the old mother in her arms, returning to all she had cast away, and casting from her all she had yearned to possess.

Look! a flash of light on the edge of the wood. Along the bank, between the trees and the river, it shines, and vanishes, and shines again. Making a pillow of her cloak, Passe Rose laid Jeanne's head gently upon it, and stood up, shuddering. The light came nearer. She watched it glimmering under the branches, fascinated. Something told her that the hour had come.

XIX.

As she looked, two forms emerged into the starlight, approaching the tower from the ford. One was slender, with a long robe whose hood concealed the face; the other wore a casque rimmed with metal. It was this casque which flashed in the starbeams.

"This should be the place," said one, as they passed out of sight under the tower wall. Passe Rose knew the voice well, — the prior of St. Servais. "Look within," she heard him say.

The answer came up the stair: "Bah! a rat's hole. But thy maid is not here."

"I would I were as sure of the Greek," rejoined the prior.

"He will come, he will come," replied the other.

"If he left Pavia the same day with thee, he should be here now."

"He will not fail, he will not fail," said the soldier confidently.

"What vexes me," pursued the prior, "is that I have no message from the duke. He promised to send me tidings by one of the clerks the pope sent the king. All is ready. Beyond the Elbe a spark will kindle the fire, and once lighted it will spread throughout Saxony. At its signal the emir will cross the Ebro. Pepin should be here now, and in his absence the Lombards will join the duke. The fleet has set sail for Tarentum, if only thy Greek" —

"By heaven," retorted the other hotly, "if he fails I will take his place myself."

"And taste the girl's knife?" sneered the prior.

His companion laughed. "Believest thou she will have the courage to strike?" he asked.

"If she but scratch him, it is enough," said the prior. "I have a poison for the blade. The plan is simple. Bid the Greek not to strike her till after the king is slain, till he is about to leave her. She must have time to use her own weapon. Though she strike not first, she will defend herself. If thy Greek can kill a king, he can stab a girl in the dark; and if she scratch him not before he is done, then a wild-cat hath no use for its claws."

"By the gods," said the soldier, laughing, "it is so well conceived. They will destroy each other. I laugh whenever I think of it. So she hath claws, thy wildcat. Hath she whiskers also on her chin?"

"One would say an angel of God, a toy to play with, her face hath such sweetness in it," replied the prior. "Wait, thou shalt see." There was a moment of silence, and Passe Rose slid softly to her knees, holding her breath. Reinforced by the echoing walls, every word seemed uttered in her ear. "I would I knew the reason of her haste," muttered the prior. "She said the third night. Hist! some one comes. It is she."

Passe Rose raised her head softly above the parapet. Two others were approaching along the bank, a woman and a man. She could hear their footsteps in the dry leaves. At the edge of the wood the woman stopped, whispered something to her companion, then advanced alone from under the trees. Passe Rose heard the prior greeting her.

"Who is with thee?" he asked.

"I will tell thee later. Come within; the night grows bright," was the reply.

"Rothilde!" said Passe Rose, recognizing the voice of the Saxon who sat beside Agnes of Solier in the supper-room at Immaburg, and whose conversation she had overheard in the wagon at the ford.

At the entrance of the tower, Rothilde, perceiving the soldier, paused, and drew back.

"A friend," said the prior; "enter. What brings thee here? The Greek is not come."

"I thought surely it was he," murmured Rothilde, her eyes fixed upon the prior's companion.

"Truly, the face of a saint," said the soldier to himself.

Impatient, the prior repeated his question. "Thou saidst the third night," he whispered.

Rothilde stepped from the door into the shadow, where she could observe the prior's face. "Listen," she said, watching him. "Gui of Tours was hurt to-day by the boar in the wood of — Hark!" she exclaimed, turning her head.

"A bat's wing," said the prior, listening also.

"I was there," she continued. "His corselet was loosened to give room to breathe, and within were the papers I sent thee by the monk who brought the missal to Immaburg for the queen."

The soldier uttered an oath.

"Peace," said the prior; "what papers?"

"How should I know?" replied the girl, her eyes riveted on the prior's face, over which a pallor was spreading. "A clerk from Beneventum gave them to me, and I sent them by the monk, as thou badest me. Have they to do with the death of the king?" she asked boldly.

The prior sought in vain to find the girl's eyes in the darkness. "Nay," he answered quickly, "they were of other matters."

"Thou liest," thought Rothilde to herself. But she gave a sigh of relief. "God be praised!" she exclaimed. "I felt the cord at my throat. When I saw them the seal was unbroken. None gave heed to them, — they were seeking the wound; a moment more and I had them safe in my hand; but they bore him away, thrusting the women aside. I remembered them well because of the seal" —

"Thou gavest them to the monk?" interrupted the prior. She saw that his composure was affected.

"Aye, but after setting out he returned again, — for what purpose I know not. I saw him after supper, with a dancing-girl. Knowest thou one called Passe Rose? The captain said she was of Maestricht. When I saw the papers in his bosom, I said to myself 'the girl got them of the monk and gave them to her lover.' She might well bewitch a monk, having first bewitched a captain. Ask Agnes of Solier, who trembles now for her morning-gift. But if the papers matter nothing — God! I shall sleep sweetly to-night; I thought to be strangled in bed."

The prior laughed nervously. "Why shouldst thou fear? The papers do not concern thee. Thy time is not come."

"Liar!" thought the girl, watching his face. "I will give thee this night to the king."

"Come, let us go," said Sergius, raising his hood.

"Wait!" whispered Rothilde, laying hold of his arm. "Thou sayest the papers put us in no jeopardy; a stone is lifted from my heart. But I said I would tell thee who is with me."

"Who is he?" asked the prior, with ill-disguised impatience.

"Fool!" thought Rothilde, "thou art in haste." Then aloud: "Dost thou remember the footsteps we heard in the chapel, in the church of St. Marcellus?" The prior, turning back, scrutinized her face. "There was one listening, — thy servant, the Saxon serf. I saw his eyes, — like a ferret's. I watched to see whither he would go. He ran before me to the palace, asking for the king. Blessed be God, the king slept last night at Frankenburg. But this morning the Saxon came again, asking for the queen. The guard refused him entrance, for he would not tell his errand" —

"By hell's demons," exclaimed the soldier, "hast thou him here?"

"For what reason should I bring him?" said the girl significantly.

For a moment the three were silent. The soldier, looking at the prior, drew his sword.

"Go," said the latter gently.

"Be not rash; he is brave," whispered the girl.

" Tut," said the other, hiding his weapon within his cloak, " I will bring thee his tongue on my sword's point."

Peering above the parapet, Passe Rose saw him cross the open space and disappear in the wood. Her thoughts whirled in her head like leaves caught in the wind and carried up to vanish no one knows where. The papers, — those she had got from the monk, and the other found on the road by the abbey pond, — she had missed them indeed, but since that night when her love stood revealed she had thought no more of them than of her collar or anklets. They must have fallen from her bosom when she swooned in the chapel at Immaburg, and her lover had taken them. The death of the king! Had she then unwittingly brought her lover into peril? A fear overspread her thought and dulled her power to reason. She remembered no more Jeanne, the garden by the square of St. Sebastian. " Gui of Tours was hurt to-day by the boar in the wood," — these words she repeated to herself over and over, as if not understanding them, seeing all the while Gui stretched before her on the trampled grass, his corselet torn open, and within, the papers, more to be feared than the boar's tusk. Forgetting all else, she rose up, trembling in every limb. Jeanne was still sleeping, her head on the cloak. Be-

low, everything was silent. Rothilde, leaning
against the wall, her eyes closed, still held the
prior's arm. Then a horse neighed in the wood ;
there was a cry, an oath — and silence again.
At this cry Rothilde drew a quick breath and
opened her eyes. A pleasure so fierce shone in
them that the prior recoiled.

"What ails thee ?" she said. "Thou desirest the life of a king. I wished only for that of
a serf. The blood of a slave for that of a king,
— that is not much." Her voice was insolent
with joy, as of one drunk with wine. "Bring
me now thy Greek, and I will show him the way
to the king's bed."

"She-devil!" muttered the prior to himself.

The girl laughed and let go his arm. Without, the soldier was wiping his blade on the grass.

"Is it done?" she asked.

He held up his sword in the light. She made
no reply, and entered the wood alone. The
horses neighed as she approached. Near by, a
black bulk lay in the reeds. She stopped and
listened, advanced a step, then, hurrying forward, stooped, searching with her hand. Aye,
it was done. Her course was free. Now for
the king ! Rising to her feet, she loosed the
rein from the branch. The trembling horse
snorted with terror. "Peace, peace," she whispered, laying her cheek to its nostril, and hug-

ging its neck with her arms. "Now, for the king!"

"Said I not the duke had messages for thee?" the soldier was saying to Sergius. "Ask her where this captain is to be found."

"Nay, it will alarm her," replied the prior, "she said at Frankenburg." Notwithstanding Rothilde had come to apprise him of the miscarriage of the papers, an involuntary mistrust tormented him. Had Friedgis indeed followed him to the church of St. Marcellus? It was not probable. Some other motive had prompted a vengeance so swift. How her eyes shone when he cried from the wood! "She has tricked me," thought the prior. Like the Roman emperor, he feared his own legionaries. As for the papers, doubtless she was right; the captain had got them from Passe Rose. He recollected the captain's inquiry for the goldsmith's daughter at the abbey, and the presence of the latter with Brother Dominic at Immaburg explained everything. "Cursed monk!" he muttered, half aloud.

"Waste no words on him," said his companion; "let us seek the captain. There is yet time. She said the seal was unbroken. A wounded man hath always need of a priest. If he knows the content of the letters, which is not probable, and the boar's work is not well done

—a wound often reopens. If he knows nothing, we will have them by fair means. If he
hath given them to others, it is already too late
to fly. Come, let us go."

"Where is she?" asked the prior. His natural energy seemed paralyzed.

"To the devil with her; time presses."

"Hush! she comes."

Leading her horse by the bridle-rein, Rothilde
advanced from the wood. Above, Passe Rose,
standing erect in the full starlight, dared not
move.

"Wilt thou go with us," said Sergius. He
appeared unwilling to lose sight of her for an
instant, and she read his disquietude in his face.

"With thee! Where is thy wit?" she exclaimed. "What! a priest and a girl to be
seen entering the gate alone at midnight?
Moreover, I rode from Frankenburg at the
queen's command, to tell Agnes of Solier of her
lover's hurt. I had a page for company," she
laughed, "and left him on the way. Perchance
I shall find him again, for I must join the
queen."

"Come," whispered the soldier impatiently.

"Thou dost not fear to ride alone?" said the
prior, reluctant to leave her, and eying her suspiciously. She shrugged her shoulders disdainfully. "Have a care, then, to thy face," he
said. "Farewell."

When they were gone, Rothilde led the horse to the tower, sitting down on a stone near the door, while the horse browsed beside her among the reeds. She could scarce wait to hear the hoofs on the distant road. She proposed to take the other, the one skirting the city through the wood. "Robert of Tours returns from Hungary to-morrow with Pepin. In an hour I will tell the king." This was all her thought. She stroked the horse's ears and smiled.

Suddenly, above her head, something stirred. It was Jeanne turning in her dreams. "Aye, I believe thee," said a voice; "only show me first the way." Passe Rose, dumb with terror, knelt down and pressed Jeanne's hand. She heard a noise below, then on the stair, but before she could get from her knees, or even think what she would do, Rothilde stood before her.

Afterwards she could remember nothing, only that she heard a cry as of a wild beast, and saw the flash of a knife in the girl's hand. Now she was alone, on the edge of the parapet, panting, and below in the river something struggled. She had grappled with the girl; the knife was now in her own hand, and her fingers were cut. Seigneur! what had she done?

"Mother, little mother," she whispered, stooping to Jeanne's ear. Jeanne opened her eyes. "The time is come, — the time is come."

Jeanne, sitting up, smiled. "The sun is not yet up," she said.

"It is time," urged Passe Rose, pulling her by the hand to her feet. Her mouth was set and her eyes were fixed, like those of the statue in the porch of St. Sebastian indeed. Down the stair, along the river, dragging Jeanne after her, she hurried. "Oh, my Gui!" she murmured.

"Thou art in haste," said Jeanne, half awake. "But it is well to start before the sun, the way is so long."

"Aye, long," murmured Passe Rose.

At the ford Jeanne paused. "Thou saidst this way."

"Nay, I swear to thee, this is best."

"I believe thee," Jeanne answered calmly. "Thou hast a good face, — lead on." And the two, close together, disappeared between the tall trees hemming, like a giant hedge, the road to Aix.

XX.

The night was far gone when Passe Rose, Jeanne's hand still clinging tightly to hers, reached the city gate. Overwhelmed by the revelations she had heard, tortured by her fears for Gui, she knew not what to do, whither to

go. Her heart ached with trouble and sus-
pense. But life perplexed her no more. All
was simple and clear. It was for love's sake
she had leaped from the wagon, and now followed the road she had abjured. It was for
love's sake she would have forgotten love in that
peaceful garden whence peace had fled. It was
her love which had turned for solace to Jeanne
— dear Jeanne, whom she dragged along the
path as a mother urges her tired child, Jeanne
whom she was deceiving — "Nay, nay," cried
her heart, "there is no right, no wrong, nothing,
but to reach *him*."

So the stream, issuing first from the wood,
runs aimlessly, now east, now west, turned aside
by a tuft of grass, divided by a root, dashed to
spray by a stone. Afterwards, swollen to a flood
and conscious of its destiny, disquieted no more
by obstacle or circuit, it floats unvexed, knowing that east or west it nears the sea.

The city was asleep. They followed the street
leading from the gate to the great square before
the palace. Jeanne, deeming it to be the square
of St. Sebastian in Maestricht, looked to see
the tower and her garden wall. After her
weary wanderings the thought of home, of finding there her child, had given her strength and
courage. Disappointed and alarmed by the
strange aspect of this silent city, she began to

ask questions, like a child unreasonable over delay and incapable of understanding. Passe Rose answered these questions as best she could, saying she knew not what, consoling, encouraging, promising, — how can one explain everything to a child? — having always before her eyes the wound the tusk had made, and in her ears the cry of Friedgis from the wood.

Before the palace gate she saw the guards chatting together. It was said that the Kan of the Huns would come with Pepin, as a hostage, and that a great hunt would take place the following week. They would show this pagan how one amused one's self in the woods of France. Would he had been with the king to-day! Such a boar was not to be had for the whistling. One who had been present when the beast was found dead beside the captain was telling its weight and the length of its tusks. Passe Rose drew near, listening.

"Was the captain hurt?" she asked.

The speaker turned. He was the Gascon who had aided the captain in carrying her to the wagon at Immaburg.

"He hath a slit in his groin the length of a skewer" — then, seeing the girl's shining eyes between the folds of her mantle: "Ho, pretty dear, thou art late abroad." And seizing her by the waist, he endeavored to snatch away her cloak. Jeanne, holding timidly to Passe Rose's hand, suddenly transformed, sprang to her rescue.

"Have a care for the hag's claws," laughed the others.

Passe Rose, taken unawares, struggled in the embrace of her assailant. "May the Devil spit me on his fork," he cried, clasping her fast, but unable to free his neck from Jeanne's arms. "Hold the old witch," he called to the others; "her fingers are like hooks." Loosing the girl's waist suddenly, he grasped her arms, and forcing them slowly back, approached his face to hers.

"Tell me where the captain is, and I will give thee thy kiss," gasped Passe Rose. In the struggle her cloak had been torn from her head, and her face, bent over backwards, was uncovered to the starlight.

"The captain's demon!" exclaimed the Gascon, letting go his hold and recoiling.

But Passe Rose held fast to his arm. "Tell me, — where is he? — it is for thy good."

"Leave go; the captain is at Frankenburg — the road is before thee — Ah, sorceress!" And wrenching his sleeve from her fingers, he drew back, signing himself. "Loose her," he cried to the others who still held Jeanne. "I had sooner kiss the Devil himself." And drawing his sword, he brandished it in circles above his head.

Jeanne, set free, was about to renew the encounter. "Come," said Passe Rose, seizing her hand and drawing her away. "Come," she whispered, — "come."

Bewildered and out of breath, but filled with rage, Jeanne obeyed reluctantly, muttering to herself and turning back to shake her clenched fist. "I will tell the abbot, — certainly I will tell the abbot, — the rascals!"

"Hush," said Passe Rose, pressing her hand tighter and hurrying her away.

"Have we yet far to go?" asked Jeanne.

"Not far," replied Passe Rose.

Passing the king's basilica they heard the voices of the choir intoning the midnight chant. The priest, bowing before the altar, had just said, "Let us pray for Karle, king and servant of God;" and the clerks were replying in unison, "O Christ, save Karle." The road forked without the gate, but the darkness was so intense that Passe Rose did not perceive it. As they hurried on she was almost trampled under foot by a horse which issued from the road branching to the right, and which she had not seen till the form of its rider, a woman, holding an arm aloft, was outlined above her against the sky. Recoiling, she plunged forward again, drawing Jeanne's hand closer within her cloak. Then she heard a cry such as no night animal utters, the human cry of distress. Was it the voice of her own fears, or did the rider call to her? Once more it came, a cry of mingled agony and rage, recalling to her that of the Saxon on the tower when leaping at her throat. Dieu! how like it was! And without turning back, she quickened her pace.

The stars were beginning to disappear in the east when the tower of Frankenburg rose from the trees. The morning had not yet come, but one felt that it was near, and that it would be beautiful and serene. The thin fog, colored by the waters of the lake, commenced to stir, making ready to go, though the sun was yet below the horizon. From the border of the wood a bird sallied forth, uttering its first short song; and a rabbit, startled from its form by the approach of footsteps, erect in the dewy grass, shook the moisture from its ears. A column of blue smoke rose from the roof like another tower.

"We will rest here," said Passe Rose, "and eat."

"Aye," replied Jeanne, faint and tired, "let us rest here. The way is long."

Following the direction whence the smoke rose, through an opening in the hedge, Passe

Rose perceived a small wooden cabin built against the outer wall. Still holding Jeanne's hand in hers, she entered the inclosure and drew near the house. Within, fagots were crackling and a woman was preparing her morning meal. Seeing strangers approach she came to the door. Her face was comely and inspired confidence.

"A little food and rest," said Passe Rose, pointing to Jeanne.

"Aye, enter," replied the woman. "The pot is nearly done. Sit thee down here," she said to Jeanne, drawing a bench to the fire; "thy feet are wet with dew."

"Christ bless thee," murmured Jeanne, taking the proffered seat and spreading her hands to the blaze.

Passe Rose sat down beside her. The woman lifted the pot from the fireplace, gazing curiously at the pair as she continued her preparations. "My sister is milking," she said. "I will go fetch her, and we will eat together."

Passe Rose looked about the room. It was small but clean. The fire sparkled brightly; a savory steam escaped from the pot. The warmth and the smell of food overcame her. She did not know till now that she was faint and exhausted. She watched the escaping vapor in a sort of stupor of physical enervation and content. Jeanne, leaning against the chimney wall, was ready to fall asleep. Presently the woman was heard returning. Passe Rose started to her feet. For a moment she had forgotten everything. A young girl was with the woman, and they bore between them a large pail banded with iron, from which the milk froth dripped.

" Where is the captain," whispered Passe Rose in a low voice, holding her finger to her lips, and indicating Jeanne, — " he who was hurt yesterday in the wood ? "

" The captain ? " repeated the woman, setting down the pail and regarding Passe Rose with surprise.

" Gui of Tours.   They said he was here."

" In the grange yonder," answered the woman, — what would the girl with the king's captain ? — " beyond the pond, in the wood," pointing over the hedge.

" Show me," said Passe Rose.

" Go with her, sister. Thou wilt not eat first ? "

" Come," said Passe Rose, taking the child's hand, and leaving the woman gazing wonderingly after her.

" This way," said the child as they passed through the hedge ; and looking up into Passe Rose's face, — " I will show thee. They would have brought him hither, to the castle, but his wound was grievous, so they left him yonder in

the grange ; it was nearer. Thy fingers bleed !"
she exclaimed, scrutinizing Passe Rose with a
child's curiosity, and observing both the collar
of gold and the torn dress under her cloak.
" Art thou his kinswoman ? " Passe Rose shook
her head. " Nay, that could not be," continued
the child wisely. " I heard it said yesternight
how the king loved him because he was betrothed to his daughter, — not the queen's, but
another's. Oh, but the queen was distressed
before the king returned. I sat in the hedge
when she passed by. They say a queen cannot
weep, but I saw her eyes, and when the king
came she embraced him before them all. Why
should not a queen weep, since she can smile ?
They say the other never smiled, — the one
whose ring is in the lake. Dost thou see the
ripple there in a straight line between the two
oaks ? It is there the ring is hidden. When a
bird flies over the spot it loses the power of its
wings, and falls like a stone. Beyond the point
where thou seest the rocks glisten the boar was
killed. That was near, eh ? They brought it
hither, — four horses could scarce drag it, —
and I touched it with my hands. I am not
afraid when it is dead. I had a father once
who was killed by a stag. I have another now.
He tracks the boar for the king the day before
the hunt. Never did he see such an one as

this. Its tusk was bent like my finger. That was because it was old. But it was fierce. Holy Virgin! it was fierce. A boar hooks like a bull. It stamps also with its feet."

"Is it far?" asked Passe Rose.

"Nay, two bow-shot. My mother is at the grange. She knows herbs to close a wound and drive the blood inward. The queen bade her care for the captain till she sent her own physician. Yestermorning my mother said some evil would befall, for a sheep left the flock and passed through the hollow of a tree. It is a sure sign of death. It happened so when my father was killed. This is the spot. Wait here. I will go fetch my mother. The queen gave her a gold sou not to leave his bed." And the girl disappeared on tiptoe through the door.

Steadying herself against the door-post, Passe Rose looked out through the wood where the lake lay. The sun, just risen, was breaking through the mist. In the trees the birds quarreled noisily. Golden bees buzzed among the vines. But she saw nothing, heard nothing. She had forgotten all those terrible secrets repeated by the echoing walls of the tower. Overcome by the thought that she was about to see Gui, that there were no longer any barriers between her and him, she was saying to herself, "It is true. It is real. I am here." She heard a footstep approaching, but could not turn her head. Her limbs trembled as with cold, yet her heart burned.

" What wilt thou?" said a voice beside her.

She made an effort, faced about, and lifted her eyes. "The captain, — Gui of Tours."

The woman looked at her in silence, examining her from head to foot. Would she never speak? Was she perchance going to refuse, thought Passe Rose; and with the desperate strength of fear : "Take this collar to him," she said, unclasping it from her neck. " If it avails nothing I will go." But in her heart she knew it would avail everything, that she would never go.

" He sleeps," replied the woman, hesitating.

Passe Rose did not stir. The eyes of these two women rendered words useless. One was saying, " You know it cannot be otherwise ; " the other replied, " I understand."

Clinging to her mother's robe, the child looked from one to the other wisely. " Follow me," said the woman.

On reaching the room where Gui lay she stood aside to let the girl pass, but remained in the doorway, the child still holding to her robe. Passe Rose crossed the room, and knelt down beside the couch in the farther corner. She forgot that they watched her. At that threshold she had left every human sentiment but love.

Gui was asleep. There was nothing to terrify. The chest rose and fell slowly and regularly; a pink flush colored the tanned face, turned upon its cheek. Passe Rose smiled, a smile of which she had no consciousness. This was the moment of which she had dreamed in her turret chamber at Maestricht, in the dark wood of Hesbaye, in the sheepfold beside the Wurm. Her eyes saw everything, — the hands which had fastened her collar, the arms she had felt about her at Immaburg when her senses fled, in whose clasp she had left a part of herself, which she now found again. Underneath the covering was the wound, but the thought of it terrified her no longer. She was there, rich in health, courage, love. What could take him from her? Death? It was not possible. When death comes one sees in the face the vain struggle against extinction; one feels in one's own heart the vain revolt of its unsatisfied desires, and hears the outcry of its deathless passions; there is a terrible presence against which rebellion is futile, which glides between us and life, its splendors and seductions. Nay, he was sleeping, and her heart was running over with projects and dreams; peace filled the room, and without the sun was rising above the trees, the birds sang, and the golden bees flew in and out among the flowers. It seemed to her that he, too, smiled. Was he dreaming of her?

Did he know she was there? His hand hung over the edge of the bed. She longed to touch it, but dared not — he would wake. She would fix her eyes on his till they opened, like flowers to the sun. Nay, that were a sin. Sleep was precious to him. She would lay her head beside his hand and wait. O God, what a blessed moment when he should wake! And with an impulse she could not resist she laid her cheek in his open palm.

Seigneur! What had she done! She held her breath. He did not stir. The hand was warm; she could feel its pulse next her cheek. She did not dare to move again, so she lay still, timing her breathing to his, and listening to the pulse in her ear. It seemed to her that in a moment she had entered some blessed precinct fenced about from peril. Those terrible realities of the night, the voices in the tower, the cry of Friedgis in the wood, the sudden apparition of Rothilde, the sickening moment of fear and struggle, the splash in the water below, and Jeanne, dear Jeanne — all these things were close at hand, but outside her refuge, and came to her thought only as the cries of pursuers reach the ear of the fugitive safe within the sanctuary.

On a chest against the opposite wall she saw a tunic and leather *braies*, a linen shift and belt. She looked at them for a long time without being able to make up her mind to rise. Then a noise at the door caused her to lift her head: it was only the woman in the outer room. Passe Rose glanced at Gui: he was sleeping. Softly, her eyes fixed upon his face, she went to the chest. The linen was clotted with blood, the leather stiffened by the waters of the marsh. These things were unutterably dear to her; in touching them it seemed as if she touched him. She lifted them noiselessly, searching for the papers. They were not there. She raised the lid of the chest. Within was a hunting-knife, its handle set with shining stones; a sealed packet, aye i and the paper she had found by the pond near the abbey; and beside these, a little ball of crimson wool and a brass pendant, like those which hung from the border of her dress. She took the papers and hid them quickly in her bosom, but the ball and trinket she held in her hand, going back to her place beside the couch, and laying her head down on its edge. The wool was matted with blood: the trinket, too, was discolored; they must have been torn from her dress at Immaburg. Tears filled her eyes. Until now she had been happy in loving, but now, — O Blessed Mother, whose image she had thrown down, pardon, pardon! for surely the gods listen, — now she was happy in being loved; and unable to restrain herself, she reached out her arms and drew her lover's head to her bosom.

"Mother," said the child, "the captain is awake; they whisper together. Shall I fetch the drink?"

"Aye, go fetch it," replied the woman, looking in at the door, over the child's head.

Running to the spring hard by, the little maid returned presently with a bowl, from which she wiped the moisture. Holding it carefully in both hands, and watching the rim lest the contents should spill, she crossed the room.

"My mother says thou hast need of refreshment," she began; then stammered and colored, she knew not why, and, setting the bowl on the chest by the couch, ran from the chamber. "Surely the captain is better," she said to her mother.

"Aye, indeed," muttered the latter to herself, as she drew the child from the door; "love and sage in May."

"I thought thee lost," said Gui. He held Passe Rose's hands in his.

"I thought thee dead," she answered in a whisper.

That was all. They could not speak, pressing each other's hands and exchanging radiant smiles. The questions which had tormented him, — why was she wandering alone in the wood of Hesbaye,

why had she fled from the wagon, — he could
not ask them; and she had forgotten the papers
in her bosom, Agnes of Solier, and the boar's
work, — her wound and his.

"Dost thou remember when I first saw thee,
in the wood?" She nodded. "And at thy
door, as I rode by? And in the meadow?"
Her hands pressed his for answer. She no
longer withdrew them, nor turned away her eyes.
The very blood in her veins seemed still, she was
so calm and contented. Have you seen the in-
coming sea toss the flags in the marshes? But
when the tide is full, what peace, what stillness!
— not a stem trembles. At this moment she
remembered what the Greek merchant had said
to her at the fair of St. Denis : "The gods made
thee to delight their eyes." The words which
had angered her then now made her smile with
happiness. "Tell me that thou lovest me," said
Gui.

Love him! Could he not see? Did she
shrink away, as in the meadow ? Then, she, the
weak, was his; now, he, the strong, was hers.
An indescribable sense of security possessed her.
Love him ! Without, the wood rang with the
songs of birds issuing from its sunlit borders,
mounting skywards from its silent glades, shaking the dew in little showers from their ruffled
feathers, trying their wings, audacious, their tiny

throats trembling with melody. Can one call them back to their nesting-places after the sun is risen? As well seek to call back from the face what the heart sets free. Love him! Could he not see? And then suddenly all those shy and modest spirits which guard the inmost sanctuary rose in mutiny and alarm, and she hid her face on his breast.

"Rose, Passe Rose," murmured Gui, endeavoring in vain to lift her head; for she clung the closer, burying her face in the covering of the bed. His arm glided under the robe which enveloped her shoulders, drew her to him, and he kissed the head, whose fine hairs trembled at every breath, close to his lips.

"Nay, it is not possible that I am here," she thought. She forced herself to imagine that she was far away, that night was coming on in the great wood of Hesbaye, that she hid in the sheepfold by the Wurm; shutting her eyes to better feign her past fears. How cold and wet was the moss next her cheek, and the wind, how it sighed! What darkness, and what sounds! Feeling all the while his breath stir her hair, and saying to herself, "It is true, it is true."

"Where is thy wound?" she asked, lifting her head quickly.

"It is nothing," replied Gui.

"Show me," she said, kneeling beside the couch, and uncovering his limb.

At the touch of her fingers he blushed, turning away his head and closing his eyes. The bandage, stained by a yellow ointment, was drawn tightly over the thigh. At the sight of it, Passe Rose remembered a terrible valley strewn with corpses and filled with groans. Where, when, she did not know. Till now she had completely forgotten it. But she saw herself distinctly, a little girl, stumbling under the jar of fresh water on her shoulder, running from group to group under the trees where the wounded were laid: one, a clear-eyed boy, — she remembered him well, — to whose lips she held her jar, while a monk washed the wound with white wine, stanching it with the miraculous salve which he took from the flask at his girdle, and who, when he had done, traced a cross upon the linen band, and repeated the four names of God containing the seven vowels. She wished to pronounce now those names of the Blessed God, but she had forgotten them; so she drew a cross quickly upon the bandage with her finger, and repeated those of the four Evangelists in their stead. Relieved and comforted by this act, she covered the limb again gently, and, taking the bowl from the chest, held it to Gui's lips.

"Thy hand bleeds," he said. .

"Drink first. I will tell thee."

He obeyed, interrogating her face. For the
first time he asked himself how she came to be
there. As he sipped the liquid in little swallows, a horn sounded without; then came the
neighing of horses and the chatter of voices.
Passe Rose listened. The woman was at the
door, beckoning her. "They are here. Seigneur Dieu, come away!" she whispered.

"Do not go," said Gui, endeavoring to raise
himself. His eyes were fixed upon Passe Rose
imploringly, and he sought to retain her hand.
She stooped to his ear, saying something which
caused him to smile. He let go her hand, and
she went out. Through the door she saw a
company of women, escorted by horsemen. The
sun sparkled in the fringes of the harness, and
glittered on the spear - heads, and pages in colored capes stood at the palfreys' stirrups. The
women were dismounting, among them Passe
Rose recognized Heluiz of Hesbaye, then Gesualda. She searched for a third, Agnes of So-
ier, but could not discover her. There was also
a monk in the black habit of the Benedictines,
having a sprinkling-rod in his hand. "He must
be the physician sent by the queen," thought
Passe Rose. She stood watching them as they
approached, till she heard the voice of Gesualda
above the others, when she sprang to the door
in the rear, and hid in the shrubbery which

masked the out-buildings. Having waited till the company had entered, she stole behind the hedge to where the horses were tethered, and putting aside the branches softly, looked between the leaves. The soldiers were sitting in groups in the shade; near by, the horses browsed, their bridle-reins thrown over the lances planted in the ground. The little maid who had shown her to the grange ran among them, stroking their glossy necks, and timidly offering them grass from her hand.

"Have a care; that one bites!" cried a soldier stretched on the moss, and laughing at the quick withdrawal of the extended hand.

"Thou art jesting," said the maid, looking from the speaker to the steed, which arched its neck, trembling with desire, and blowing the froth from its nostrils.

"On my faith, have a care."

Studying the brown eye and the ears pricked forward, the girl advanced her hand again slowly till the velvet mouth just grazed her palm, and cast a triumphant glance over her shoulder.

"Wilt thou mount?" asked the soldier, rising.

"Aye, willingly!" cried she, clapping her hands.

He lifted her in his arms, and set her in the

saddle. "So now, softly. Sign thyself and say thy prayers."

The child laughed, her eyes sparkling with pleasure. "Heu!" she said, taking the rein.

The soldier looked at her admiringly. "Amuse thyself, but go not far," he called after her as she made her way between the trees.

Gliding along the hedge, Passe Rose ran towards the angle where the path from the grange entered the road. The little maid, her bare feet pressed against the horse's flanks, her fingers grasping the tufts of hair hanging from the saddle-bow, did not at first perceive her, being occupied in personating the Queen of Sheba coming to Jerusalem, with a very great train of camels bearing spices, gold, and precious stones. Holding her head erect, she endeavored to impress upon her features, radiant with joy, the dignity befitting her station, talking to herself as she rode.

"Thy mother calls thee," said a voice, just before her. Queen and camels and spices vanished. She looked up and saw Passe Rose. "Run, quick! I will care for the horse."

The child slid to the ground in terror, her thoughts divided between the reality and the dream. Would her mother then punish the Queen of Sheba? and gathering the skirt of her dress in her hand, she ran with all her might towards the house. She had not disappeared under the leafage of the oaks before Passe Rose was in her place, and the feet of Gesualda's palfrey were echoing on the road to Aix.

XXI.

At the foot of the tower by the ford of the Wurm the waters lie still and deep. A lance, hurled by a strong arm into the heart of the pool, disappears its entire length, then rebounds, falls sidewise, turns slowly in the eddy, shoots into the channel next the bank, past every root and hollow where it would pause, till it reaches the crescent of sand below. Here the waters, tired of their toy, cast it up on the bar, and hurry on over a broad slant of pebbles. This year's blossom or last year's leaf, the dead or the living, the Wurm treats all alike.

Reeling from the edge of the tower, it seemed to Rothilde that the river leaped up to embrace her. She put out her hands, turned in mid-air, saw the sky twinkling with stars, — then everything disappeared. Her feet were entangled in her cloak. She straightened her limbs to free them from its folds, shutting her mouth and bracing the muscles of her chest and throat against the pressure which strangled her. At last the stars appeared again ; she could breathe once more. Her hands were free, and she struggled blindly for the shore. But the river was not done with her. It whirled her round like a straw in its eddy, sucked her down where it left the pool, drove her past root and stem at which she clutched, till, tired of its plaything, it pushed it aside on the shallow, and ran rippling over the shingle.

The instant her feet touched the sand she knew she was saved. Those terrible visions which crowd upon the eyes confronted by sudden death, and which for the moment seem the only realities, were gone, and all the energy of life, its hopes and fever, were hers again. Breathless and spent, shivering with the chill of the river, bewildered, as one waking from a nightmare, but safe, she crawled to the top of the bar, laughing hysterically. "Nay, not yet, not yet," she repeated to herself. She unwound from her feet the cloak which trailed behind her, leaving a glistening track upon the sand, and wrung the water from her silver-braided dress. The tower rose among the trees, — what a leap! The girl had worsted her. "Wait, wait," she cried through her chattering teeth, loosening her clinging dress, "my time is not yet come." As she broke her way through the bushes which fringed the shore, a sharp pain

smote her in the breast, — the chill of the water,
she thought. If the horse were still there, she
would warm her blood with such a gallop as the
page never dreamed of. Dieu, the pain again!
Her bosom was wet, not with water, but with
something slimy, which stuck to her fingers.
Had the girl struck her? It was not possible;
she felt herself strong, — the strength of ten
lives! Crossing an open space, she held up her
hand in the starlight. Aye, it was blood; it
ran down her wrist. She opened her dress to
see whence it came. A mere scratch, — let it
bleed: it was blood shed for the king; every
drop the heart lost would buy what it desired.
She tore the shreds of her neckerchief from her
throat, rolled them together, and pressed them
within her robe, hurrying on through the wood.
As the tower appeared between the trees, she
paused to listen. The horse was still there, —
she could hear it browsing in the grass; there
was no other sound, and she stepped out cautiously from behind the trunk of a tree. The
horse lifted its head and neighed. She held out
her hand, speaking softly, cajolingly, till the
rein was in her grasp. In a quarter hour she
would be with the king! She led the horse
along the bank, for the space between the river
and the trees was narrow and the branches
hung low, and on reaching the road sprang for

the saddle. But the hand which grasped the
mane gave way, and she fell back with a cry of
pain. The blood trickled into her palm again.
Had the girl cut her arm? She had felt nothing, yet it was from there the blood came. Rolling back the sleeve, she turned her arm to the
light. Aye, the wound was there. She tore a
strip from her dress, and, holding one end between her teeth, knotted it above the wrist,
twisting it tightly with a broken branch. With
but one hand, she could not fasten the knot se-
curely. In spite of every effort it slipped and
loosened. Abandoning the attempt, she stepped
upon a stone, and climbed to the saddle. The
horse, feeling the pressure of her knees, bounded
forward. It was not so easy to hold her seat as
when galloping with the page. She turned the
mare's head into the road which led to Frankenburg, through the wood, and which joined
the highway without the eastern gate, where, if
need were, she might enter the city. What secret apprehension, what presentiment of peril,
brought this to mind she would not confess;
she only knew that at every leap a lance-like
pain caught her breath. Holding her arm close
to her face, she strained her eyes to see how it
fared; but the shadow of the overhanging trees
was so dense she could discern nothing. She
could endure the pain no longer, and drew the

rein to slacken the pace. From time to time,
a feeling of sinking made her fingers clutch the
mane, and a horrible misgiving that she was
fainting, dying, oppressed her. The horse was
walking now; if she could but reach the gate!
Cursed blood! oozing through the bandage,
running into her palm, dripping from her fingers, like a living thing. God! was it possible?
to vanquish the river only to see life ebb under
her eyes, drop by drop! The thought of her
arm filled her with rage; she wished to strike
it, to cut it off. Hark! the midnight bell in
the king's chapel. The gate must be close by.
Aye, she could hear the voice of the watch crying the hour in the palace court. With a desperate calm she rewound the bandage and tight-
ened the knot, then held her arm aloft to dimin-
ish the flow. As the gate loomed up before her,
the horse started back, nearly throwing her from
her seat, and she saw two forms hurrying away
in the darkness. "Help!" she cried, turning
in the saddle. The tones of her own voice,
wavering beyond control in her throat, frightened her. "Help!" But no answer came
back. "Cowards!" she muttered through her
set teeth, and still holding her arm aloft, clinging to the saddle with the other, she passed
under the gate. Not a soul was in sight, and
the echo of the horse's feet beat back and forth

between the walls. The pain was gone, but a sensation of suffocation oppressed her. She had forgotten the king now; all her desire was for instant relief. It seemed to her that she could not longer retain her hold; that she must slide to the ground, where she might fix her arms against something firm, to get relief for her laboring lungs. The horse was turning into the square, and she fastened her eyes upon a light shining before her. It looked so far! Feeling no rein, the horse wandered from the direct course, lifting its head intelligently for some sign. She made an effort to guide it with her knees, and at the same instant a spasm of suffocation so terrible attacked her that she cried out, forgetting everything, and sliding to the ground, where she supported herself upon her hands, like the wounded gladiator dying from loss of blood, and lifting himself with a last gasp for air above the sand of the arena. At that moment, from the basilica where the light shone came the response of the clerks: " O Christ, save Karle." Refreshed as by a draught of wine she raised her head and opened her eyes. Where was she ? Overhead a single star gazed steadfastly at her; and about it, in narrowing circles, swept its myriad fellows, — oh, so fast, so fast! a whirlpool of stars, shouting in her ears, " Christ, save Karle!" long after her wide-open eyes had ceased to see.

It was then that Brother Dominic, returning from midnight service in the king's oratory, as he hastened across the square, saw a horse trembling with fear, and sniffing at something lying at its feet. Hurrying to the spot, the monk stooped above it. Jesu! the woman of Immaburg! Her eyes stared at him fixedly. Distraught, not knowing what to do, Brother Dominic wrung his hands, ran a little space, crying, "Succor! succor!" returned, lifted the body in his arms, and staggered towards the palace gate. A groan escaped the woman's lips. He had taken her awkwardly, and she slipped from his grasp. He laid her down, bending his ear to the bloodless lips. Faint with horror and fasting, he began to run once more, crying, "Succor! succor!" Men with torches were issuing from the guard-room under the archway. "Ho! this way! Succor!" cried Brother Dominic, out of breath.

The Gascon was first on the spot. "God's wounds!" he exclaimed, holding the torch above his head, and recognizing Rothilde.

His comrades crowded about him with excited speech : —

"Loosen her girdle."

"She is dead."

"I saw her enter with the page."

"Nay, she rode out again."

"Stand off, — give her air!" cried the Gascon, pushing them back. "Fetch water, quick!"

"She hath water enough," said one, aiding him to unfasten her girdle.

"Look, she bleeds. Hold thy torch here. Some one hath stabbed her!" exclaimed the Gascon. "The monk, the monk!"

Brother Dominic had not stirred from the spot where he stood. To his sensitive vision, a supreme egoism, the egoism of a soul which sees in every phenomenon the interference of God in its behalf or the effort of Satan to entrap it, rendered every event a phase of that fierce struggle between the powers of good and evil for his possession. He watched with anguish this desperate combat, whose issue involved his spiritual destiny. To his soul, concentrated upon itself, alert to every influence, impersonating its own impulses, penetrated by the sublime conviction of its dignity, life was an expanding circle centred in his own individual experience. For God had opened his eyes. He had been environed by wonders, and he had not known it. Spirits, palpable, visible, surrounded him, and he had not seen them. They were within him, rousing every evil desire, and bringing to shame a life of consecration. They were without him: by the wayside as he journeyed; in the goldsmith's daughter, who took from his very hand the papers with which he had been intrusted; in the woman of Immaburg, whose compelling presence enslaved his will, distilling sweet but noxious perfumes from her hair, lighting in her garnet girdle unholy fires, luring him through her lips with unhallowed promises. Aye, God had opened his eyes; he, who thought himself the least of all with whom he mingled, was the prize for which they contended. Glad to escape from that spacious chamber which had formerly been his pride, where lingered the odor of a *cendal* tissue, whose walls were ever whispering to him, " Be discreet, and I will pay thee in what coin thou wilt," he had consecrated himself anew in the gloom and chill of the king's chapel. Even while he prayed, struggling to put his foot on the neck of his infirmity, a pearl chaplet gleamed before his shut eyes; and when he raised them aloft, imploring succor, the brooch shining on the mantle of the shadowy form in the king's tribune seemed the eye of God fastened upon him. Above all else he yearned for his narrow cell at Maestricht. Sitting at his desk by its window, he had often longed to follow the birds, resting for a moment on the apple branch within reach of his hand to disappear in the far mysterious horizon. The way had appeared hard then; but it was the way to heaven. Horrified as he was by the spectacle before his eyes, he

felt that God had come to his aid. The pride
of beauty and the lust of flesh, — these had almost gotten the mastery of him; and he saw
them prostrate in the mire of the street. Surely
God trampled his adversaries under-foot. The
joy of an immense deliverance broke into praise
at the very moment when the soldiers seized
him, and every emotion was swallowed up in the
exultation of spiritual victory.

"Bind him fast," cried the Gascon; "let him
not escape!"

Brother Dominic, offering no resistance, was
smiling. Would God indeed measure the depth
of his repentance as he had tried the faith of the
martyrs? For through stripes and suffering
even those who had offended him became his
friends, and thus the martyrs had gained their
crowns.

"Aïe, aïe," said the soldier, binding his
wrists, "a monk stab a woman!"

XXII.

On dismounting at the ford of the Wurm,
Sergius and his companion had left their horses
to browse in the forest. Feeding quietly among
the reeds, the latter had strayed to the pool
where Passe Rose had set her jar, for there the
grass, moistened by the trickling water, grew

rank and tender. Close by lay the body of
Friedgis.

Suddenly the leader drew back, trembling, its
nostrils inflated, ears bent forward, and tail extended ; then wheeled, communicating its terror
to its fellow, and plunged through the brakes.

One would be at a loss to know what death
is, were the representations of the mind, com-
plex and mysterious as is the mind itself, its
only witnesses. A gasp for air when the spirit
lies in stupor ? A liberation from the wants of
the body ? An usher at a door? A realmless
king, slighted by love, mocked by ambition, defied
by a swaggering nobody ? An enemy, before
whose approach " life is an organized retreat,"
turning to victory at the final rout? But death
will wear none of these guises. To-day, as on
the first day, it appears under one simple aspect
— the corpse upon the bier, a form no longer
human, not yet material, inspiring the same terror which the horse felt when the nameless odor
of this which had once subjugated him and
which he had loved reached his nostrils in the
wet grass, and he bounded panic-stricken
through the wood.

" This way," said the soldier, stumbling over
the uneven ground.

" Where art thou ? " replied the prior, groping behind in the darkness.

"Here, to thy left. Have a care, — there is a pool. Damnèd horses! they have escaped us."

" Listen," said Sergius, turning his ear to the wind ; " we have passed the spot."

" Nay, nay, this way ; I remember," cried his companion, continuing his search, and uttering an oath at every obstacle.

Embarrassed by his robe, Sergius followed in the direction indicated, till, caught in a thicket whose stems stabbed his face at every movement, he was forced to stop. " Where art thou?" he asked again. Receiving no answer, he made another effort to extricate himself ; then paused again to listen. At some distance he heard a noise of breaking bushes, but the sounds seemed behind him. The leaves trembled in the fresh air of night, and the water from the spring trickled between the stones. " It were best to follow the stream," he thought to himself; "it must lead to the river ;" and, stooping, he felt his way with his hands. But the gurgle of the water was lost in the leaves' rustle, which resembled the murmur of the river, now before, now behind him. " Hola!" he cried, rising to his feet, bewildered. In a space which a swallow traverses with a single beat of its wing he was lost as completely as in an immense wilderness. No longer knowing whither he went, he hurried forward, changing his course unconsciously at every barrier, and stopping from time to time in a vain endeavor to reason.

At last his feet sank in the marshy ground, and he observed that reeds had succeeded the thicket. He must be near the river. As he advanced cautiously over the miry soil, the trees became more scattered and a clear space of stars opened overhead, his foot struck the sand, and he heard the wash of water. Traversing the wood parallel to the river, he had struck the latter far below the ford. He hastened to the bank; for a moment the Wurm appeared to him to be flowing in the wrong direction. He struggled slowly through the dense growth which lined the shore, not daring to trust himself beyond hearing of the water, following the windings of the stream. When he reached the spot where Rothilde had dragged herself from the current, signs of dawn were in the east. So slow and exhausting was his progress through the bushes which choked the bank that, seeing the opposite bank was more open, he crossed over by the bar jutting out into the shallows. From the meadow the tower was visible in the gray dawn. At every sound he paused to listen. Where was his companion? Fool! they should have kept together. When the wind sighed

and the rubbing branches creaked, he thought
he heard the whinny of a horse, — a horse which
followed his voice as a dog hugs the heel of a
shepherd, and which had deserted him like a
wild colt when minutes were precious! At the
ford he plunged in unhesitatingly, although the
water was deep. "It is not far," he thought,
shivering, for the stream was cold.

When he reached the gate, day was come and
the streets were filled with people. He sought
his lodging by circuitous ways, for his robe was
torn, and its skirt wet and stained with mire.
From the preparations he saw on every side he
divined the coming of Pepin. From the court-
yard of the abbot of Fontenelle issued a tumult
of voices. Profiting by the confusion, and resolved upon first interrogating Brother Dominic, he drew his hood over his face, and, slipping through the crowd unobserved, gained the
monk's chamber. The room was empty. A
candle, burned to the socket, stood on the table;
the bed was undisturbed. From the window he
saw gathered the abbot's followers, and, not
daring again to risk observance, determined to
wait till the train should pass out. As he
barred the door he saw at his feet something
which glistened, — a black pearl! That it was
one which belonged to Rothilde's fillet he was
sure. He endeavored to recall her as she stood

at the tower door in the starlight: had she
worn the fillet that night? Holding the pearl
in his hand, he felt the perspiration start in
beads from his forehead. The night's mischance,
like a little cloud before the sun, casting a
shadow out of all proportion to its size, had
filled him with anxiety and alarm. Tortured by
uncertainty, every event assumed importance.
What devil's imp directed them! He had taken
a serf for a servant, and this stolid fellow,
with the shoulders of an ox, had the eyes of a
ferret; or did the girl lie? Her mocking smile
haunted him. He had chosen her for her wit;
had she outwitted him? He had sought to turn
her passion to his purpose; had she purposes
of her own? With what eagerness she demanded Friedgis' life, like a tigress lapping
blood! Did she really fear him? If, as she
asserted, he had followed her to the church of
St. Marcellus, why had she gone to the hunt?
What! he tracks her from the church to the
palace, asks for the king, and again for the
queen, and she rides unconcerned to the chase
at Frankenburg? It was incredible. Why then
did she thirst so for his life? They were of the
same race; did they perchance know each other?
thought the prior. And the Greek failed him at
the decisive moment! But for his delay this had
been the very night; and now the papers were

in the hands of the king's captain. What fiend's luck had sent this captain to Maestricht! And a multitude of forgotten details crowded upon the prior's recollection, — Gui's inquiry at the abbey for Passe Rose, the latter's disappearance, her presence at Immaburg, where Rothilde had seen her with the monk. "So," thought the prior, looking at the pearl in his hand and thinking of Brother Dominic, " thou also hast passions and purposes."

Without, the tumult had ceased, and he resolved to gain his own room. The day was passing, and he had much to do. Not to risk something was to lose everything. He had drawn the bolt and his hand was on the door, when it trembled under the blow of a sword. He recoiled a step, his fingers closed on the pearl ; the door was thrust open, and the Gascon stood on the threshold. His sword was in his hand, and others pressed behind him. The prior stood speechless ; he had the appearance of a mute, whose emotions betray themselves only by convulsive expressions of the face.

" Ah, Monseigneur," cried the Gascon, uncovering himself as he advanced, " we were seeking thee everywhere. The monk that was with thee hath stabbed a woman of the princesses' household. We have him fast, and he sends for thee."

For a moment the prior experienced an intense joy, the satisfaction of having escaped an imminent peril, before which every preoccupation vanished. "It is not possible," he said, with a foolish smile. "What woman?"

"If thou wilt come with us, Monseigneur, I will show thee," pursued the Gascon, leading the way, and eager to relate his story. "We were of the watch at the palace gate. There came a cry from without" —

"What woman?" repeated Sergius, following the Gascon's hurried step. His agitation had returned again.

"The Saxon whom the queen brought with her from Ehresberg. Dead, Monseigneur, dead. She came from Frankenburg with a page after sundown. The page says she went out again. Well, there was a cry, and we ran out. She lay in the square midway, between the gate and the church; the monk stood over her. Her garments were soaked with blood, like water, — aye, and there was water, too. We bore her to the guard-room, and laid her on the trencher, thinking her dead. Suddenly her eyes opened, like a spring. I asked her who had done her injury. With that she raised herself, and cried, 'The king! the king!' Then her lips curled from her teeth, and she fell back, dead, Monseigneur, dead, like that," and the Gascon

clacked his tongue, making a quick gesture of
the hand.

"Dead?" repeated Sergius. "It is not possible, — it is not possible."

"Aye, and from a little cut on the wrist, no
bigger than a thorn would make. But the
water, Monseigneur, the water, — how explain
that? She was drenched, like a ewe fallen into
a pit. The monk answers nothing, yet his robe
is smeared with blood. The devil is in it, — I
will tell thee why. There came a girl to-night,
with an old woman, asking for the captain, Gui
of Tours, the same who was hurt by the boar
yesterday. For a jest, Monseigneur, just for a
jest, thinking her some wench late abroad, I
caught her by the waist, and I swear to thee
her touch was fire. Before I could loose her
she had gotten from me that the captain was
at Frankenburg, — the words slipped from my
tongue like a tear from an eye. But I saw her
face, — oh, I saw it well. Dost thou remember
the day I came with the captain to Maestricht,
— when this monk returned with us? As we
went down the hill, a demon appeared to him in
the hedge by the roadside, — a demon having
the form of a young girl. It is likely enough,
for when the captain returned from pursuing
her he was like a man in wine. I tell thee,
Monseigneur, this selfsame girl — witch or girl

I know not — came to Immaburg, whether for the captain or the monk, I cannot say. As I stood in the court waiting for the women — it was the night we came hither — the captain issued from the chapel with the girl in his arms. I thought her then certainly to be flesh and blood, and made a place for her, as the captain bade me. But on the road, by the ford of the Wurm, she escaped, like a smoke. For two hours we searched; not a trace. Hard by is a tower, where, they say, demons congregate. Well, — wilt thou believe it? — it was this girl that came to-night. Here, Monseigneur, this way."

The court of the palace was thronged with people gazing at the horsemen of the king's guard, drawn up within and waiting for the order to set out on the road to Colonia, by which the King of Italy was approaching. To escape the crowd, the Gascon entered the guard-room by a side door. A few soldiers and attendants, on whose faces were blended expressions of curiosity and apprehension, were whispering together in low, excited tones as they entered. Seeing the prior's robe, those nearest him drew back, signed themselves, and ceased their conversation. Following his conductor, Sergius advanced without regarding them. At the threshold of the adjoining room the Gascon paused.

" Enter, Monseigneur," he said, lifting the curtain. The prior took a step forward, and stood still. Before him was a table surrounded by women, and on the table a body, partially naked. Seeing the priest, one of the women spread a cloth hastily over the body, and drew it to the chin. Vessels of water and spiced wine stood on the floor near the wall. Sergius saw everything, yet he had not taken his eyes from the heap of clothing on which they were fixed : a dress soaked with water ; a sandal, its silver lacings soiled with mud, protruding from an under-tunic stiffened with blood ; and fragments of a tissue veil. And suddenly, out of that stained, disordered heap, Rothilde rose before him, as he had seen her sitting on the lid of the king's sarcophagus, warm with life, the veil about her throat, the fillet in her hair, her eyes shining upon him from between the folds of her head-cloth. As if fearful of awakening some one asleep, the women drew back on tiptoe, transformed by the presence of death, — death, so common yet so wonderful, so simple yet so mysterious. With a deep-drawn breath, the prior looked up to the face on which the candles shone. No trace of terror, pain, or passion disfigured it. A serenity no sleep can counterfeit, no emotion could disturb, reigned there. Yet this face, this form outlined under the sinister drapery of the linen drawn over the limbs, had no reality for him ; he saw only the slender, supple figure balanced on the edge of the king's sarcophagus, the face insolent with joy, whose eyes menaced him by the tower on the Wurm.

" Monseigneur," said a voice behind him.

At its sound these visions vanished, and the reality was before him — clay to be washed and anointed with spices. *She* was not there. Where, then ? Did she see him now ?

" Monseigneur."

The prior turned quickly. The Gascon stood in the doorway, and behind him the chief of the king's pages. Why did they observe him so ? They stood aside as he passed out, and he crossed the guard-room to the door by which he had entered. Against this door leaned a soldier, who looked at the wet skirt of his robe as he approached.

" Show me to the monk," he said, turning to the Gascon. He thought the latter followed him, but now he perceived that he was alone in the middle of the room.

" Monseigneur," said the Gascon, with a politeness which affected him strangely, " it is no longer the monk who desires to see thee."

" Who, then ? " stammered the prior.

" Monseigneur, the king."

XXIII.

The king had risen from table and entered his cabinet.

One might have known this from the murmur of voices in the dining-hall, indicating that the officers of the palace had succeeded their royal master at table ; for when the king was eating, the silence of the room was broken only by those who served, and by the voice of the clerk on the estrade, reading from the Frankish chronicles or the works of the saints. One might have known it also from the demeanor of those who crossed the court without. The boldest inmate of the palace, seeing the curtain drawn aside from the circular window over the south portal, hurried about his business with the conscious air of one who is observed; for this window was like the lens of a telescope, and this curtain like the cap which covers the lens. When the curtain was drawn aside, one knew the king's eye was there.

A single door, covered by a tapestry sown with lions and bordered with marigolds, gave access to the room from the royal sleeping-chamber. A chair standing habitually in the embrasure of the window, a stool and reading-desk near the chair, a wooden bench beside the fireplace, and two cushions of silk on the floor were its only furniture. Smoke had darkened the rafters overhead, their gilded edges and the rosettes painted in orange on the pale sea-green of the intervening spaces being scarcely visible. A single window, too, lighted the room; but this window redeemed it. Gloomy and dark within as the tube of the telescope, through this its lens one saw, below, the court; above, beyond the roofs, a green circle of wooded hills; and, higher still, the heaven-fields, which the king loved to scan at night, when the watchman cried the hours to the stars.

Spread open upon the reading-desk lay the king's favorite book, the City of God of St. Augustine, from which a clerk was reading aloud in slow, monotonous tones, glancing between the periods from the immobile figure in the chair to a young girl, who, seated on the cushion at its feet, caught every word as it fell from his lips. A tunic of white silk shot with silver threads, which glistened like frost, reached to her feet, and descended in rolls to the wrists, where it ended in broad bands of fine pearls. A like band terminated the garment at her throat, and still another, narrower, but with larger pearls, spaced at equal intervals, confined a thin veil about the temples. This veil, covering the hair and shoulders, and embroidered with flowers of a lustrous white silk, sparkled in the sun, which, now nearly vertical, began to enter the window, creeping slowly up the carved pillars of the king's chair to the crystal balls which terminated its arms. Her hands clasped about her knee, her eyes riveted upon the reader's face, the young girl listened intently, unmindful of the king's gaze, her whole attention absorbed by what she heard.

"Who, indeed, can enumerate all the great grievances with which human society abounds in the misery of this mortal state? Who can weigh them? Hear how one of their comic writers makes one of his characters express the common feeling of all men in this matter: 'I am married: this is one misery. Children are born to me: they are additional cares.' What shall I say of the miseries of love, which Terence also recounts? — 'slights, suspicions, quarrels.'"

Sighing at these words, as if they were her own utterance, the listener lifted her eyes to the king, and, seeing his clear, penetrating gaze fixed upon her, blushed, and turned her face to the window.

Her body was frail, and slender as a flower's stem, and his rugged and robust, like a stout blade beaten into shape under the blows of a forging hammer; the eyes of each were great and gray, but hers soft as a falcon in mew, and his keen as a hawk trussing; her skin, softer than the tissue of her silken garment, was scarcely less white, and his, bronzed by many winds and suns, was darker than the brown moustache, which, thick and strong like the brows and hair, overshadowed the firm lines of the mouth. Where the subtle likeness between the two hid were hard to say, though it struck the shallowest observer at a glance.

His hands resting on the crystal balls, the king watched the averted face, while the voice of the reader pursued its even way: —

" Who ought to be, or who are, more friendly than those who live under the same roof ? And yet, who can rely even upon this friendship, seeing that secret treachery has often destroyed it, producing enmity even more bitter than the amity was sweet " —

"Turn over some pages," said the clear voice of the king. It was scarcely four years since the conspiracy of his first-born.

Startled by this interruption, the clerk hastened to obey, fumbling the leaves of the manuscript between his thick fingers, and casting furtive glances from its yellow pages to the king, — that king so imposing to the historian, the creator rather than the product of an epoch, greater in authentic annals than in the epics to

which his greatness gave rise, a sun shining between the two nights of barbarism and feudality.

At the sound of the king's voice, the young
girl had looked up quickly, but the eyes she
sought were far away upon the hills. Of what
was he thinking? Of that nest of Bavarian
hate and perfidy mothered by Luitberg, who
had never forgotten his insult to her race in the
divorce of her sister and the overthrow of the
house of Lombardy? But this nest of conspiracy had been destroyed, and its inmates had
followed the Lombard kings and the dukes of
Aquitania into the tomb of the monastery. Did
he hear beyond those hills, from the heart of
Germany, the sullen murmur of moving peoples?
But this murmur was hushed. One by one his
environing enemies, Saxon, Tartar, and Slav on
the north and east, Lombard, Saracen, and
Aquitanian on the south and west, holding
France as in the jaws of a vise, had been reduced to vassalage. The Saxon dream of inde-
pendence was over, and their tireless leader, discouraged at last by reverses, had been baptized
at Attigny. Thrice conquered, the Huns lay
powerless between the newly constituted duchies
of Frioul and Bavaria. Not in vain had the
Holy Pontiff appealed to the Frankish monarch;
he feared no longer to see the Saracen under the
walls of Rome, or the galleys of Irene in the

Bay of Tarentum. Irene herself trembled in
her palace of Byzantium; for the tread of
Frankish horsemen was heard on the banks of
the Save, and terror reigned in Thrace and
Macedonia.

Although the clerk, having discovered a more
agreeable chapter, continued tranquilly his reading, the king was apparently not listening. Did
he see beyond those hills the shadows of great
disasters yet below the horizon? But the Western Church and State were unifying, their Eastern rivals disintegrating. If this church was
still blinded by superstition, if this monarchy
was still weighted by abuses, yet decay had
given place to organization, sterility to life; if
this kingdom was yet to be torn in fragments,
its hitherto fluctuating boundaries had become
fixed. The sun rose on a world of hope. The
prophetic dream of the Thuringian Bazine,
mother of Clovis, on the night of her nuptials,
had been fulfilled, — her race had descended into
the cloister, then the sepulchre of incompetency
and fallen greatness; and now was being accomplished that other prophecy, of Strabo, who foresaw in Gaul the seat of a great empire.

Ordinarily, the king observed with interest
what was passing in the court below, now filling
with the motley concourse of strangers come to
witness the approaching *fêtes*. The vast build-

ings surrounding the palace, erected for the accommodation of those who for any cause of interest or shelter flocked to the royal residence, overflowed with visitors from every part of the kingdom, curious to see the booty and captives which the young King of Italy brought his father. Never had the city swarmed with so many people, never had so many illustrious personages gathered in the capital of the western world. Neustrian and Austrasian lords, who for so long had mutually despised each other, the one for his effeminacy, the other for his barbarism, now united under a single sway, mingled freely with polished Southern nobles and blunt warriors from provinces beyond the Rhine. The most extravagant stories of the riches of the *ring*, plundered by the victorious Pepin, circulated from mouth to mouth; descriptions of the Hunnish captives, their savage appearance, braided locks, and dress of furs, were on every tongue. One could scarcely wait to see these spoils of conquest, to gloat over these haughty prisoners. Tables were being placed in the streets, before the doors of the houses; the buildings were being decorated with colored cloths; and from the lofty poles erected between the palace and the gate of Colonia were to be displayed enormous paintings, representing the history of the world from the temptation of Paradise to the present time.   Already workmen were preparing in the great square the tribunes from which the court was to witness the entry, and trenchers at which the army was to feast by torchlight after the Te Deum in the basilica of the Mother of God. These streets were soon to be strewn with flowers, these tables to be covered with chased dishes filled with meats and running with wine, this square to resound with shouts of rejoicing; and every eye was beginning to glitter with the feverish light of impatience and expectation.

So many people circulated about the gate and filled the court that none gave heed to a girl, who, pressing through this concourse of curious loiterers, made her way to the door under the south gallery, where the guards with difficulty prevented the crowd from invading the palace itself.   She had dismounted from her horse in the street, and, guided by the exclamations and fragmentary sentences of those about her, advanced resolutely to the bronze gates, where the crowd was densest.   These gates opened upon the spacious stairway leading from the gallery to the audience chamber.

"They say the king is there," said one, pointing to the window above.

"Is it true the army is but a day's march — Seigneur! take thine elbows from my ribs!" exclaimed another to his neighbor, who was forcing his way excitedly towards the soldier guarding the door.

"Let him pass!" cried a third, holding back. "I heard him tell an officer that his wife was lost in the press."

Passe Rose turned, and saw Werdric. He also recognized her, but at the same moment a cry arose from behind, and the surge of the crowd swept them asunder. This cry was due to the opening of the gates leading to the stables, whence a troop of horse issued into the court, already thronged. It was the royal guard going out to meet the young king on the road to Colonia. Beset by the swaying mass and excited by the tumult, the horses threatened to trample those nearest them under foot, and their leader called to those about the gates to clear a passage with their lances. Seeing the attention of all diverted and the bronze doors momentarily deserted, Passe Rose pushed the heavy panel far enough to slip within, and without pause or deliberation ran up the broad stairs she saw before her. At their summit extended a long corridor, down which she advanced hurriedly, till the clamor of many voices and the metallic ring of dishes caused her to retreat. Passing thus quickly from the noise and light without into the gloom and solitude within, she heard every heartbeat, and felt her courage desert her. At the sound of approaching footsteps, she began to run, and at the first door she met glided behind its tapestry screen. This door gave access to the great hall where the noble youth of the kingdom assembled to listen to the teachings of the school of the palace, and adjoined the private apartments of the king. Passe Rose had no sooner lifted the curtain than she saw a page, who, sitting on the floor at the entrance of the passage to the king's chamber, was amusing himself with a parchment, from which hung a multitude of tasseled strings. Seeing that she was observed, she went forward timidly, gaining courage, however, at sight of the pretty face of the boy. The latter, whose duty it was to summon the chaplain when the king had finished his reading, occupying himself with no business but his own, evinced only a lively curiosity in the young girl, whose presence promised to relieve the tedium of his waiting. Passe Rose, on her side, having no fear of a boy, approached with all the unconcern she could affect, smiling, her eyes fixed upon the silken fringe, but alert for every sound.

"What hast thou there?" she asked, stooping over the parchment in the boy's hands.

"The Oracle of Truth," he replied, looking up into her face.

"The Oracle?" whispered Passe Rose, glancing sidewise through the doorway. "Pray what is that?"

"Choose one of these strings," said the boy. Passe Rose reached out her hand. "Nay, shut thine eyes, then choose, and I will tell thee what will befall."

"Canst thou read?" asked Passe Rose, observing the characters on the parchment.

"Nay, but I know the answers by heart. This one with the blue string reads thus: ' Beware: after honey, gall!' But choose; only close thine eyes."

Forgetting for the moment her purpose, and fascinated by the mysterious parchment, Passe Rose shut her eyes, and, first signing herself, touched one of its pendent strings. "What is it?" she asked, opening her eyes and bending forward with anxiety.

The boy clapped his hands, laughing. "The yellow, the yellow! What luck! See,"—pointing with his finger, — "' A great happiness is on its way to thee.'"

Passe Rose stood up, her eyes dilating, her bosom swelling. She could not speak. This great hall was not large enough for her to breathe in. Stooping quickly, she kissed the boy's face, then disappeared in the corridor which led to the chamber of the king.

"Ho! Knowest thou not he is within?"

called the page. Passe Rose neither paused nor
turned. "Ho, I tell thee!" he called again,
springing to his feet. But Passe Rose had already disappeared. "Seigneur!" cried the boy,
terrified by such audacity, and running across
the hall to tell the chief of the pages that a
strange girl had entered the sleeping-chamber of
the king.

On emerging from the obscurity of the passage-
way into the light, Passe Rose was still smiling.
She paused a moment on the threshold of the
chamber, then stepped upon its mosaic floor, and
stood still again. The room was empty, yet, as
when gazing at the altar in the chapel of Immaburg, sure of some invisible presence, she
searched its length and breadth, her heart beating fast with expectation, and her members numb
with awe. Before her was the king's bed, low and
wide, with its ermine cover and pillows of broidered silk, partly concealed by curtains hung from
swinging rods. On the floor beside it stretched
the red skin of a fox, and upon the table stood
the king's cup and the candelabrum, whose six
candles of wax indicated the hour of the day;
for the king had not yet received the famous
brass water-clock, damaskeened with gold, pre-
sented to him by the Caliph Aroun-al-Raschid,
whose falling balls sounded the hours night and
day. Three of these candles were already con-

sumed ; it would therefore be more than an hour
before the king would send for his chaplain.
From the bed Passe Rose's eyes followed the
tapestry which hid the wall to the height of her
shoulders, and above which a carved shelf made
the circuit of the apartment.   Behind the objects
upon this shelf the walls displayed flowers,
painted in red and yellow and other colors, of
such marvelous forms and hues that Passe Rose
could think of nothing but the beautiful fields of
Paradise.   Moreover, above the door opposite
her she saw an image of the blessed St. Martin,
who divided his cloak with a beggar ; and the
face of this image, rudely carved though it was,
certainly smiled upon her, while its lips, albeit
of wood, moved visibly, as if saying, " A great
happiness is on its way to thee."   Persuaded
that the saint really addressed her, she approached, her two hands crossed upon her bosom, when she perceived that the sounds came
from within the door, and suddenly —

" Turn over some pages," said a clear voice,
as it were at her very side.

She started back, but catching sight again of
the encouraging countenance of the saint, murmured a quick prayer, and advancing to the door
laid her ear close to the golden lions of the tapestry.   Some one was speaking.   She held her
breath, and listened.

" But now as regards loftiness of place, it is altogether ridiculous to be so influenced by the fact that the demons inhabit the air, and we the earth, as to think that on that account they are to be put before us ; for in this way we put all the birds before ourselves. But the birds, when they are weary with flying, or require to repair their bodies with food, come back to the earth to rest or to feed, which the demons, they say, do not. Are they therefore inclined to say that the birds are superior to us, and the demons superior to the birds ? But if it be madness to think so, there is no reason why we should think that, on account of their inhabiting a loftier element, the demons have a claim to our religious submission."

This passage excited in Passe Rose so lively an interest that she forgot everything. Her face flushed redder than the fabric next her cheek, and in her eagerness to catch every word she parted the fringe, revealing to the reader a pair of dark eyes, which glistened like dew-drops among the silk marigolds of the tapestry. Disconcerted by this apparition, the clerk paused.

" Read on," said the king sharply.

The clerk would have obeyed, but the place was lost ; in vain did he seek it with his finger, for he could not wrest his eyes from the girl's face ; so that the king, following his gaze, and turning quickly, discovered Passe Rose standing terrified in the doorway.

Whether because his face inspired confidence (for in the presence of some we are at our best, as in that of others every good quality deserts us without reason), or whether because her courage rose when put to the proof, no sooner did the king's eye meet hers than her terror left her, and with a firm step she advanced into the room, rendering gaze for gaze. She had taken no thought of what she should say, but, going in, she remembered how, when a little girl dancing before Queen Hildegarde at the Easter *fêtes*, a young chamberlain came with a message, and, bending upon one knee, said, "In the name of God, who suffered for us, I salute you;" and how the queen made answer, "In the name of God, who was our ransom, hail." These fine words came back to her and were on her lips as she approached, when, just beyond the king's chair, she saw Agnes of Solier, and stopped, mute and staring. A hundred times the space in which Passe Rose stood thus trembling like a tense bowstring would not suffice to tell all she felt and saw in that moment of silence, though in reality it was but the length of two breaths. All which before had seemed sure and easy became suddenly hopeless and of no avail, while every evil fear she had once lightly set aside was uppermost. How could she contend with a king's daughter? She had killed the queen's favorite! What if, as the prior had said, the papers were of other matters? Who would then believe her? Where were her witnesses? It was perhaps a dream, and she made a little movement of the fingers to feel whether the wounds caused by the Saxon's knife were still there; seeing at the same time the white hands of Agnes of Solier and her own, brown with toil and stained with blood. A confused recollection of what the clerk had read crossed her mind. "Demon of hell," whispered a voice in her ear, "the abbot, the prior, the monk, will swear to it, and the captain also, whom thou hast possessed." "Aye, whom I possess," she replied; and she heard the page saying to her, "A great happiness is on its way to thee." She repeated the words softly, "A great happiness, a great happiness," as if they could conjure away her fears, clinging with her eyes to the king, and resisting with all her strength the challenging gaze of Agnes of Solier. The latter, no less surprised than Passe Rose, stared back in wonder.

"Who art thou, and what dost thou wish?" asked the king, astonished at her sudden appearance and agitated face.

At the sound of his voice, the words broke like a torrent from Passe Rose's lips: "This one I found by the fish-ponds," — she had thrust the papers in his hand, — "and this the Saxon gave

the monk for the prior. Read, read!" and drawing the cord through the wax seal with her trembling fingers, she spread the parchment on his
knee. "I was in the tower; there came two,
the prior and another, — then the Saxon maid
who sat at supper at Immaburg. I heard what
they said. Look! there are the prints of her
knife! the knife was for thee."

"Peace!" exclaimed the king, rising to his
feet, and crushing the parchment in his hand.
It was a cry rather than a command, for inco-
herent as were the words he heard, they were
sharper than any knife to his pride. He stood
for a moment in doubt, and then, as if convinced
by the girl's fearless manner, sank back into his
chair, opening the papers slowly, and fixing
from time to time, as he read, a searching look
upon Passe Rose. Her heart was beating violently, but her fear was over, and she watched
the king's face boldly. Every trace of anger
and distress had fallen from it, as a mantle falls
from the shoulder to the ground. He neither
started nor frowned, as she had thought to see
him do; nevertheless, she was content, for his
eyes were good to look at, and she felt the happiness of which she had been foretold running,
as the tide runs in the sea-meadows, to her finger-tips. She wished to laugh aloud, to dance,
to sing, and at the same time tears of which

she could give no account dimmed her vision, causing the garnet in the clasp of the king's cloak to swell and glisten like a bubble of blood. She heard the clerk closing his book and retiring softly behind her, but when the king turned to Agnes of Solier with a sign that she should go also, Passe Rose reached out her hand.

"I pray thee let this lady listen," she said entreatingly.

Surprised beyond measure, the king knit his brow, looking from Passe Rose's eager face to the flushed countenance of Agnes of Solier, who had risen to her feet, and stood beside his chair, her hand resting upon his.

"Speak on," he said, feeling the hand trembling upon his own.

Anxious lest his patience should be exhausted, divided in her mind as to what was trivial and what important, Passe Rose began, — relating her meeting with Gui of Tours in the wood of Hesbaye, her adventure in the abbey and consultation with the sorceress (though this were a forbidden thing), and then her return to the abbey at midnight to tell Friedgis what the gospels had said, and how the captain had promised to seek the Saxon maid in the household of the king. "It was going down the hill after the prior was gone that I found the paper," she said, pointing to the parchment, "for the moon came up while I was hid."

So candid was her speech and so eager her haste that the king listened in silent wonder, though he saw her oft bewildered between two stories, one for him and one for Agnes of Solier. But here she paused, and a sob rose in her throat.

"Father and mother have I none," she continued, "because of the pest; and they being dead, I went wherever the wind blew, with dancing-girls and jugglers, — it was then I danced at Chasseneuil, before Queen Hildegarde, — and afterwards with merchants. But I parted from these at the fair of St. Denis because of a certain Greek," — here Passe Rose looked full at Agnes of Solier; "for love is like God's winds, coming at no man's bidding and dispelled by no command, except it be the Christ's, as told in the gospels. Afterwards, till now," — for the first time she hesitated, — "I lived with Werdric, the goldsmith of Maestricht, and his wife, Jeanne, till — till I came to Immaburg."

"What brought thee to Immaburg " — interrupted Agnes of Solier quickly.

The question was rude, and Passe Rose grew hot and cold by turns. A defiant light flashed in her eyes, but she kept them fixed upon the king. "If one should mock thee to thy face, what wouldst thou do ? " she said, lip and voice quivering together.

"By the Lord of heaven!" cried the king startled by this unexpected question, but liking well her boldness, "were I the stronger" —

"Nay, the weaker."

Perplexed, the king observed her in silence.

"When I returned from the abbey," continued Passe Rose in a hard voice, "the night was far gone, and the goldsmith met me at the garden gate. 'Wanton!' he said. For that reason," looking at Agnes of Solier, "I left my home, wandering two days in the wood of Hesbaye, and came to Immaburg, as thou sawest, not knowing where I was. There it was I first saw the Saxon maid. She came by stealth into the strangers' hall, and gave these papers to the monk as he sat by the fire, bidding him deliver them to the prior. Why I took them from him I know not, except it were God's will, for I thought no more of them till yesternight, being distraught at what the page told me."

"What did he tell thee?" asked Agnes of Solier.

"That thou wert a king's daughter, and betrothed to Gui of Tours."

The king's face flushed red, but Agnes of Solier, pale as the holy napkin, neither spoke nor stirred.

"What happened at supper thou knowest," continued Passe Rose.

" But what happened afterwards I know not ! "
cried Agnes of Solier, torn between her jealousy
and her pride.

" I am come to tell thee," answered Passe
Rose with dignity. " When thou wert gone, I
said to the captain, ' Though I were the meanest
slave in the kingdom, what God hath given the
king's daughter he hath given to me, and I
yield it to none except at his altar.' With that
I ran to the chapel to pray and seek counsel of
the priest. But because in my anger I had cast
down the image of the Virgin above my bed,
God would not listen to me; the priest at Immaburg is witness that he took away my senses,
and when I got them back I was in the wagon
on the high-road. Dost thou remember how the
stream was swollen at the ford? I was there,
and while they sounded the water I heard the
voices of women in the wagon next to mine.
One said that the heart of the captain was
plainly mine, and could not be had of me for
all the gold of the Huns."

" Insolent ! " murmured Agnes of Solier,
tightening her fingers on the king's hand. But
the king, chary of words, waited.

" Another," pursued Passe Rose, " replied
that it were easier for a dancing-girl to give herself to a captain than for a king's daughter to
forget an injury. ' Mark well what I tell thee.'

she said: 'one hath his heart; the other will have his head.' 'Liar!' I said to myself. 'What a king's daughter will do I know not, but what a dancing-girl can do I will show thee.' So, when the ford was passed, I cut a hole through the skins with my knife, and went mine own way."

A gesture of surprise escaped the king, who had risen from his chair, and was pacing slowly to and fro between the door and the window. At this moment the troop was filing through the archway into the square, and the Gascon, followed by the prior, was opening the wicket gate leading to the room where the body of Rothilde lay.

It were idle to deny that Passe Rose was conscious of the greatness of her action, for even the angels serve God with pleasure; and if it be that they rejoice over the sinner's repentance, some echo, as it were, of this rejoicing is borne to the soul which doeth well, for its encouragement and satisfaction. Yet so little did Passe Rose think to win applause that she mistook the king's gesture for a sign of impatience. "I am coming to it fast," she said, pointing to the parchment, and hurrying on to tell how she hid in the sheepfold, how Jeanne came bereft of reason and without the power to know her own, and all she saw and heard from the tower while Jeanne slept.

Not once during this recital did the king cease his walk or lift his eyes from the floor till Passe Rose told how Friedgis was slain; "I heard a sword drawn, and the rustle of leaves under foot; afterwards, from the wood, a cry — and then the Saxon maid said " —

She stopped short. The king stood before her, his brow knit as with pain and his face gloomy with suppressed passion. "Well, what said she?" he asked, fixing upon Passe Rose his piercing eye.

" ' Bring me now thy Greek, and I will show him the way to the king's bed.' "

The king drew himself up to his full height. For a moment he was silent, his eyes shining with points of flame. Then he struck his palms together, whispering a few words to the page who at this signal came in haste from the adjoining room, and, returning to the window, gazed thoughtfully into the court.

Passe Rose, motionless, stood speechless. It was one of those silences which one does not dare to break. "Continue," said the king at length, in a calm voice.

"When the Saxon was gone into the wood, the prior concerted with his companion how they should get the papers from the captain that night, by fair means or foul," pursued Passe Rose, stealing a glance at Agnes of Solier.

" ' Ask her where this captain lies,' said the soldier. 'Nay,' replied the prior, 'it will alarm her. Hist! she comes.' "

" Aye, she comes," murmured the king, beckoning to Passe Rose. "See."

Obeying his motion, she approached, holding her breath with the presentiment of impending shock. The throng had followed the troop into the square, and the court was empty. From the farther angle a litter, borne by soldiers, issued from the shadow of the gallery. Over the litter a cloth was spread, and on the cloth a cross glittered in the sun.

Passe Rose, leaning forward, drew a quick breath. "The Saxon!" she whispered.

"Slain, yesternight, by the monk."

"By the monk!" gasped Passe Rose.

"Yonder, in the square."

"Nay, it was I!" she cried vehemently, grasping the king's arm. "Look, the marks of her knife! My mother spake in her dreams when the prior was gone. I laid my hand to her mouth, but it was too late. Before I could get to my knees, she " — pointing to the bier — " was on the stair. I caught the blade in my hand as her blow fell, and then we locked, without breath to speak, she above, and I below. God is my witness I had done her no harm but that I knew she or I must die, and die I would not till the captain was warned, for the prior's words were in my ears. Time was lacking to pray, but I saw the stars, and strained leg and arm till her fingers gave way and my throat was free. Then I stood up alone — how it happened I know not, but I heard the waters splash, and, once, a cry." She stopped, her bosom heaving, her eyes fixed upon the litter. "Jesu!" she murmured, her voice falling to a whisper, " it was I."

The king regarded her in a stupor of wonder and admiration. He strode back and forth from wall to wall, looking now at Passe Rose, and now, uneasily, at Agnes of Solier, who, pale and speechless, stared back with eyes of stone. Suddenly, with an abrupt gesture, he stopped before Passe Rose.

" If the King of heaven gave thee thy heart's wish, what wouldst thou ask?"

"The reason of my mother Jeanne," said Passe Rose.

The king started. " I will ask it this day in my prayers. And of me " — his voice trembling — " what wouldst thou?"

"To give me leave to go in peace to Maestricht, and then to send thither my mother, whom I left in the house by the gate at Frankenburg; for if she see me in the garden combing wool, in my own attire, her reason will return."

"Afterward," said the king, a shadow of vexation passing over his face. Indeed, it were hard to say which was suitor to the other, for his voice faltered, and hers was firm and clear. "That is not all. Afterward," he repeated impatiently.

The color deepened on Passe Rose's cheeks, she trembled violently, and, no longer able to support his gaze, she turned her shining eyes to Agnes of Solier, and threw herself at her feet.

"By the Mother of God!" exclaimed the king, taking Agnes of Solier's hand and seating her in his own chair, "thou art right. She is a king's daughter. Ask her, and thou shalt see what a king's daughter can do." And stooping to Agnes of Solier, he kissed her on the forehead, and left the room.

If love and death could be made subject to will and reason, so that instead of loving love and fearing death, as nature and instinct compel us, we should love death and fear love, then had Passe Rose never gotten from her knees when the Saxon's knife threatened her, nor thrown herself at the feet of Agnes of Solier. But in concerns of love and death nature is stronger than reason, and impulse will countervail consideration; and though at the king's going Passe Rose felt shame drying the source of her tears, and pride nipping the buds of her heart's promise, yet, " If I rise," she said to herself, " all is lost ; " and thus bowed down by the weight of her love, before lesser motives could sway her she felt warm arms pressed about her neck, her face was drawn upwards, and she saw two eyes shining in tears like her own. No word was spoken. They thought no more of their grief and joy than of the coarse wool and silken tissue which clothed them, but like two naked souls fresh from God's hands gazed at one another.

" Thou hast seen him ? " murmured Agnes of Solier. Passe Rose's eyes answered. " And he loves thee — he has told thee " — Passe Rose buried her face in the broidered dress, her shoulders shaken with sobbing. It seemed to her that she could not bear the kiss she felt upon her hair, nor the arms' tender pressure.

" By the Blessed Jesus," she exclaimed, struggling to her feet, " would I might die for thee ! "

XXIV.

On the day Passe Rose appeared before the king, the twelve psalms were recited at nones, and prayers were said in commemoration of Christ's death, in presence of the royal house-

hold, the king himself chanting the epistle before the congregation, who wondered at his ·
fervor. And though no mention is made by
the chronicler of Passe Rose, who knelt beside
Agnes of Solier in the queen's tribune, I had
given less to hear the king's voice than to know
what Passe Rose and Agnes of Solier said to
God at the moment indicated by the rubric in
these words: "Here speak thyself to God, and
explain to Him thy need as thine heart shall
prompt thee."

The night of that same day, also, when the
lights of the palace were extinguished and the
city slept, the king rose from bed, walking to
and fro like one troubled in mind. But I had
given less to know his thoughts than to know of
what Passe Rose was thinking, as she lay in bed
that night with Agnes of Solier. Was it for joy,
or for the novelty of all about her, or for awe and
love of her bedfellow, that she could not sleep?
For my part, I think it was because of an image
of an angel standing within the curtain rail,
whose wings were of silver plates so cunningly
riveted that they seemed ready to beat the air;
and that in her dreams she took this image for
the priest coming with his swinging censer to
bless her nuptial bed. Else why, when day was
come, did she lie abashed, not daring to move,
watching a full hour its silver wings?

There was marveling among the queen's women to see this stranger with Agnes of Solier.
Gesualda's eyes were big with wonder, and her
tongue could scarce keep pace with her conjectures or with the gossip whispered around her.
It was said the king had recognized Agnes of
Solier to be his daughter, and had forbidden
her marriage through excess of affection, as in
times past he had refused Bertrade to Ethelwold
of Mercia, and Rotrude to the Emperor Con-
stantine. One pretended that, having proclaimed
her his own daughter, he would wed her with a
greater than a simple captain ; and another,
that Gisla, the king's sister, had persuaded her
to leave the world, and that to this end the king
would give her the abbey of Poictiers. Whether
any of these rumors were true or all were false,
this is certain (for Gesualda had it from the
chief of the pages, while waiting for the queen
to go to mass on the morning of Pepin's coming): that after the prayers above mentioned
the king, being alone with the queen in her
apartments, sent for both Agnes of Solier and
Passe Rose ; that these two came hand in hand,
and were kissed in turn by the queen ; and that
the king pressed Passe Rose to ask his favor on
whatever her heart desired. Whereupon she
made answer that, of all things she had ever
desired, to do her own pleasure freely for a

whole hour was the greatest. "At this," said the page, "the king laughed, and gave her his signet ring till night, to work her will with it as she pleased, bidding me to wait upon her."

"Holy Virgin!" gasped Gesualda. "What did she?"

"First, she sent for the young page Gerald, and caused to be written for him an order on the king's treasury for a hundred sous, 'because,' she said, 'of the truth spoken by the oracle.'"

"What oracle?" asked Gesualda.

"All I know I tell thee," replied the page. "At the same time," he continued, "she had another written for a woman living without the gate, by the ford of the Wurm, of the value of a young Breton colt lost in the king's service. Then she inquired for a certain Gascon, captain of the watch, and bade me fetch him. Thou shouldst have seen the fellow when he saw her! For she pretended anger, and, showing him the ring, asked if, being bidden by the king, he would now kiss a demon. At this he began to tremble and stammer, and she to laugh, saying that although her mouth were as full of kisses as her heart with joy, they were not hers to give, but that she would forgive his rudeness if he would bring her a certain goldsmith, by name Werdric, living in Maestricht, but now scarching for his wife Jeanne in the city. While the Gascon was gone she went to the new basilica, leaving me at the door to wait till she was come out again. But I followed her, — an easy matter, because of the crowd, — and saw her at the altar of the Virgin, laying there a collar of gold which she had about her neck."

" I remember, I remember," said Gesualda.

"Listen," continued the page, lowering his voice. " As we came back, the streets being full of strangers, — what thinkest thou? She laid her hand upon one who passed near us. ' Art thou not the Greek expected by the Prior Sergius from Pavia?' she asked. I tell thee the fellow's eyes shone with pleasure at seeing her. But before he could answer, 'Thy mission is known to the king,' she said. 'Get thee gone, therefore, if thou wouldst save thy life, and endeavor also to save thy soul. This I do for no love of thee, but because thou once lovedst me,' — and left him white and staring."

" Oh, oh ! " murmured Gesualda.

" Afterwards the Gascon came, saying he had the goldsmith below. 'Knowest thou the monk who stabbed the Saxon yesternight ? ' she asked. At which he replied that he knew him well, having seized him in the act. 'Go loose him,' she said, showing the king's signet again, ' and say to him that, being by age and learning a suitable person, the queen is pleased to write the abbot to make him deacon, that he may the better serve God at the altar. . . . I would have him prior,' she said, turning to me, ' but he is not fit; it were better, therefore, to leave this to God.' Then came the goldsmith, and this man also began to tremble and change color when he saw her, and suddenly fell on his knees, crying, ' Pardon ! ' ' Speak no more of it,' she said; ' the curse is turned to blessing; but get thy mule ready, for on the morrow I would go with thee to Maestricht, and Jeanne will follow.' "

" Hath she truly gone ? " asked Gesualda.

" This very morning, as she said. Here, thy rein ! " cried the page, for he stood at Gesualda's stirrup. " The queen comes." As he spoke the doors were thrown open, and Liutgarde appeared with the king's daughters.

" Is Agnes among them ? " asked Gesualda, raising herself on the point of her toe.

" Aye, behind, to the left. See," said the page, steadying the girl with his arm. " Adieu." His eyes lingered on her face. " Adieu," he repeated, seeking her hand under the saddle fringe.

But Gesualda's eyes were fixed upon Agnes of Solier. " By Heaven ! " she said to herself, " she hath been weeping."

Who will may read in the chronicles how

Pepin entered Aix with files of captives and chariots loaded with treasure; how the Kan Thudun was baptized and his nobles forswore their idols; how the army feasted under the toss of torches; what largesses were distributed to the Church and among the king's vassals; and how, in memory thereof, Leo caused to be executed the mosaic representing the king receiving from the hand of St. Peter the standard of the empire. But since Passe Rose rode that morning from Aix with Werdric, it were not our business to paint a fleeting pageant. And if any one should deem it strange that she should ride to Maestricht, and not to Frankenburg, where her lover lay wounded, let him remember that in all times, when the road is rough and dangers threaten, a woman will win her way in spite of them to the side of her lover; but that when the road is smooth and open, when the wedding train is ready, the horses neighing in the street, and the priest waiting at the parvis door, she will dally at her toilet table and linger with her maids before descending.

If ever a man had paid dear for a hot word spoken in wrath, that man was Werdric, the gold-beater of Maestricht. Had Jeanne flown at him with reproaches, that morning when the madness of a shameful suspicion got the better of love and reason, grief had been easier to bear.

But to see her stealing up the turret stair, listening at every footstep without the gate, and looking up eagerly at the sound of a latch; to see her wits departing with her hope day by day, and yet, from force of habit, her hand still turned to her tasks; to feel her eyes, as he worked on the holy image, watching hungrily its beauty grow under the tool's edge, was almost beyond endurance. Many a man will breathe God's air, close his eyes in sleep and open them again to the sun, without the knowledge of what these things mean; wrongly believing that in the gold which swells his purse or the wheat which bursts his barn lies the bulk of his happiness. Thus Werdric had lived in joy and peace with his wife Jeanne, not knowing wherein his content lay, till, one morning, he found the kitchen fire dead, and the bench, where she was wont to sit, empty. But now, returning home from Aix, he thanked God for every breath he drew, and for every sunbeam struggling through the trees; for Passe Rose rode before him, as on the morning when he found her, coming from St. Denis' fair, and Jeanne was following but a day's journey behind them.

"It is firmly fixed in my mind," said Passe Rose, as they journeyed side by side, "that if the pot is put to boil, and all things made to appear as if nothing had happened, our mother will recover her reason."

At these words, tears filled Werdric's eyes and coursed down the furrows of his cheeks; but there was no bitterness in them. For his heart was swollen with happiness, and when this is the case one has great confidence in God.

Never was Passe Rose so surprised as when, opening the garden gate, she saw the geese un-pastured and the boy lolling with the maids in the grass. It seemed as if every stick and stone knew of Jeanne's absence. The weeds were growing insolently in the path; the leaves had assembled in companies under the wall, and chased each other at will over the beds; the very pots were dull, as with spleen, and spiders wove in the corners. But forthwith Passe Rose set the boy at the weeds and the maids at the pots, and, leaving them to marvel, went up the turret stair to her own chamber. There was the open chest, with the dress she loved flung therein; there among the fragments of the holy image lay her purse on the floor, where it had fallen when she hurled it in her rage at the Blessed Mother of God; and there, too, was the print of her face in the golden sun broidered on her bed-cushion. Surely Jeanne had often come by stealth to gaze at these things, and now for the first time Passe Rose saw that this desolation was the work of her own hand. She who had given her pardon to Werdric needed now pardon for herself. "Seigneur Dieu!" she cried, falling on her knees and stifling her sobs in the golden sun, "I was more cruel than he." Whether she prayed while sobbing so heavily I know not, but just then a sound of distant chanting came as it were an answer from heaven itself. She raised her head, listening. "That should be the monks of St. Servais," thought she; and, rising quickly from her knees, pushed wide her window of horn. A flood of sunshine enwrapped her. "Why sing they at this hour?" she cried to a passer-by.

"Knowest thou not the abbot hath gotten his health? The monks give the praise to God."

"Aye, aye, God be praised," said Passe Rose, drying her tears.

XXV.

The next morning came a messenger from the hill to Passe Rose, saying the abbot desired to speak with her, much to the astonishment of Maréthruda, who observed everything from her window. For while it was publicly said that Werdric had found Passe Rose in the king's palace, as the sons of Jacob had found their brother at the court of Pharaoh; that Passe Rose had won the king's favor, and would wed the newly appointed master of the stables, — Robert of Tours being dead in Hungary, — these rumors, so far from appeasing Maréthruda's curiosity, like stones dropped in a water-jar, only caused it to overflow the more. On hearing, in the market-place, that Passe Rose was betrothed to the captain of the king's horse, she had shrugged her shoulders contemptuously, declaring she would credit it when wolves preached to lambs, and cabbages had the smell of roses. But when Werdric showed her a samite cloth woven of six threads in Sicily, the gift of Agnes of Solier for a bridal robe, for the tressed silk of whose girdle he was fashioning two dragons' heads with gaping mouths to hold the strands, she could doubt no longer. "God pardon us!" she thought, as she watched Passe Rose go forth mounted upon one of the sleek monastery mules, remembering how she had joined her neighbors in declaring the girl to be a demon.

Half-way up the hill Passe Rose bade the messenger ride on before her. "The motion fatigues me," she said. "I will rest here a little, and join thee at the gate." When he was gone she slipped from her seat, tying the mule by the roadside, and went in through the thorn-thicket to where Gui had found her fastening her sandals. There she lingered awhile, listening to the brook's tumble; then went down among the mulberries, to the place where she had sat with her lover. Did she feel nearer to him among these mute witnesses of her first confession? At her approach the mulberry leaves ceased their whispering, and she, observing them all tenderly, stood still in their midst, as if ashamed at all they knew. Regaining the road, she met the herdsmen going with the pigs to the oak feeding-grounds, and citizens coming from the sale of new wine, held every autumn without the abbey gates; and these, intent upon their own business, went their ways, with only a glance or word of common greeting, when it seemed to Passe Rose that every one should stop to gaze at her. A sense of superiority lifted her above them all, and she looked with pity to see such sordid cares on the faces of God's creatures. Indeed, the mulberry-trees were far more congenial companions, and, though ignorant of the price of new wine, were better judges of the fruits which God has planted in his garden.

There were no stars in the water-mirror as she neared the pond, but the sun shone there, making a golden whirlpool where the waters eddied about the sluice. Her guide, angry because she dallied by the wayside when the abbot was waiting in the orchard, stamped his foot impatiently to see her now gazing stupidly into the pool. But Passe Rose, occupied by her thoughts, ob-

serving first the bush where she had lain concealed, and then the small gate whence Friedgis
had issued, paused again under the wall of the
Saxon's cell ; at which her companion muttered
so loudly that she drew a long breath, and followed him in silence. At the orchard gate he
left her, and she perceived the abbot on the seat
near the cliff's brow, beckoning to her. Advancing under the king's gaze, in his cabinet at
Aix, she felt less trouble than now, remembering
how this holy man had thought her certainly to
be a devil, once dwelling within him. Her step
trembled and her cheeks burned, and she covered
these with her hands as she knelt down before
him. Yet never did penitent bow with greater
assurance of pardon, for between her fingers she
saw upon the abbot's knees a parchment missive
stamped with the king's signet. There was a
silence, and then, —

"God has sent thee much sorrow," said the
abbot.

"And great joy," she replied, lifting her head.
The evidence of it was on her face, and Passe
Rose was convinced that the abbot knew all that
she had ever said or done, for immediately he
added, —

"In sorrow we curse God, and in joy we forget him." Then he pointed to Maestricht,
spread below on the plain, where the river shone,

saying, " When Christ was yet young, as thou art, Satan took him up to such a place as this " —

" Aye, father," murmured Passe Rose quickly.

" Thinkest thou the Tempter showed him lands and gold and honor only, and not love also?" said the abbot.

Though his voice was gentle and his palm rested on her hair, Passe Rose stood up, trembling.

" If thou takest away my love, thou takest the staff from my hand."

The abbot turned away his head, and then, after a little, " God make it to blossom like that of Aaron."

" And give it rain and sun, that it may bear fruit to his glory," added Passe Rose candidly.

" Thine is the age of ready promise," said the abbot, looking at her with a show of severity.

" And great courage, father."

Vanquished by her sturdy confidence, the abbot turned his eyes again to the plain. The sun was struggling with the autumn wind to make the day fair, breaking at times from behind the clouds with a burst of its springtime power. Certainly it did not occur to Passe Rose that, like the sun, she could open to the abbot a vision of spring ; for who, in the shadow of a mighty tree, would ever think that its stubborn trunk had once swayed to May winds, or that so rugged a bark was ever smooth and fair? What Passe Rose saw was the king's letter close under her eyes, yet as far from her comprehension as had been the gospel page on the altar of St. Servais. " I will ask leave," she was vowing to herself, " to come to the abbey school, that I may master this mystery ; " and at the same time she remembered the ivory tablets sold by the Greek merchant, also an alphabet designed to hang from the girdle, and thought how well they would become her.

Surprising her gaze fixed upon the letter, the abbot took the missive from his knee. " The king," he said, " hath sent hither the silver pyx from his chapel at Aix. Into whatever place this pyx is carried, there the sick are healed, the barren bear, and reason returns to the witless. Art thou able to fast " —

" Oh, willingly ! " cried Passe Rose.

" And to pass the night in prayer " —

" That is nothing," she interrupted eagerly.

" For to-morrow thy mother returns. At the third hour, by the king's command, the brotherhood will assemble to chant the litanies of Marcellus, which the Virgin taught the saint from her own mouth at Embrun. At that hour the bell will ring in the tower of St. Gabrielle, and, at its sound, lift thy voice also to heaven." He raised his hand, and Passe Rose knelt again. " The peace of God and his angels guard thee."

Passe Rose did not stir. When at last she raised her eyes to the abbot's face, they were shining as never stars shone in the pond. She rose to her feet, yet did not turn to go. A scarlet flush overspread her face. She retreated a step, and paused again, with a wistful glance at the letter of the king.

Opening it, the abbot began to read : " In the name of God and of our Saviour Jesus Christ, Karle, by the will of the Divine Providence, king, to Rainal, abbot of St. Servais : Be it known that our will is that you make preparations to come, the xv of the calends of January, that is to say six days before Noel, to our palace of Aix, there to celebrate the espousals of our faithful vassal, Gui, Count of Tours " —

Here the abbot looked up from the missive.

But Passe Rose, who had gone with her dagger to the Saxon's cell, who, though bred among dancers, bore herself courteously with a king's daughter, had fled ; and going down the hill, now walking, now running, sang aloud the *salut* she had sung to Queen Hildegarde, when she danced at Chasseneuil : —

" God give thee joy,
And great honor.''

XXVI.

Since the world was made, the wise pretend to set Art over against Nature, showing how the latter proceedeth by law, repeating herself by a blind necessity, without admixture of will or purpose. Yet no man twining his hovel with vines, clothing his nakedness with fineries, or fencing his life about with ceremonies, can compare with Nature in enchantments and illusions. No painter will make the flat appear round with greater nicety, no coquette hide a blemish with such delicacy. With a moonbeam she will out-do fancy, and, splitting the sun's rays, weave her-self garments of such beauty as puts imagination to shame. When age is written on her face she will wear her gaudiest ribbons, and no flower of the field under the autumn stars would dream that the drops gathering on its petals were the sharp points of her frost arrows. Has any one failed to observe how, like an old woman who tries her wedding dress when her wrinkles are as plenty as its creases, Nature will put on her spring gown when leaves are falling and the ribs of rock appear in the mountain pastures; how she will draw about her passing comeliness a veil of mist so full of glamour that one is forced to believe her youth restored, and winter far dis-tant?

In Jeanne's garden the leaves of the carnelian cherries were yellow and specked with black, and their branches ready to shiver at the least breath of the wind; the plum-trees were tired of growing, and no longer strained to reach the top of the wall; shallot and parsley were withered into brown tufts of shrunken leafage; and the apples on the kitchen wall were pinched and lustreless. But none of these things could contend with Nature, bent upon counterfeiting a spring morning. Purple hemp-nettles bloomed along the wall, — one might think they were May harebells; asters and yellow celandine nodded to each other across the path, as neighbors passing in the street might greet each other with wishes for a long life; hairy heads of grass jostled each other under Maréthruda's window; and everywhere the loriots and the sparrows preened and plumed their feathers wisely, as birds will when the young are grown, and all the screaming and chirping, the worry and fuss, of spring loves and summer cares, are over. Under the open kitchen roof the fire blazed on the stone floor, with fagots fit for use hard by; a fleecy steam rose from the pot, and the spoon protruded above the rim ready for the hand to seize; the geese were at pasture, the two maids washing at the river; Maréthruda was leaning from the window as formerly, when she had news to tell;

through the open door came tinkling sounds of tools where Werdric was at work; and by the wooden post under the eaves Passe Rose herself sat in the sun, combing wool and watching the shadow of St. Sebastian's tower creeping up the path.

At every sound in the street, Maréthruda, her eyes fixed upon the garden gate, started. " Dieu!" she called to Passe Rose, "my tongue cleaves to my mouth; it will not move even to a prayer."

" Leave prayers to the monks," said Passe Rose, drawing her comb through the wool, but trembling inwardly; " thy business is to speak some common word as thy wont is when she returns from market."

"As true as I live, I can think of nothing," replied Maréthruda.

" Say that the abbot hath sent her a tun of beer in exchange for the cheeses."

" That had not occurred to me," said Maré-thruda. " Is it sour or honeyed?"

Passe Rose cast a quick glance of scorn at her neighbor; then the comb dropped from her hand in the wool, for the bell struck in the tower of St. Gabrielle, and immediately the gate opened and Jeanne entered.

Passe Rose could neither stoop to take her comb nor lift her eyes. Every beat of her heart was like the stroke of the bell's hammer. She wished to run and clasp to her bosom the form she knew was standing in the door, and at the same time a cruel thought, " If I show her over-much love, she will mistrust me," took all her courage.

" Thou art late, so I put the pot to boil," she gasped, regaining her comb with a desperate motion.

Her eyes riveted upon Passe Rose, Jeanne stood immobile in the archway. In her fin-gers she held the ragged skirt of her garment. Whether she heard the pot steaming on the tripod, or the click of Werdric's tools, or the burden of the monk's hymn, " Alleluia, song of sweetness," I cannot tell; but at the sound of Passe Rose's voice, she advanced a step timidly, then stood still again. In her eyes one could see the struggle of contending passions, distrust, desire, fear, and the hunger of love's famine. With a rapid glance about her, she took another step forward, and, seeing Maréthruda, smiled faintly ; then, hesitating, retreated again, like an intruder.

It seemed to Passe Rose that God and Maré-thruda deserted her; and forgetting both, as also the silver pyx, she rose in her own strength, and went to meet her mother. I know not what mixture of sweet cajolery and commanding willfulness was in her face and motion, but as she drew near Jeanne began to smile, and then to laugh, — a laugh so strangely pitiful that Passe Rose burst into sobbing, and caught her about the neck.

When Maréthruda, hastening from her window, reached the spot, Passe Rose was seated on the garden walk, holding Jeanne to her bosom, and Werdric knelt beside her. "See, her lips move!" cried Maréthruda, beside herself.

Passe Rose bent her ear and listened.

"What says she?" asked Maréthruda excitedly.

And Passe Rose, looking up through her tears, whispered, "That she dreamed the geese had gone astray in the meadow."

He who, before he returned to Paradise, opened by a word the sealed ear to the sounds of his world, and the closed eye to its beauties, might doubtless have set Jeanne's wits aright instantaneously, without leaving them, as it were, to grope first among the geese, and to set themselves in order little by little with the growth of her bodily vigor. But such is the general course of his Providence, — to proceed by gentle stages, and not after the hot desires of our own wills. And if through much longing Passe Rose chafed at the delay in her mother's restoration and the healing of her lover's wound, yet she gathered more happiness by the way than if God had granted her wish as the fays do, in a point of time. Thus a man enters the temple of his joy as he would go to the church of St. Servais, on the hill above Maestricht, seeing first the tower of Gabrielle from a distance, then hearing its bell faintly, afterwards losing all sight of its walls among the oak-trees, till, having passed the ponds, they appear again close at hand, and at last, gaining the steps of the parvis, he lifts the curtain and goes in to the shrine. And it was so that Passe Rose, when Jeanne had left her bed, and the time of the espousals drew near, went up to the public mass said in honor of the silver pyx which had worked her mother's cure. The service had commenced when she reached the church door, so she went forward on the points of her toes, listening to the priest reading the epistle. His voice quivered like a flame; she recognized it well, though it was new, and as she passed the last pillar she perceived the celebrant was Brother Dominic. Remembering what terror she had thrice caused him, she remained in the pillar's shadow, observing him.

His face had grown thin, changed in some marvelous fashion like his voice. Fascinated, she advanced unawares, and their eyes met.

His look passed from her face as the wind leaves
the cheek, and his voice soared higher : —

"Love not the world" —

At these words Passe Rose started, as at a
blow.

"— neither the things that are in the world.
. . . The world passeth away"—

But Passe Rose, looking up, smiled.

For love abideth forever.